RETURN OF THE LIVING DAD

DOCTOR WHO – THE NEW ADVENTURES

Also available:

THE NEW

ADVENTURES

RETURN OF THE LIVING DAD

Kate Orman

First published in Great Britain in 1996 by
Doctor Who Books
an imprint of Virgin Publishing Ltd
332 Ladbroke Grove
London W10 5AH

Reprinted 1996

Cover illustration by Mark Wilkinson

ISBN 0 426 20482 4

Typeset by Galleon Typesetting, Ipswich
Printed and bound in Great Britain by
Mackays of Chatham PLC

For Jon Blum

Prologue

Once upon a time there was a hermit.

He never talked much about why he was one, but he was. Some people said there was a woman . . . or a whole bunch of weird sisters, depending on who you believe. But no matter who or what brought it on, he knew he didn't want to live the life he was meant to. The life his name and address had laid out for him long before he was born.

All he really wanted to do was wander the world, and forget the responsibilities his name carried, and meet all the people he could never get to see otherwise.

Well all right, he was a very social hermit.

But before he left home, he broke his name. Broke it into thirty-eight tiny pieces. It made a lovely shattering sound, like a wineglass tossed into a fireplace.

He swept up all the pieces of who he was and tucked them away in an inside pocket. And over the years, as he met people who ended up sharing the road with him, travelling with him for a while, he would quietly give each of them a piece of his name.

And once they went their separate ways, his name continued to grow within them, and made them into something better, something bigger, than they were before.

Or just something different.

Most of the time he didn't think about what grew as he passed. Most of the time he didn't know. But he did know that, with all the jigsaw pieces of his name scattered about, they wouldn't be able to get all of him when they came to take him away.

PART ONE

BIG TROUBLE
IN LITTLE CALDWELL

The point of archaeology is to carefully recover the past – not disintegrate it.

The Doctor, *Battlefield*

1

Find

The planet Youkali, 2587

'Death has no name.'

Jason Summerfield-Kane looked up at his wife. She was lying on the step above him, face pressed to the ancient stone. 'What?'

'It says here, *Death has no name*. Very suggestive.'

Bernice Kane-Summerfield sat up, brushing the dust off her denim jacket. Jason leant up and kissed her. She smiled at him, hugging him awkwardly, her hands full of pen and paper. He plucked a cobweb out of her long dark hair.

'Look.' Benny pointed with her stylus at the complex hieroglyphs carved into the stone. Jason hunched, put his face close to the ancient words. '*Name not has Death*,' translated Benny, running the pen along under the words. '*Therefore steals She ours*. Death was a female figure on this world. Also very suggestive.'

'Are you just going to sit there making suggestive remarks?' asked Jason. 'Or do you want to tell me what it means?'

Benny sat up on the step and looked around the site. The sun had come out from behind the clouds, poking orange fingers down through the canopy, a mix of native and Earth trees. Archaeologists and students buzzed around each staircase or crumbled building.

'Youkali witnessed the battle between the Osirans and Sutekh,' she said. 'Over five and a half thousand years ago. The

5

planet was laid waste. Cities burned, economies collapsed, cultures mutated . . . there are incidental similarities between these hieroglyphs and the ancient Egyptian language.'

Jason took the pad and pen off her. Benny had been making painstaking transcriptions of the hieroglyphs. 'So what about the Egyptians? Did they have a name for Death?'

'They had a couple of death gods,' shrugged Benny. 'But that's not quite the same thing . . . the Osirans influenced the culture on hundreds of planets. And, thousands of years after them, the Exxilons took their own version of Osiran culture and spread it even further . . . But there were people before the Osirans.'

'So they were influenced by someone else before they went off influencing everyone.'

Benny grinned at him. 'I'm sorry, you're getting a lecture.'

'I like listening to you talk.' He closed her notepad. 'So is this going to be helpful for your thesis?'

'More than helpful.' *They Sit Above in Shadow*, said the notepad's cover, *Archaeological Echoes of the Universe's First People*. 'I wish I could have talked to the people of Youkali. There's so much guesswork. It's like trying to get to know someone by reading the phone book.'

'Would the Doctor have taken you back?'

'What?'

'Back then, I mean?'

Benny ruffled her husband's hair. Dark roots were showing under the blond. 'He might have, at that. He took me to some amazing places, some awesome times. But it wasn't so much archaeology as tourism. I suppose I like the puzzle-solving, trying to work out the picture without being given all of the pieces.'

'If you don't like what you find, you can always make something up,' said Jason.

Benny frowned. 'What makes you say that?'

'It was a joke. Sorry, it wasn't a very good one. I'm no good this early in the morning.'

Benny planted a kiss on the top of his head, and looked up. An elderly woman, well-wrapped in a black coat and scarf, was watching them from the base of the steps.

She couldn't be a student – no dirt – and Benny didn't recognize her from the seminars on board the *Henrietta Leavitt*. A cold wind was suddenly blowing.

'Hello!' called the woman. Dried leaves blew around her feet. 'Is your name Summerfield?'

'What can I do for you?' said Benny, standing up.

'Professor Truszkowski said I'd find you somewhere around here,' said the woman. 'I knew a Summerfield once, but it was a long time ago, a very long time . . .' Benny started walking down the steps towards her. 'You didn't have an uncle or perhaps a grandfather named Isaac?'

Benny sat down on the steps, hard. Jason was by her side in a moment. 'Oh my dear girl,' said the woman. 'What have I said?'

Jason squeezed his wife's hand. Benny was staring through the woman as though her eyes had stopped working. 'Admiral Isaac Douglas Summerfield?' she said.

'He was my commanding officer,' said the woman. 'Forty years ago.'

'He was my father,' said Benny. 'And he disappeared. Forty years ago.'

'Your father,' repeated the old woman. She squinted at the young couple. 'My name is Admiral Groenewegen. I think you'd better come back to my tent.'

Benny sat on a box, looking at a photograph of her father.

Jason put his hand on her shoulder, just to let her know he was there. She gave the hand a reassuring squeeze. The Admiral's tent was warm and cosy, a massive affair like something out of a Foreign Legion movie, all poles and cushions and interesting boxes.

Benny held the photograph in her hands. Sepiatone, a wooden frame; genuine artificial antique, a craze half a century out of date. Her face was dimly reflected in the dusty glass.

She didn't look anything like him.

He was standing next to Groenewegen in the photo, a much younger Groenewegen, with short dark hair, her uniform in disarray and her eyes twinkling above a smile.

He . . . wasn't exactly handsome, but striking: strong jaw,

very pale hair, very grey eyes. The photo was different from the holograms in Spacefleet's records, real, *alive*. Groenewegen had a mug of beer, while he was holding a shot glass of dark fluid.

'Turkish coffee,' said the Admiral, handing her a cup of tea. Benny stared at it in confusion. 'He used to get through endless cups of that stuff. I don't know how he managed it. It still gives me palpitations.' Groenewegen's eyes were misty with remembering. 'He had his own *cezve*, this pot with a long handle to make the coffee. He used to carry it everywhere. For good luck.'

Benny said, 'When I was four, maybe five, Mum told me that he didn't drink. I laughed because I didn't understand what she meant.'

'He was always stone-cold sober.' Jason shook his head as the Admiral waved a chipped mug at him. She poured herself a cup. 'How much do you remember about him?'

'Just little bits and pieces. I remember the last time I ever saw him . . .' She closed her eyes. The light glinting off the badge of his cap. 'I remember the cologne he wore; I always associate that smell with childhood. One of the reasons I became an archaeologist was because I thought I might find him. Somewhere, out beyond the edge of civilization. Trapped on some backwater world amongst the scum and villainy. Or fighting a top-secret war against the Daleks. Or taken prisoner and bravely holding out against torture. Or something.' She gave a little choked laugh. 'Silly things. I haven't thought about him for a long time, not like that.'

The Admiral shook her head. 'I don't know if it means anything to you, but I protested the official report of his disappearance.'

Benny brushed a speck of dust off the photo. 'That was good of you.'

'Whatever Isaac was doing, he wasn't running away.'

'I don't know. I suppose I'll never know.'

Groenewegen said, 'I do know. I knew him. And besides, I was there.'

Benny's eyes shot to the Admiral's face.

'I was only a captain then,' said Groenewegen. 'There were

a flock of us – those clunking old Fury-class fighter-ships. The Dalekbusters. Huge ships, huge guns, small crew – mostly automated. So much of Dalek strategy is repetitious, predictable ... Admiral Summerfield's ship was the *Tisiphone*, the lead ship. It was just us, a dozen or so Furies, between a trio of Dalek planet-rippers and Bellatrix. My ship was the only one that survived the battle, and that was luck, not brilliant tactics.'

Benny said levelly, 'The report said he turned and ran.'

'He certainly turned. Surprised the cruk out of us – 'scuse my language. Was he running? No. Not Isaac. Hell, to someone who could drink that coffee, the Daleks must have seemed like a pretty minor health hazard.' She barked a laugh. 'Hang on a minute.'

The Admiral got up and went to one of her boxes, tapped her fingers on its lid, chose another box. 'Half of this stuff is Mel's,' she said apologetically, rummaging. 'More than half, actually. And she's off shopping again. We're going to need a bigger tent. Aha!' She pulled a small black cube out of the box.

'What is it?' asked Jason.

'The *Clotho*'s flight recorder.' She turned the datacube around in her hands, thoughtfully. 'When they decommissioned her after that battle, I kept this as a souvenir. Captain's privilege. It's in an archaic format, but it's still intact. If you plug this into the right software, it'll show you the whole battle as a tactical hologram. If you want to see it.'

'What kind of software?'

The Admiral put the cube into her free hand. 'You're sure?'

'No,' said Benny. 'No, I'm not sure. I am less sure than something very unsure indeed.' She looked down at the cube. 'You've been so kind. I don't know –'

'Goodness, girl,' said the Admiral, grinning. 'If you do ever find him, get him to look me up. He still owes me five credits.'

The first time Jason woke up, Benny was lying with her back to him. His left arm had gone to sleep under her shoulder. When he moved it, he realized she was still awake, staring into the candle beside the bed.

He hugged her, gently. 'You don't have to decide right away,' he said.

'I won't be able to stop thinking about it until I do decide,' she breathed. 'I've never been so close . . .'

'We could stay here,' said Jason. 'You could finish your credit unit. Then we could go back.'

'I don't think I could stand it,' said Benny. The candle flared, turned blue for a moment, lapsed back into steady yellow. 'And then there's that.'

'Is it really bothering you? I didn't realize.'

'Our ghost?' She laughed softly. 'That's just a running gag, meant to scare the newbie students. The atmosphere is full of exotic charged particles. That's bound to produce all sorts of weird effects. Problem is, some of the students take the ghost stories too seriously.'

'Oh,' said Jason, clutching her interestingly. 'I was rather hoping it was the spirit of an ancient Youkalian, come to terrify the grave-robbers desecrating its world.'

Benny rolled over, kissing his stubbly chin. 'Very funny.'

'I don't want to see your future messed up by something from your past. That's all.'

Behind her, the candle flared again, giving her a soft blue halo. 'I keep thinking about Groenewegen. About Dad, retired instead of vanished, wandering about in a rickety spaceship and pitching his tent in holiday resorts.'

Jason stroked her hair, working his fingers down her scalp and right to her shoulders, over and over, wanting to get at the tension inside her. 'Maybe Groenewegen is a Dalek agent,' he whispered. 'Come to lure the last of the Summerfields to her doom.'

'Can't you take this seriously even for a moment?' muttered Benny.

'Hey, shh, I'm sorry . . . I thought you needed cheering up.'

Benny hugged him back. 'I'm sorry. I'm frightened, I think. Look, let's go to sleep. I'll work out what to do in the morning.'

The second time Jason woke up, Benny was sitting at the foldup table in the dark. Rain was spattering down on the

10

roof of the tent – a soothing, drumming sound.

Benny was watching a hologram floating above the table. A loop of maybe ten seconds kept repeating itself, the glowing outlines of the tiny ships making the same manoeuvres over and over.

Three big orange shapes must be the planet-rippers. Six small blue ships blipped into existence at the edge of the hologram, made desperate turns as their brave attack became a rout, exploded into symbolic blue puffs as they were destroyed. The timescale must be hugely compressed, maybe a second for every real minute.

Each time, a tiny blue ship at the front of the fleet veered suddenly, turned completely around, and sped out of the hologram's field of reference.

'What were you doing, Daddy?' Benny whispered.

'Maybe it doesn't tell you the whole story.' Her face snapped to him, one cheekbone an orange crescent of light. 'Maybe there's something out of the frame which we can't see.'

Benny reached down and snapped off the hologram. 'I can't work it out,' she said, suddenly invisible again. 'What am I going to do?'

'Whatever you decide,' said Jason, 'I'll be right there; I'll back you up.'

'I really want to get this degree. I want to be able to point at a piece of paper and say, see, I really *do* have a PhD.'

'You do that anyway.'

'Cheeky.' She picked up a cushion from the floor of the tent and threw it at him. 'I've really enjoyed the last couple of months, you know. Despite the ghost and the wet weather. Just staying in one place and really working on something . . . tidying up one of the loose ends of my life.'

'And then along comes another one.'

'He's dead,' said Benny. 'Occam's razor. Surely he's just dead.'

Jason didn't know what to say.

Benny got back into bed. 'I want to talk to Groenewegen again in the morning,' she said. 'Assuming we don't sleep in until lunchtime.'

* * *

11

Noon.

Benny put down her brush. The hieroglyphs were emerging slowly and surely from the dirt, speaking to her a little at a time. The past slowly coming back into the light.

The Admiral was distracting a bunch of the trainees. They were supposed to be cleaning up one of the staircases so a translation team could move in, but they'd ended up sitting on them instead, listening to her talk about fighting Daleks.

Benny had been around that age when she had gone AWOL from Spacefleet. Crammed into an escape pod, praying her computer modifications would hide her hasty exit from the troop transport. And that if they didn't, the captain wouldn't just have the deserter shot out of space.

Woman overboard.

God, that was a long time ago.

Her life had had such a muddled beginning. What was it like, to just grow up and go to school and get a job, like those kids? Not to be orphaned at seven? Not to run away from school and live in a forest? Not to be shanghaied into military service? Not to fake your academic credentials?

Not to meet the Doctor?

She smiled to herself. She wouldn't have given any of it up. Not even the moments of horror, the brushes with death. Not even the doubts and betrayals and the heart-thumping moments when she remembered that she was travelling through space and through time with a man who only looked like a man. Human on the outside, alien to the core.

Through space, and through time. The TARDIS could go anywhere, anywhen. And somehow they'd never landed anywhere near her father, never made a concerted effort to look for him. Somehow, they'd just never got around to it. Because, of course, he was just dead.

The students were laughing now, at some joke the Admiral had cracked, their young voices echoing across the mossy plaza. Youkali had been colonized centuries ago, though only a couple of bases had been built. When they'd realized that you couldn't throw a stone in a Youkalian jungle without hitting ruins, someone had slapped a protection order on the place. They were still sending teams here; budding archaeologists

12

inevitably did a Youkali tour. And so did haggard old ones who were working on their 'second' doctorate.

Why did she want to find Dad? Who was this man? She could remember the sound of his voice, but the photo had shocked her. It didn't match her blurred, child's memories.

For one thing, he was a lot shorter than she remembered.

She put down her bits and pieces and strode across the clearing, her hands in her pockets. The Admiral looked up. 'Good morning, my dear!' she said. 'These young people have just been telling me about the ghost that's following you around.'

Right on cue, a chilly wind blew through the clearing. 'It's supposed to be the phantom of a trainee who disappeared here about five years ago,' said Benny. 'No one knows what happened to her, but they say she haunts this site, trying to complete her honours project. Personally, I think the mutant flying funnel-web spiders probably got her.' A couple of the students bought that, eyebrows raised and mouths opened. Mwa ha ha. 'Admiral,' she said, 'I need a word.'

Groenewegen detached herself from her audience. She followed Benny to one of the little catering tents at the southern edge of the clearing. 'What can I do for you, my dear?'

'I need to extract the exact coordinates of that last battle from your flight recorder,' said Benny. 'The precise time and place. I didn't want to start messing around with your only copy.'

The Admiral nodded seriously. 'I'm still very sorry about the shock I gave you. Two teas, please,' she told the Caxtarid in the tent. 'If you want to know the mathematics, I can easily sort the numbers out for you. But I'm a little worried . . .'

'I want to reconstruct the battle. Let's say I want to clear the family name.'

'Fair enough.'

Benny had brought the flight recorder; she handed it to the Admiral, who started up the hologram. The tiny ships flew around her head as she folded down the miniature keyboard and tapped in some instructions. 'There,' she said, after a moment. Benny's hands were filled by the cups. Her father's ship had

13

frozen in place at the very edge of the field, the moment before it disappeared from the recording. Numbers appeared over it. 'That's the last recorded position of the ship.'

Groenewegen shut down the hologram and folded the flight recorder back up. She swapped it for her tea. 'I want you to keep that,' she said. 'You might be tilting at windmills trying to actually find Isaac, but it'd be worth it just to prove that he wasn't running away.'

'I have to know,' said Benny, surprised at the intensity in her voice. 'I really have to know.'

The Admiral patted her arm. 'There's precious little honour in being a soldier, love,' she said. 'That inquiry took away your dad's honour. There are probably only a handful of people left alive who remember, but –'

'History remembers,' said Benny. She took a large swig of the tea. 'Fixing history used to be my job.' Whatever Groenewegen made of that, she said nothing as the younger woman looked around the clearing. 'This isn't what I should be excavating. It's me. *My* archaeology. My past.' She held up the flight recorder, its black surface shining in the morning light. 'My dad.'

Jason stretched, yawned, sneezed and realized it was lunchtime.

He dragged himself out of bed. Benny had probably been up with the dawn. She –

He looked around the tent. Everything was gone, the tent was empty. He yelled, involuntarily, and ran outside in his pyjama bottoms.

He nearly ran right into Benny, who was standing amidst neatly packed boxes and backpacks, doing up a shoelace.

He gaped at her. She had cut her hair, a little roughly, so that it looked the way it had when they'd first met. Her fringe hung down into her eyes as she tied off the lace and straightened up.

'Fold up the bed,' she said. 'We're off to see the wizard.'

2

Earth

Death has no name.

The Doctor lifted the mop and dipped it into the bucket, operating the little handle that squeezed the rollers.

The old fairy tale had been in his thoughts a great deal over the last week, and no surprise. *Death was born when the gods had been drinking; they accidentally gave her name to someone else. No one remembers —*

He moved the bucket to one side and glanced at his watch. Chris and Roz were due to pick him up at about twelve. He only needed to finish this floor, and it would be over; his last day here. *No one remembers what her name was, or who it was given to. 'Everything and everyone has a name,'* she lamented, *'except for me.'*

Neither of his companions had really understood why he wanted to come here, but they'd accepted it, the way they'd accepted the last couple of months. The three of them had stayed on Earth, in the late twentieth century, just doing . . . small things. Nothing important on a cosmic scale. This last week had been spent in Sydney: movies and coffee, art shows and museums.

Volunteer work in a hospice.

So Death takes our names. She finds out what we are called, and takes our names away.

The Doctor squeezed his mop out for the last time.

15

'Why don't you just stop it?' Chris had asked him. The young man's voice had been very serious. That was a week ago, just before they went their separate ways. 'All those twentieth-century diseases. They're so simple, anyway. Why don't you just cure them?'

'You know why,' the Time Lord had said.

Chris had sighted down the arrow, trying not to squint at the straw target. 'Tell me anyway,' he said.

The Doctor hesitated, as though appraising the young man's stance and aim. 'Should I go back and put a stop to the Black Death?' he said.

Chris let the arrow go. It sliced through the air, thudded into the TARDIS wall behind the target, clattered to the floor. He made a face. 'That'd be easy,' he said. 'You'd just work out where and when to be with a bottle of penicillin, right?'

'But then Europe's population would rise instead of falling dramatically. Labour would become cheaper instead of scarce and precious. Feudalism might continue for centuries.'

'So it's too big to stop. Too much a part of history.'

'And changing that history would mean erasing the thirtieth century you and Roz come from.'

Chris nodded to himself, flicked his yellow hair out of his eyes, and nocked another arrow.

The Doctor said, 'This is a well-worn discussion.'

'It helps to hear it from you,' Chris had said. 'If you're certain, then I'm certain.' The arrow had bounced off the wall. 'This is really starting to bug me!'

The Doctor emptied his bucket into the laundry sink. He couldn't change history on such a massive scale. Not Earth's history. His voyages through time and space had taken him from one end of the little blue planet's story to the other, from the beginnings of life to long after its destruction. But he always ended up back here, in a narrow band of time stretching from the middle of the nineteenth century to around the end of the twentieth. His home away from home.

He sighed, putting the mop away in the cupboard. He couldn't rebuild the house, but he could do a little cleaning.

* * *

16

Christopher Cwej was playing chess with Roslyn Forrester in Hyde Park. Roz's (genuine 1996) watch made a dull electronic noise. 'Time to go,' she said, standing up.

Chris looked at her, face level with hers. 'Just when I'm winning!' he said.

She grimaced in annoyance until she saw that he was joking. He grinned at her, tumbling the pieces into a bag and stuffing them into his backpack.

They walked along in silence, enjoying the sunshine. Yesterday they'd gone to the Three Sisters and walked down the side of a mountain. The day before that they'd gone to a film festival.

They had seriously chilled out over the last couple of months. Not that there hadn't been enough excitement, between the bungee jumping and sneaking on board the Greenpeace mission. But not once in the last month had his life been at risk, or had a whole planet depended on him or Roz or the Doctor.

He felt alive again. Very alive.

He risked a glance at Roz. Her deep brown skin glowed with health; her dark eyes flashed in the sunlight. She was wearing a denim jacket over a tight T-shirt and jeans. She was old enough to be his mother, and she'd probably shoot his head off if he so much as contemplated holding her hand, but . . .

A bus sounded its horn as he almost stepped in front of it. Chris jumped back onto the pavement with an embarrassed yelp.

He looked around, feeling his ears turn red, but Roz hadn't noticed. She was staring up at a building. 'This is it,' she said, nodding at a sign.

Chris looked around. 'I don't see the Doctor.'

'Do you want to go in and see if he's there?'

'Okay.' Chris paused in the doorway, but Roz was pretending to read a billboard. He frowned and went inside.

The Doctor was waiting for him, sitting at the end of a row of orange plastic chairs. He held his one-of-a-kind white fedora in his lap. He was wearing one of his old shirts and a pair of oversized, worn trousers. Work clothes.

Chris glanced at the receptionist, busy with paperwork, and went over to the Time Lord.

The Doctor stood up. 'Hello, Chris,' he said, peering up at the Adjudicator. 'How have you been?'

'Oh, fine.' Chris glanced at the door. Outside, Roz looked away quickly. 'We've been down in Sydney for the last couple of days. We spent some time at a seminar on law enforcement. It was fascinating, really primitive stuff . . .'

The Doctor jammed his hat on his head. 'You'll have to tell me all about it.' He nodded at the receptionist, moved towards the door.

'Er,' said Chris.

The Doctor stopped with his hand on the door handle, looking out at Roz, who was watching the traffic.

'When you phoned,' said Chris, 'you said there was some-one you wanted us to meet.'

'There was,' sighed the Doctor. 'There was. Come on.'

It took a couple of hours on the train, and a half-hour walk, to get to the beach house. Chris had wanted to rent a car, but, given what had happened to the last two, they'd decided against it.

At last they wound their way through the scrub to the house. It was miles from civilization, surrounded by an overgrown garden that segued into the bush. The sun was going down behind the mountains as the Doctor pushed open the front door. He never seemed to lock the place up.

'Whose turn is it in the kitchen?' said Chris. Roz and the Doctor both smiled at him. 'Oh . . .' he murmured, heading inside.

Roz pulled her boots off, shook the sand out of them. The ocean was a dark, glassy mass. A single white smear appeared down the centre as the moon's reflection brightened. She sat down on a foldup chair, put her bare feet up on the railing and closed her eyes, listening to the white noise of the surf.

After a while she opened them again. The Doctor had come out onto the porch, silently. He had changed into his more usual outfit – the linen suit and the silk shirt – though he hadn't bothered to put on a tie. His feet were bare. The sea breeze ruffled his dark hair.

He noticed that she'd noticed him, and handed her a tiny

T-mail datacube, the sort the TARDIS console spat out. She thumbed the switch on the base. A tiny Bernice appeared on top of the cube.

Hi! I'm on the planet Youkali Six, in the jungle not ten kilometres from the Archaeological Institute, with Jason. It's the year twenty-five eighty-seven. The precise time and coordinates are appended.

Roz twiddled a dial to make the image a little larger. Benny's face was cool as a cucumber, her eyes glittering with cheerfulness, like a suspect who was sweating on the inside.

I've just found someone who was with my father during his last battle. She is, effectively, the last person to see him alive.

Doctor, if it's possible, I want to go back to the battle. I've thought about this a lot. I know we can't change anything, but even if we just watch from the distance, I need to find out what happened to Dad.

Please drop in when you have a moment spare from saving the universe. Hope everyone is well.

The holographic Benny laughed.

Help me, Obi-Wan Kenobi, you're my only hope.

She vanished, replaced by a string of digits.

'We'll leave tomorrow morning,' said the Doctor. He sat down in one of the other chairs. 'You disapproved.'

'Sorry?' said Roz.

'You disapproved of my spending that week working in the hospice.' He didn't look at her, but gazed out over the ocean.

'I don't know about "disapproved",' said Roz. She put her hands in her pockets. 'It just seemed tokenistic.'

'Tokenistic?'

'Self-indulgent,' said Roz. 'You were only doing it to make yourself feel better.'

The Doctor's face took on a thoughtful expression. 'I suppose we all do that, from time to time.'

Silence for a bit. 'So, did they work you hard?' said Roz.

'No, it was very ordinary work – cleaning, mostly. A little cooking. A great deal of talking and a great deal more of listening. There was a young woman . . .'

'Chris said something about your wanting us to meet someone.'

'Quite young. I had hoped to say goodbye to her this morning.'

'I'm sorry,' said Roz. 'Did you get to know her well?'

'As well as two strangers can come to know one another in the space of a week. I told her rather more about the future than she probably should have known. She would have loved to have met you. Human beings from the future . . . it helped her, I think, to know that there was a future.' The lines around the Doctor's eyes stood out in the dim light.

You couldn't understand, could you? thought Roz. She was dying, a dying human being, and you couldn't understand her.

There was something about it that made her feel oddly proud.

As if reading her mind, the Doctor turned to her and said, 'Why does Benny want to find her father?'

Roz said, 'Good grief.'

The Doctor made an agitated movement with his hands. 'People growing up together, living together, yes, I can understand how that would create a bond, but this seems . . .'

'Arbitrary?'

'She hardly knows him,' said the Time Lord.

'If it was your father,' said Roz, 'what would you do?'

'On Gallifrey –'

An aproned Chris wandered out onto the verandah, completely missed the atmosphere, and gave them a cheery smile. 'I've decided to make tofu surprise,' he said.

'Oh yes,' Roz smiled back, despite herself. 'What's the surprise?'

'We're out of tofu,' said Chris.

3

On Youkali, a cold wind was blowing

It blew through the forest, making the leaves hiss like the surf. It found the camps at the edge of the trees, and snuffed out an ancient kerosene lamp, making an elderly xenobiologist curse and fumble for the matches.

It curled around the base of the staircase Benny had been excavating that morning. It blew across the clearing and stopped to ruffle the hair of a late-working trio of trainees, sending chills down their backs.

It tugged at the Doctor's hat, but couldn't lift it. He was standing at the base of the steps, leaning on his umbrella, reading the hieroglyphs. The wind bit through his silk shirt. He'd taken off the tweed jacket in the afternoon warmth. Now he shrugged it back on, not taking his eyes off the glyphs.

'One day,' he read out loud, 'she will find the person who was given her name. And then there will be no more dying.'

'Oh, you don't want to worry about her,' said a voice nearby. 'She's only a ghost.'

The Time Lord turned. An elderly woman was watching him. By her bearing, she had once been a soldier. 'She was an archaeologist. Or, properly, she was one of the students. She wandered off into the jungle about three years ago, and didn't come back. Now they say she roams the planet, looking for her classmates. I expect she gobbles up little first-year students who don't finish their reading lists.'

He doffed his hat, smiling. 'I'm the Doctor. And this is my

21

friend . . .' he looked around bewilderedly for a moment.

'Admiral Groenewegen,' said the woman, shaking his hand. 'And you're looking for Benny.' The Doctor nodded. 'Well, you're in entirely the wrong place! She's been waiting for you at her camp for nearly a whole day. I'd take her a present if I were you. Come on, I'll point you in the right direction.'

The Doctor found himself trailing obediently after the little woman. He put his hands in his pockets and smiled at himself.

Benny yawned, looked at her watch again, and said, 'Buggery bollocks.'

Jason didn't look up from his paperback. He was lying against the pile of boxes and bundles that his wife was sitting on. 'The message hasn't reached him, has it?'

'Possibly not,' said Benny. She blew out her cheeks in frustration. 'It's more likely that he's too busy defeating the Vermicious Knids to bother with me.' She looked at her chronometer again.

'A watched pot never boils,' said Jason.

Benny stuck out her tongue at him. He grabbed her ankle and pulled her off the boxes. She yelled, laughed and kissed him, pinning him to the grass. The paperback waved about in the air behind her as he pretended to struggle.

After an interval, someone coughed.

Benny looked up with a start. There was someone immensely tall and blond and embarrassed standing over them.

Benny let out a whoop, and jumped up, throwing her arms around the big man. Roz was standing behind her partner, eclipsed. Benny shook her hand awkwardly while Chris hugged her. 'I'm so glad to see you!' she said. 'Are you well? Where's you-know-who?'

'Your coordinates plus some wonky TARDIS widget or other landed us in the institute's garden,' said Roz, helping Jason to his feet. 'Well, in the fountain, actually. We decided to send out two search parties to find you.'

'Do you want something to drink?' said Jason. He rummaged in the luggage, pulled out some foil packs of Crimson Star beer.

'How'd he take it?' said Benny.

Chris was trying to tear the foil with his teeth. It took Roz a moment to puzzle out what Benny meant. 'The Doctor? I think he's worried about you.'

'*He's* worried!' Benny grinned weakly. 'This was the last thing I expected, Roz. I'd always had a sort of mad belief that I'd just stumble over Dad one day . . . but this is different. We'll be going back to the moment he originally disappeared. Or maybe the moment he died. The moment of truth, anyway.'

'You know – I don't think he *has* a father.'

Now it was Benny's turn to be puzzled. 'Oh, the Doctor. I'd picked up bits and pieces – that the Time Lords are all test-tube babies or something or other. I expect they're just too clever to manage it the old-fashioned, unskilled way.'

'We should talk!' interjected Jason. Benny hurled his paperback at him.

Roz shook her head. 'My parents were always very annoyed that I didn't want kids. To pass on the genes, you know.'

'You should have a couple with Chris,' joked Benny, 'and really give them a surprise.'

'Well,' said Roz, her grin vanishing, 'we can't hang about here all day.'

Benny bit her lip. 'Right,' she said. 'Er, why don't you lot stay here, and I'll go and see if I can spot the Doctor.'

'He headed for the dig,' said Roz. 'We might take some of your stuff to the TARDIS in the meantime. Off you go.'

Benny nodded, decided not to say anything, and went.

Only a few of Benny's and Jason's belongings were left now: just a big wooden chest with a flat top, a few chairs and a bag or two. The cold wind had become a steady icy breeze, barely stopped by the row of trees at the edge of the clearing.

The Doctor had deactivated the alarm field they'd left to guard the bits and pieces. He'd improvised a tablecloth from one of his cleaner handkerchiefs, and rummaged through the bags until he'd found a chipped ex-UNIT enamel mug and a mug with the message MY PARENTS WENT TO SKARO AND ALL I GOT WAS A LOUSY PAIR OF GENES.

Groenewegen had insisted on helping him pick out the champagne from a travelling merchant's wares. The Lacaillan, a blue humanoid with cropped white hair, had spent five minutes rummaging through the coins and notes from the Doctor's pockets until he'd found one he liked.

They clinked their mugs together as the sun began to set.

Benny took a long drink and sat down, swinging her feet up onto the wooden box. The Doctor copied her, watching the sunset as he took a careful mouthful of the wine. He was still into the silk shirts, she saw, but the burgundy-coloured waistcoat made a nice change. The tweed jacket made him look like an eccentric university tutor.

For a little while they just sat there, quietly, letting the night settle in.

' "Drink! for you know not whence you came, nor why," ' said Benny, at length. ' "Drink! for you know not why you go, nor where." '

The Doctor tilted his head to one side. 'The *Rubáiyát*,' he concluded.

'It's good to see you.'

The Time Lord raised his mug to her.

'Well, what do you think?'

'We have two options,' said the Time Lord. 'One is to watch the outcome of the battle from a nearby safe bit of space. The problem with that is that we might not learn much more than we already have from the hologram.'

'What's the other option?'

'We could materialize aboard your father's ship a few minutes before the disappearance.' He looked at her sternly. 'They might have been blown apart by a Dalek energy bolt.'

'I understand. But won't we, well, give them a bit of a surprise? Appearing on their ship out of nowhere?'

The Doctor reached into a pocket, pulled out a plastic sheet with blueprints stamped on it. 'The Fury-class ships were massive, all engine and weapons systems, with a tiny cone at the front where the crew of six sat.'

He traced his fingertips over the blueprint. 'There were access corridors running through the bulk of the ship, like tunnels in a warren. We could materialize the TARDIS in one of those, and take a quick look around.'

But Benny was shaking her head. 'Not us. Me. I can't ask anyone to risk themselves for this.'

'Asking isn't required,' said the Doctor, drumming his fingers on the blueprint. 'I'm coming with you.'

Benny took another swallow of the champagne. 'I'm not planning to try and save him,' she said quietly.

The Doctor looked up at her. 'The best-laid schemes of mice and Benny . . .' he said. He held up a hand before she could speak. 'I have a responsibility to history. We have this responsibility, Benny, each time we step out of the TARDIS.'

'I mean it,' she said.

'Of course you do.' The Doctor watched the bubbles rise in his champagne. 'We reassure ourselves that we'd give our lives to protect it all. But anyone can die. Living with the responsibility is much more difficult. How long before we're wondering what little exceptions we can make? Whether solving one problem, saving one life, would spoil some great eternal plan? From time to time, I need to reassure myself that I can still do it.'

'Do what?' said Benny.

'Let someone die.' He ran a finger around the rim of the mug.

'I understand,' said Benny.

The Doctor's eyes bit into her. 'Do you?'

She held up her thumb and forefinger in a mimed pinch. *Just a little*.

The Time Lord shook his head. 'What have I done?'

The Doctor had spent an hour rummaging through the TARDIS for baby things, and had come up with a magnificent Victorian wooden cradle, a food machine capable of producing nappies, and a Martian hatchling's spinning top. Out of his own pockets he'd produced a teddy bear and a chewed copy of *Little Miss Star*.

The cradle needed a few repairs. Benny handed the Doctor the hammer. He'd managed to avoid his own thumbs, for the most part. A handful of nails were sticking out of his mouth.

'It's very different,' she said. 'Living one day at a time. I'd nearly forgotten what it was like. Monday comes after Sunday, the seasons change in order . . . and you can make plans.'

'I make plans,' the Doctor mumbled.

'I mean plans that last a lifetime. Getting a degree. Finding somewhere to live. You know, the sort of things the rest of the human race spends their time on.'

The Doctor plucked the last of the nails from his mouth. 'I see . . .'

Probably not, thought Benny, but never mind. She sat back, looking around at her old room. It wasn't even dusty.

Something furry brushed up against her. 'Wolsey!' she said, delighted, gathering the tabby up into her arms. 'You fluffy creature. How are you?' Wolsey miaowed and gave her a cat kiss, nostrils flaring as he took in the alien scents she had accumulated.

'Meeting Admiral Groenewegen must have thrown quite a spanner into your plans,' said the Doctor.

Benny rubbed Wolsey between the ears. 'I suppose so.'

'I know how important finding your father is. How much it has defined your life,' said the Doctor. 'Or rather, I know how important it once was.'

'Hey?'

'I still carry the snapshot of your mind I took when we first met. You're . . . the only other person inside my head like that. From time to time I like to take the picture out, and look at it. You've changed, Benny.'

'Let me see,' she said. 'May I see?'

He put down the hammer, took her hand, brushed her fingertips across his temple. It took only a moment, but it was like phoning an old friend, someone you haven't seen for years but who you can talk to at once, as though the two of you had never been apart. It was like catching up with a younger sister.

'Oh,' said Benny, lowering her hand. 'Oh, you're right.'

'Are you sure you still want to go through with it?'

'Yes.' She rocked the cradle, experimentally. 'Doctor,' she said, 'why are we fixing this?'

He waved at her vaguely. 'We don't know how long you'll be staying.'

She laughed. 'It'll have to be a long time. We've been trying for most of Youkali's autumn.' More seriously, she said, 'Actually, that is one reason I need to find out about Dad.'

'Clearing the family name, yes.'

'Bugger Spacefleet and all that. When little Keith or Dorothy finally arrives, when they're old enough to ask about their grandfather, I want to be able to look them in the eye and tell them not to believe what anyone says. That Admiral Isaac Summerfield wasn't a coward, he was a good man.'

'We'll be materializing in a few minutes,' said the Doctor softly.

'Then we'd better get up to the console room,' said Benny, spilling Wolsey from her lap as she stood up.

'I'll be with you in a minute.' The Doctor fussed about with his toolkit, spilling a packet of screws across the floor.

Benny kissed him on the forehead, startling him. She smiled, and went out of the room.

He leant his head against the cradle, eyes closed, listening to her footsteps recede.

'But what if he wasn't?' he said softly.

'Now,' Benny said. 'The Doctor and I are going to go aboard the *Tisiphone*. We'll have at least four minutes before the ship blows up, or does whatever it does.'

She wore jeans and a denim jacket with big pockets – adventuring clothes. There were lines of tension around her mouth. She looked so businesslike that Jason didn't dare to hug her. It had taken almost an hour to persuade him to stay behind.

'We're just taking a quick look round,' said Benny gently. 'We won't stay for the whole show.'

'I'll be waiting for you,' said Jason, almost keeping the bitterness out of his voice.

Chris and Roz stood about, looking awkward. The Doctor said, 'We'll be materializing aboard the *Tisiphone* in thirty seconds.'

Benny nodded. She gave Jason a quick kiss. 'I'll talk to you in five minutes,' she said.

She couldn't help smiling as the old, familiar noise of the TARDIS materialization ground through the console room. The Doctor put his hand on the door control. 'Are you ready?' he said.

Benny gave him a quick nod. He tugged on the door control, and the big double doors swung open.

Benny stepped out onto the *Tisiphone*, and nearly walked right into her father.

4

From Here to Paternity

Aboard the *Tisiphone*, 2543

Stay calm.

The TARDIS had parked itself in a narrow corridor, an access tunnel curving through the inside of the big ship. Dark walls were covered in stencilled lettering. The floor shook. The air stank of burning electrics and smoke.

Benny steadied herself against the TARDIS, staring at her father.

He looked just like he did in the photo. Except for the battle fatigues. And the soot and the blood. And the blob of grease over one of his cheekbones. And the faintly puzzled expression.

He looked her up and down with those startling grey eyes, raised an eyebrow at her, and walked quickly away down the corridor.

Benny jumped as someone put their hand on her shoulder. She was light-headed, unable to call out after her father, unable to move. *Stay calm*, she told herself, *stay calm*.

'He just pretended we weren't here!' she whispered, blinking back tears in the smoky air. 'That's insane. Why?'

The Doctor shut the TARDIS door. 'We still have three and a half minutes to find out.'

They followed Isaac through the ship, which tossed and rolled like a sailing boat in a storm. There were tremendous clanging noises, missiles or energy bolts striking the outside hull. If there was a breach, they might be trapped in a sealed section as the air whooshed out into space.

He glanced back at them, once. Benny opened her mouth to call out to him through the noise, but he had already turned around, fighting his way along the corridor.

The ship rolled almost onto its side as they reached the entrance to the brilliantly lit cockpit. Seen through the front screen, the battle was a video game, all blips and lines of coloured light. Playing out the hologram Benny had watched.

'Reeve and Lawrie aren't answering their intercoms because they're dead,' her father was telling his bridge crew. 'Engine containment looks stable, but the lateral stabilizers are a mess.' He struggled back to the captain's chair.

'We're good for another ten minutes at the most,' said the African woman at what Benny guessed was the engineering panel. 'After that, the emergency stabilizer system's going to lose power, and – what the hell!'

She'd seen them. Benny almost took a step backwards into the shadows, but the Doctor's hand kept her in place.

'No,' said Isaac. The African was nearly out of her seat. 'The Daleks' hallucinatory weaponry. Don't let them distract you, lieutenant.'

The other members of the crew swung around, glanced at them, turned back to their controls. Only the pilot, a plump red-headed woman, was still staring. 'Admiral,' she said, 'how do you know they're hallucinations?'

'Because,' said Isaac, without looking around, 'that's my wife.'

The Doctor and Benny glanced at one another. 'Just pretend you're not really here,' said the Time Lord.

'Why not?' said Benny, more hysterically than she would have ideally liked. 'That's what they're doing.'

The pilot yelled as the controls caught fire. She snatched an extinguisher from a hidden panel.

'Options,' shouted Isaac.

'We can make another attack run,' said the lieutenant. 'But it'll leave us helpless. We can pull out of the battle – we might be able to limp back home.'

'Right,' said Isaac. 'I have a better idea.'

The Doctor raised his head suddenly, frowning, as though listening to something.

'The Daleks will expect us to retreat. So we'll give them a surprise.' He was moving his hands over the controls, inputting a course. 'What do you think, helm?'

The redhead grinned, fanning away the smoke from her controls. 'Worth a shot, sir.'

The ship lurched once more as they moved onto their new course. And suddenly Benny saw what it was that had been outside the picture.

There was a fat purple moon behind them, its surface flowering with red mushroom clouds. The Daleks had dropped dozens of primitive nuclear weapons onto it – one of their favourite brute-force tactics. How many people had they killed?

The radiation would help to mask the *Tisiphone* as she shot around the back of the small planet, used its gravity to increase her speed, and attacked the Dalek ships from behind.

He hadn't been running away.

He *hadn't* been running *away*!

Benny whooped. The Doctor turned to say something, but suddenly the ship rolled madly, throwing them both to the ceiling.

Benny tumbled down the wall and hit the floor with a thump that knocked the breath out of her. She felt the Time Lord grab her, pull her upright. 'That's four minutes!' he yelled, over the strained roaring of the engines. 'We've got to go!'

Benny mutely pointed to the front screen.

There was a large yacht sailing past one of the Dalek ships.

'I think you're right about those hallucinations, sir!' shouted the pilot.

'We have to go!' shouted the Doctor. He caught Benny's arm and pulled her along behind him, winding back down the access tunnel.

She nearly cannoned into him when he stopped suddenly, a hatch slamming shut ahead of them, sealing off a breach.

Instantly he was pulling her down another corridor, stumbling through the smoke and flame, homing in on the TARDIS by instinct. He all but threw her inside.

Her ears rang in the sudden quietness. 'I would have gone!' she coughed. *STAY CALM*! 'I would have gone anyway!'

The Doctor didn't have time to answer her, hands darting over the console. Jason put his arms around her, but she shrugged him off as they dematerialized. 'What happened next?' she yelled at the Time Lord. 'What happened?'

He nodded at the viewscreen.

They were in space, watching the battle as though it was on television.

The *Tisiphone* emerged from behind the moon, cannons blazing. A Dalek ship burst like an opening flower. The *Tisiphone* flew through expanding wreckage.

A massive rip appeared in the blackness, right in front of the *Tisiphone*, venting butterfly colours.

They didn't even have a chance to turn before it gulped them down and vanished.

Benny found she didn't have the energy to get up a good yell. 'What?' she said, faintly.

'The Ants' tunnels?' muttered the Doctor. 'A Dalek time corridor?' The readouts flashed in his eyes. 'Neither.'

'Their hyperspace drive?' asked Chris. 'It might have misfired or something.'

'No, look at the energy patterns.' The Doctor glanced up at the viewscreen. A smudge of colour still hung in space. 'Whatever it is, it's still there.'

Benny grabbed his arm. 'Can we tell where they went? Can we follow it?'

The Doctor turned to her, took her hands. 'We can try,' he said. 'But they may not have gone anywhere. That wormhole could terminate in a black hole, or the heart of a sun, or nowhere at all.' He squeezed her hands, gently, as though he was frightened of breaking them. 'We'll be protected in the TARDIS. Do you want to know?'

Benny nodded fiercely.

'All right then,' said the Doctor. 'We can try to follow the ship's transponder signal through the wormhole.' He closed the viewscreen. 'Hold on, everyone.'

5

Little Caldwell appreciates careful drivers

And they landed in December, outside a post office.

6

Dad on arrival

Little Caldwell, Berkshire, 10 December 1983

Joel woke up an hour before his alarm was set to go off.

He rolled out of bed, knocked a pile of comics off his clock radio, and switched it on. Static.

Joel closed his eyes, breathing hard. This was stupid.

He pushed his thumbnail into the grooves of the tuning dial and moved it until the noise turned into the strains of 'Safety Dance'.

He sat back on the bed, breathing out a cloud of white mist, letting his thumping heart slow back down. Civilization as he knew it was still there, or at least Radio One.

Joel reached under the bed and fished out a packet of cigarettes. His hands shook a little as he lit up the first smoke of the day.

It hadn't been the nightmare that had woken him up. Some big noise, outside. He found his glasses, wandered over to the window and looked down into the street.

'Holy priceless collection of Etruscan snoods, Batman!'

He nearly burned his nose off trying to pull the T-shirt over his head while holding the communicator up to his ear. 'Tony!' he yelped, snatching the cigarette out of his mouth. 'Yeah, it's me. I *know* it's seven in the morning. Go take a look at what's standing outside the post office.'

He dragged on his jeans and went to the window.

The police box was sitting on the grass verge at an angle,

34

the door facing towards the street. It was a dim, blue shape in the winter mist. The first few drops of morning rain spattered on Joel's window.

Tony's voice buzzed in his ear. 'Well, it wasn't there last night,' said Joel. 'I'm gonna go wake up the Admiral. You and Ms R had better get up here.' He snapped off the communicator and stuffed it into his back pocket.

The Doctor insisted that the others stay inside the TARDIS. After the bumpy ride through the wormhole, no one was willing to argue with him. Benny, however, was already outside.

'This could be a trap,' he said. 'It might be some sort of virtual reality, or the Land of Fiction. It might be a cleverly constructed replica of a sleepy, wet English village.'

Benny stood in the rain and looked up and down the main street – actually, the only street. There were a handful of houses, a café, a post office which sold groceries (or a grocery which sold stamps).

'It might be,' she said. 'But it's not.'

The Doctor looked at the question-mark handle of his umbrella. He flipped it over and opened it. He gathered Benny up, her freshly cut fringe already plastered to her forehead. 'I think we should explore cautiously.'

'I say we explore a couple of butter croissants and a cuppa,' said Benny.

'I'll tell you what,' grinned the Doctor, as they walked down the street. 'Why don't we go to the tavern and listen for rumours?'

'Do they have butter croissants in taverns?' said Benny.

She took a deep breath. Late-twentieth-century air, freshly washed. The sudden plunge back into normality was helping her brain settle back into place. 'You didn't bring me here just to calm me down,' she said suspiciously.

'Believe it or not, this is the source of the transponder signal.'

'The *Tisiphone*,' said Benny, 'is conspicuous by its absence. Unless it's in the lost property at the post office.'

'The temporal tangent may have been slightly off,' muttered the Doctor. He stopped outside the café, glancing around in irritation, as though he felt he was being watched.

THE PYRAMID, said a hand-painted sign over the door. FOOD FOR MIND AND BODY. 'It's a bookshop upstairs,' observed Benny.

'And a coffee shop downstairs,' said the Doctor. 'Shall we investigate?'

'Er, here they come,' said Tony.

Joel's voice said, 'Okay, we're staying where we are.'

'What do I do if they –'

'The Admiral will come downstairs in a minute. Just take it easy!'

'Right. Sorry.' Tony flipped the communicator shut and tucked it into his back pocket. He smoothed down his apron as the Doctor and Benny came in from the rain.

The place was saturated with the smell of coffee, that roasting – acetone – steam smell. It was wood and leather and mirrors, old and worn and comfortable. A corkboard was covered in fliers. A narrow staircase lead upwards to the bookshop.

Behind the counter, a bearded man was washing up coffee pots in hot, soapy water, steam rising around him. 'Good morning,' he said, in a soft voice. 'Sorry, I've just got to finish these – I'll be with you in a moment.'

There were two or three dozen types of coffee listed on the blackboard. Everything from cappuccino to espresso granita to chocolate-covered coffee beans. A separate menu covered pastries and sandwiches.

Benny sat down at one of the little tables, suddenly feeling wobbly. It had been four hours since she'd first entered the TARDIS, less than an hour since she'd been breathing smoke and badly recycled air aboard the *Tisiphone*.

Banged about, boggled and nearly blown up. It was as though she'd never been away.

The Doctor sat down opposite her. She could tell by the way he was studiously ignoring her that he was very concerned.

He pulled a small tracking thingummy from his pocket, pretended to fuss with it. It obstinately refused to beep. 'That transponder is here somewhere,' he said.

36

He pulled a map out of his pocket, struggled with it, flattened it out on the table. 'We're quite close to a military base,' he said, tapping the map with his fingers.

'Hey, maybe they're Hanger Eighteen-ing the ship. You said there might be some temporal deflection. How much?'

'It's difficult to – Benny, look at me.'

She frowned. 'I am looking at you.'

'All right,' he said. 'When I say "now", I want you to look to your left, and then straight back at me. Do you understand?'

'What is it?' she hissed, paralysed.

'Now,' said the Doctor.

Benny looked. Her father was standing behind the counter, talking to the bearded man.

'Grief,' she said.

'Take another look,' said the Doctor.

Benny did. He hadn't seen her yet. He was older. She couldn't tell how much. Fifteen years? Twenty-five?

They were late.

'How do we know he isn't a robot replica or a Sloathe or something?' she whispered. 'What do we do?'

'We have a *caffé latte* and two buttered croissants each,' said the Doctor, 'as insurance against the shock.'

'Right,' said Benny faintly. She looked into the mirror next to her.

He'd seen her – he was staring right at her. She couldn't help it. She turned to look. Their eyes met.

'Grief,' said Isaac.

In the TARDIS, Roz looked at her watch for the third time.

'How much longer do you think we should give them?' said Jason.

'The Doctor knows what he's doing,' said Chris.

Jason drummed his fingers on the console, trying to avoid any obvious self-destruct switches. 'I wish we knew what he was up to.'

'The eternal lament,' said Roz. 'Let's hope the natives are friendly.'

* * *

'Do you think there are any more of them?'

Joel peeked over the top of the hedge. It was bloody freezing. Thank God, he thought, for thermal socks. 'Probably not,' he told the communicator. 'He usually travels with one passenger. Almost always human and female.'

His boots squelched in the soggy grass as he tried to get a better view of the police box. It sat there, dark and quiet, like a bogeyman in the mist. Or like a badly photocopied picture in a UFO 'zine.

'Can you see what's going on in the shop?' Ms Randrianasolo wanted to know. 'Do you want me to come out there?'

'No and no,' said Joel. 'You'd better stay next to the phone. The Admiral will call us in his own good time.'

He tugged at the hood of his anorak, wondering if he could have a smoke without blowing his cover. 'Let's hope they're friendly,' he muttered.

Isaac stepped out from behind the counter. He was wearing a pair of faded jeans and a black cardigan. His face was neutral, everything held back.

An hour ago he'd been uniformed and twenty years younger.

Benny stood up, cautiously, aware of the Doctor's eyes.

Her father came closer, until he was within a few feet of her. Still far enough away to dodge back from an attack, she thought. He studied her face carefully. 'You're not Claire.'

'No,' she said, the lump in her throat rising. 'I'm Bernice.'

His mouth opened, a little. But he nodded.

She started to cry. She reached out and wrapped her arms around him. He stood there, awkwardly, while she sobbed, 'It's me, Daddy. It's me. It's Bernice.'

At last he untangled himself, looked at her. 'How old are you?'

'I'm . . . I'm about thirty-five.' She looked at the Doctor for confirmation, but he had nothing to say, quietly watching.

Isaac looked from her to the Doctor and back. 'How did you find me?'

Benny rubbed at her eyes. 'I've been looking for you for years. That is, I . . . when did you get here?'

'This is our twentieth anniversary,' he said. 'We arrived just in time for Kennedy's assassination.'

'The Doctor said there'd been a temporal tangent . . . There's so much to tell you, there's so much . . . My husband's in the TARDIS!'

'Your husband.'

The Doctor was sliding his legs out from beneath the table. 'Shall I just pop back and collect everyone?' he murmured.

She nodded, thought about it, nodded again. 'Tell Jason to come and meet his father-in-law.'

The Doctor went through the front door, leaving them alone.

Isaac sat down at one of the tables, looking up at his grown daughter.

'Um,' she said.

'Yes?'

'You're taking all this rather well. Your long-lost daughter travels through time . . .'

'Oh.' He smiled for the first time, a small smile, the tip of the iceberg. 'You're our third set of time travellers this year.'

The Doctor walked silently to the corner of the building.

'That's right,' the cook was saying. 'One of them says she's the Admiral's daughter! Well, I don't know . . . he seems to believe her. No, come on, how would *they* know about her? Well, I suppose . . . oh dear.'

The Doctor smiled up at the man and took the communicator away from him. 'I'm sorry,' he said into it. 'The mobile phone you have called has yet to be invented. Please call back.'

He closed up the communicator and handed it to the bearded man, who was blinking down at him. 'Were you one of Isaac's crew?'

The man shook his head. 'You really are *him*, aren't you?'

'Yes,' said the Doctor.

'Oh, crumbs.'

7

Taking stock

Woodworth slammed the empty boot shut.

She got into the car, reached into the glovebox and pulled the Ordnance Survey map of Newbury out from underneath the Berretta. She spread the map out on the steering wheel, double-checking the route. People had a habit of 'missing' Little Caldwell. She didn't want to be one of them.

She was forty-something, pepper-haired and green-eyed, a chunky shape inside her leather jacket. She folded the map and tucked it into the bag of equipment perched on the seat beside her.

'I don't know where to start,' said Benny.

Isaac pushed the plunger down on the cafetière. 'In your own time.'

'I wish I could be as calm as you,' she said, as they sat down at the coffee shop's front booth.

'I haven't had a lifetime to build up to this,' said her father. He poured the coffee. He raised an eyebrow at her as she heaped sugar into her cup.

'It's bitter,' she said.

'It's supposed to be bitter. So. Begin at the beginning.'

'Do you remember Sarah Groenewegen?'

'Remember her?' he said. 'I still owe her five credits.'

'She had the flight recorder from her ship.' Benny took a deep breath. The Doctor was going to take some explaining. 'Let me gloss over the details right now, but we travelled in time to your last battle, and saw the *Tisiphone* fall into the wormhole. Then we followed you here.'

'But you missed,' said Isaac. 'We arrived twenty years ago.' She couldn't put her finger on his accent. Irish? 'How did you meet the Doctor?'

Benny nearly choked on her coffee. 'You know who he is?'

'Are you one of his travelling companions?'

'I used to be. Dad –' They both started. 'Exactly what have you been up to for the last two decades?'

'You're saying you don't know?' Isaac put down his coffee. 'I'm sorry, but I find that a bit difficult to believe.'

'What are you talking about?'

His grey eyes probed her face. 'We've been waiting for the Doctor to pay us a house call for years. When he finally arrives, he just happens to have my daughter with him.'

Benny was shaking her head. 'You don't understand. None of this was planned. I just happened to run into Groenewegen.'

'Do you believe that?' he said.

'Of course.' My God, thought Benny, now I'm not sure. Is the Doctor up to something? Or have we stumbled into a trap? '*Why* have you been waiting for him?'

He poured himself a second cup of coffee.

After a bit, Benny said, 'You said we were the third lot of time travellers this year.'

'Yeh. It's been a big year for time travellers. The first one had escaped from a laboratory of enslaved physicists in the twenty-fourth century. We got her back to her own time so she could free the others. The second one we couldn't send home, so we helped him to find a place in the present.'

'You help time travellers?'

Isaac turned his cup around in his hands. 'And aliens.'

'You help time travellers and aliens?'

'Everyone needs a hobby.' He drained the cup.

The sky was lightening and the mist was beginning to clear. Tony reached up and put a hand on the TARDIS. Its paint was rough and warm under his palm, tingling with life.

After a moment he stepped back, feeling the weight of the Doctor's eyes on him. 'Sorry,' he said.

The Doctor took a key from inside his hat and unlocked the door. Tony trailed after him into the console room. It wasn't much like the descriptions he'd heard, but then those were probably speculation.

There were three humans inside. 'Chris, Roz, Jason,' said the Doctor, 'this is Tony.'

He looked at the trio. Chris was a tall blond in a T-shirt, jeans and black overcoat, Roz a short black woman in a maroon pullover, black trousers and riding boots.

Jason's clothes were anachronistic, especially the synthetic jacket with orange stripes. He was hovering anxiously. 'What's the deal?'

'Benny's father is alive and well and running a small coffee shop,' said the Doctor, rummaging in his toolkit. 'Everything seems to be what it seems to be, with one exception.' He pulled out a stubby, copper-coloured device.

The Doctor turned and tapped Tony on the nose with the metal rod. The holographic disguise burst like a bubble, revealing a short, pale-skinned alien with an oversized head and huge, slanted black eyes.

'Your hologram generator's batteries need a recharge,' said the Doctor, replacing the tool in his kit.

The alien looked down at himself, then up at the three humans staring at him from across the console.

'Sorry,' he said.

The Doctor tapped at the scanner controls. 'There are eight other alien life forms in Little Caldwell.'

'You've left her out there, then?' said Jason.

The Doctor looked at the Tzun. 'Do you want to tell me all about it?'

Benny turned in her seat as the bells tied to the door jingled. But it wasn't the Doctor, it was a man in his late teens or early twenties, with red hair and round glasses. 'Good morning, Joel,' said her father.

Joel looked between the two of them. 'Hi.'

'This is Bernice,' said Isaac. 'She's my daughter.'

'So I hear.' Joel took off his thick coat. He was thin, wearing a green *King Thunder* T-shirt and jeans. His accent was – American? Canadian? 'I just wanted to see if everything was okay in here.'

'Good. You can heat up three croissants for us.' The corner of Joel's mouth tugged up, and he went behind the counter. 'I've just been telling Bernice about the railroad.'

'Time travellers and aliens,' said Benny.

'Heck,' said Joel, as he took the croissants out of the display, 'we get all kinds. ETs, mutants, strays, greys, LGMs, BEMs, UNIT deserters, Striebs, dweebs, Stepford Wives, Midwich Cuckoos, missing persons, faraway people, peepers, buzzers, hoppers, hitchers, Leapers, Sliders . . .'

'We have contacts all over the world,' said Isaac. 'We find them, bring them here, and make sure they get home. Damage control. It's safer for them and for Earth if they quietly go home.'

'That's why you've been expecting the Doctor.'

'We've been tidying up his messes for twenty years,' said Isaac. 'I'm surprised he hasn't got around to us before now.'

Woodworth was starting to wonder whether she hadn't 'missed' Little Caldwell after all. She'd been driving in circles around Newbury for half an hour. She pulled over. The radio was murmuring something about cruise missiles.

It wasn't anything supernatural, she'd just missed the turnoff, twice. She folded up the map and shoved it back in the glovebox.

After a moment, she pulled out the gun and put it in her bag, pushing it to the bottom under the jars and bags and books.

'Breathing' started on the car radio as she pulled out onto the road. 'Third time lucky,' she muttered.

Benny closed her eyes for a moment, breathing the breakfast smells. This ought to be a barren plain on some far-flung moon, or an alien graveyard with human names scattered amongst the headstones, or the shattered shell of the *Tisiphone* suspended in space.

She opened her eyes. Tony, his hologram restored, was

cooking bacon and eggs behind the counter. Chris and Roz were working their way through a huge plate of doughnuts. At the next table, Jason was describing his adventures to a rapt (and rather too-young-to-hear-them) Joel. And at the next, a tall black woman and a plump forty-ish woman – Ms Randrianasolo and Jacqui – were listening in, amused.

Benny's heart was thumping, and it wasn't the macchiato. Jason had shaken Isaac's hand, formal as a business rival. The Doctor was even worse. He was sitting next to her, and he and the Admiral were eyeing each other like a pair of cats disputing territory.

The Doctor spread strawberry jam on a croissant, deliberately. 'How large is your crew?'

'The crew proper comprises myself, Ms Randrianasolo, Joel, Tony and Albinex,' said Isaac. 'Only Ms Randrianasolo and myself are members of the original *Tisiphone* crew.'

'What happened to the others?'

'One married, one disappeared, one died.'

'Do you know what caused the wormhole? Or why you landed here, of all places?'

Isaac shook his head. 'I've been wondering that since nineteen sixty-three.'

The Doctor drummed his fingers on the table. Benny imagined that the pattern matched the rhythm of his inner thoughts, rapid and staccato. 'Just how many fugitives have you helped?'

Isaac met his eyes. 'Hundreds.'

'So, many of them must have been hostile,' said the Doctor. 'Dangerous.'

'Most of them are frightened and miserable and just want to get home,' said her father. 'The ones who don't want our help are UNIT's problem, or sometimes the CIA. A few times we've tipped them off ourselves. There was a Lalandian safari killing people in Durham in nineteen seventy-six –'

'Grief,' said Benny. 'I was in England in nineteen seventy-six. And in nineteen sixty-eight. If I'd known I could have just phoned you.'

'They must offer you a great deal,' said the Doctor. 'Technology, funds, a lift home . . .'

44

'We're not interested,' said Isaac. 'When I joined Space-fleet, I took an oath to keep Earth and all its territories safe, and that's just what I'm doing.'

The Doctor stirred his tea. 'I've often wondered what happens to all the leftovers,' he said.

'There are rather a lot of them,' said Isaac dryly. 'UNIT's policy has always been blow it up or cover it up.'

'To my eternal frustration. This is very good tea,' he said.

'We'll have to wean you off that stuff,' said Isaac. 'It's not a patch on my espresso.'

Tony pushed open the gate to one of the little cluster of cottages. 'We only have a few guests with us at the moment,' he said. 'So you can have this one all to yourself. I hope it's okay.'

'It looks nice,' said Chris.

Tony unlocked the front door and led them into the lounge. 'I've switched the electricity back on, and there should be towels and things. Um, is there anything else you need to know?'

'About a hundred things,' said Roz.

'Oh,' said Tony.

'How have you managed to avoid detection for so long? We had a look around the place. There aren't any monitors and there aren't any weapons.'

'That's right. This village is so small and uninteresting that a lot of people drive right through without noticing it. We don't want any alien technology about the place.'

'But you have a hologram generator,' said Chris.

'Well, of course,' said Tony. 'I'm supposed to be *inconspicuous*.'

'Blasters?' asked Roz.

Isaac flicked the big red switch on the back of the PC. It ground to life, chewing on the 5¼-inch diskette in drive A. 'I'm very glad,' he said, 'that we only have to do this once a month.'

Benny was walking through the small bookshop, peering at the crammed shelves. Handwritten cardboard signs marked the different subjects: WESTERN MYSTICISM, ZEN,

45

CLOSE ENCOUNTERS, TAROT. At the far end, big front windows gave a clear view of Little Caldwell. It must be a speck on the map. 'Do you get a lot of customers?'

'Yeh,' said Isaac. 'Enough. Paranormalists come here from all over the country.'

'But wouldn't that be the last thing you'd want?' said Benny, taking a copy of *Dreaming the Dark* off the shelf.

'Know thine enemy,' said Isaac. 'Or better still, recruit them. A lot of our contacts are UFO spotters.'

'What happened to the *Tisiphone*?' She put the book back under WOMEN'S SPIRITUALITY.

'We appeared halfway between Earth and Mars, and limped as close to Earth as we dared.' He was tapping keys, bringing up the inventory program. 'Then we sent the ship on a course for the sun and crammed ourselves into an escape pod.'

'Where did you land?'

'In the Welsh countryside. We were lucky to come down over land. Hogan got married nine years ago. He's living in Upper Norwood. Beilby died of the common cold. And no one knows what happened to Langford.'

'I'm sorry.'

'That was all a very long time ago.' The PC beeped. 'This thing is ready at last. You know, the one time M'Kabel – that's Tony's real name – pulled the cover off this thing, he looked inside and just started to laugh.'

'I didn't know Tzun laughed.'

'Neither did I.'

'Grief!' said Benny, picking up a different book. '*The Shoreditch Incident*, by H.O. Macbeth.'

'Autographed,' said Isaac.

'You've *met* him?'

Isaac nodded at her across the room. 'We had dinner together last year. Don't tell me you were at Shoreditch?'

'Before my time.' Benny flipped through the pages, her eyebrows skittering up her forehead. 'I wonder how many of these are about the Doctor.'

'Dozens of refugees have landed on our doorstep because of him.'

Benny frowned. 'He's saved this world a hundred times.'

'Of course,' said Isaac. 'And I've met hundreds of the survivors. You should meet Adam Colby – he's still got the nightmares, seven years later.'

She crossed the floor, put her hands on his. 'You have to get to know him,' she said. 'He's not at all like you think he is. You know, he stood in for you at my wedding?'

Isaac looked down at her hands. 'So much of what we do has revolved around him for such a long time, and we know so little about him.' He looked back up at her. 'We dance around in a ring and suppose –'

'But the secret sits in the middle and knows,' finished Benny.

They looked at one another in astonishment.

'I used to say that when you were a child. When you asked awkward questions,' said Isaac.

He put a hand on top of hers.

'No blasters,' said Joel. 'We don't have any weapons at all. And they're not allowed inside the perimeter of the village.'

'That's not going to make the star cops happy,' said Jason. He was looking out through the door. 'There'd better be more than one bedroom in those houses.'

'Well, of course there is,' said Joel, wiping down the counter. 'Which year did you say you were from?'

Jason hesitated. 'This one,' he said.

'You're from now?'

'Yeah, but I spent a lot of time out in space. Long story. Me and Benny have been living in the twenty-sixth century.' He tested a mouthful of forgotten cappuccino. It was cold. 'You know, I'd sort of prepared myself not to say anything futuristic that might give us away.'

'Yeah,' said Joel. He threw the damp cloth into the sink with a flick of his wrist.

'But nothing about us surprises you at all.'

'It's like that Foglio 'toon,' said Joel, as Jason sat down again. 'Where all the people are running screaming from the alien, but the fan is saying, "Long trip?" '

'I'll take your word for it,' said Jason. 'Is everybody in

Little Caldwell as relaxed as you are?'

'It's just us, the crew and the guests. Except for Mr Sullivan in the post office. He's been here twenty years and he still hasn't noticed anything weird. We try not to keep lots of aliens around. London's the best place for them, or sometimes New York.'

'What about Tony?'

'Oh, he's been part of the crew almost from the start. He was a kind of backwards case – he deserted from the Tzun when they were trying to invade in the fifties. He's our computer expert. He did stuff to my Commodore 64 that'll be advanced even in ten years' time.'

'And what about you?'

'Oh . . . I'm a latecomer,' said Joel, fumbling with a packet of cigarettes. 'They needed a fan real bad. What people think about aliens mostly comes from films and TV. Thank God for *ET* and *CE3K*.'

'Why no guns?' said Jason.

'Because that way you know anyone with a gun is a bad guy. 'Scuse me, I'm just going outside for a minute. This must be about the first non-smoking restaurant in the world.'

Jason pushed the undrinkable coffee away and gloomily looked at the newspaper. 'Face it, Kane,' he told himself. 'She's going to be attached to daddy dearest like a hyperleech. Until the novelty wears off.'

'What about the professionals?' Chris was saying. 'If you get paranormalists, do you get them too?'

'Well, we've had more than one run-in with C19.'

'And that would be?'

'Well,' said Tony, 'not to, um, sharpen too fine a point on it, they would dissect me faster than you could say "von Däniken". You learn to tell friend from enemy.'

'What about us?' insisted Roz.

Tony looked between them. 'My hologram makes you a bit nervous,' he ventured.

'Oh?' said Roz. 'And why would it make me nervous?'

'Well,' said the Tzun, 'it makes you wonder who else around the place is in disguise.'

Roz grimaced. Chris said, 'How many, er, guests do you have at the moment?'

'Six. About once every two years we have to evacuate the extraterrestrials. That's my job,' said Tony proudly. 'Sometimes it's the secret service, but usually it's the military. Last year UNIT cordoned us off for twenty-four hours, as part of a "training exercise". There were unsuspecting soldiers tramping around all over the place. We sold a lot of coffee that day, I can tell you!'

'So what did you do?' said Chris.

'In the end the Americans asked them to leave.'

'And that's another thing,' said Roz. 'If I was going to choose a place to harbour alien refugees, my first choice wouldn't be next door to the air force.'

'It actually draws attention away from us,' said Tony. 'It's all in the misdirection, you see. Um, I'd better get back to the Pyramid. Just phone us up if you need anything.' He headed for the door, looking relieved. 'I hope you two will be comfy together!'

Roz gave Chris a sideways look. The boy's ears were turning red. 'Thanks a bundle,' she said.

Woodworth pulled up at the coffee shop and shut off the engine. She smiled at the sign that said THE PYRAMID, LITTLE CALDWELL. The village was real. She was here.

She got out of the car and locked it, looking up and down the street. It was barely a village, more a sort of hamlet, a handful of buildings spread out along the road; at the west end, a petrol station, to the east, a few cottages and a church. No wonder people missed it.

There was a boy leaning against the wall outside the café, smoking a cigarette. She went inside, pulling off her scarf and gloves, and the lad followed her in.

'Hi,' he said, ducking behind the counter. 'What can I get you?'

She peered at the menu. 'Just a coffee.'

'What kind?'

'No milk or sugar,' she told him. There was nothing supernatural about this place. Even the oddly dressed man struggling with *The Times* crossword was probably merely in fashion.

Woodworth pulled off her glasses and rubbed her ageing eyes. She peered at her watch. Would the village still be here if she drove away and tried to find it again? 'Will the bookshop be open tomorrow?'

'Yes, ma'am,' said the boy. He sounded American – the son of someone from the airbase? 'It's open Monday to Saturday, but not on Sundays.'

'Right then, make that coffee to go. I'll be back tomorrow.'

'No problemo.' The boy poured the steaming stuff into a polystyrene cup. She pushed a handful of change over the counter at him. 'Have a nice day,' he said.

Woodworth grimaced as she stepped out into the cold again. 'It doesn't seem likely,' she muttered.

The Doctor had spent a relaxing half-hour in the graveyard next to the boarded-up church, looking for just the right stick. The place was cozy, with a smattering of naked trees between the headstones. He chatted for a while with old Tom the grocer, who popped over every day to do a bit of unofficial caretaking.

When Benny found him he was dozing with his back to a tilted headstone, holding a stick shaped like a large wishbone. The mist had cleared, but it was still bitterly cold. He was wearing a duffle coat as a gesture towards winter clothing.

He pushed his hat back and smiled up at her. 'I thought you were asleep,' she said, pushing her hands into the pockets of her coat. 'I'm just taking a break. It's so peaceful here.'

'Well,' said the Doctor, 'it gives the impression of peace, and sometimes that's enough.' He stood up, and the stick twitched in his hand. 'How are you and Isaac getting along?'

'He's nothing like me,' she said. 'He's distant. Terribly serious. Military, I suppose. But . . .' She gestured around. 'I wish Mum could have seen this.'

The Doctor made a face. 'All right, I admit it. I'm impressed. If your father's operation didn't exist, it would be necessary to invent it.'

The tension went out of her shoulders. 'He said they'd been waiting for you. I think he expected you to . . .'

'Yes?'

'To disapprove. To shut them down. Doctor?'

He'd been looking down at the quivering stick. Now his eyes came back to her face, searching. Her mouth went dry.

'Doctor, you *didn't* know about Little Caldwell, did you?'

He replaced the piercing gaze with a happy grin. 'Not at all. But I'm delighted to find myself here.' He looked around at the graveyard. 'We all have to find ourselves somewhere. What do you think my epitaph ought to be?' Benny frowned. 'How about, "Don't just stand there, do something!"?'

'I know, " 'Pull the trigger, end my life,' was a figurative expression." '

'It'll probably end up being "Behind you!" ' He shook his head. 'I think I'd like it to be "He really did the best he could." You can't ask for much more than that, really.'

'There was something else,' said Benny. The Doctor moved his dowsing rod around in a slow arc. 'Isaac mentioned that one of his crew had died of a cold. The rest of them have been very ill at times, from minor bugs that wouldn't bother someone from the twentieth century. They don't have any immunity.' The Doctor turned slowly, holding the stick loosely in both hands. 'And it occurred to me that I haven't had a cold since the day I got into the TARDIS.'

'No . . .'

'And then there was something Ace said once, about nanotechnology, and . . .' she ground to an embarrassed halt.

The Doctor stopped in place, the stick quivering in his hand. 'This is leading somewhere,' he said, 'but I'm not quite sure where.'

'Doctor, will the nanites you injected into my system stop me from becoming pregnant?'

'Oh,' said the Doctor. 'No. They don't even notice the human genome, which means they won't protect you from cancer or autoimmune disorders, either.'

'It's just that I rather fancy giving Isaac some grand-children.' Benny pushed her hands into her jacket pockets. 'And Jason and I have been trying for so long . . . and I keep

51

wondering which bit of alien radiation or virus or whatever has got to one of us. Or both of us.'

The Doctor let the stick drop down. 'Oh, Benny. I'm so sorry. Come back to the TARDIS, we can try a few tests.'

'We thought about adopting, but between Jason's credentials and mine – i.e. none whatsoever – I'd hate it if I couldn't have kids at all. Ever. Not to even have the choice . . .'

She bit her lip as he looked down at the ground, face suddenly full of ancient sadness. She wanted to hug him. Instead she pretended to study a standing stone, an incongruous slab of grey rock in the graveyard's corner. 'I'm really grateful,' she whispered. 'You gave me my dad back.'

'We can stay as long as you like. As long as you need to get to know one another.' The stick jumped in his hand again. 'And there are a few things I want to take a look at for myself.'

'What are you up to?' she said, watching the stick move.

'My cunning plan,' he said, 'is to read the paper and drink as much tea as I can safely contain. I feel like putting my feet up for a while, and letting my subconscious churn over the question of human psi powers for a while, instead of chasing hints and shadows about . . . This is Isaac's show. We'll see how long it lasts.' He glanced around at the stones. 'I wonder what Joan's is.'

It took Benny a moment to realize what he meant. 'Oh no,' she said. 'Don't you start getting all morose. That's Roz's job.'

They grinned at each other.

Back in the café, there was a strong, acid smell of dishwasher detergent mingled with the smells of coffee and grilling. Joel looked at Benny over the counter and waved a washing-up-gloved hand.

Jason was sitting by himself at a table, trying not to look grumpy. She put an arm around his shoulders and kissed him on the top of the head. 'I haven't forgotten you,' she said.

'What's to forget?' muttered Jason, as she slid into the seat beside him. He pushed the paper away. 'Isn't this exciting?

Finding your long-lost father after all these years.'

Benny drummed her fingers on the table. 'It's not like I thought it would be,' she said. 'I mean, there was the initial complete and total blubbing and freaking out session. For me, at least.' She vaguely gestured around. 'I wasn't expecting any of this.'

Jason said, 'Isaac doesn't need rescuing.'

'My God,' she said, 'that's exactly it. He's all right. He doesn't need to be saved.'

They just sat there for a few minutes, Benny's head resting on his shoulder.

'You're so tense,' she murmured. 'Look, I just want you to know that I'm not going to totally ignore you while we're here.'

'It's not that,' said Jason. 'I hate being back here.'

'Back where?'

'Back in the English countryside in the eighties,' he said. 'I was born this year, you know.'

'My God, Jason,' she said. 'I hadn't thought about it.'

'I could go and find my dad too,' he said. 'Get on a train.'

She held onto his arm. 'Don't.'

'Nah,' said Jason. 'It's history.' He shrugged. 'He's upstairs. Go on.' He looked at her with sad eyes. 'Go on and get to know your father.'

The Doctor had followed his dowsing rod for an hour, tracing a wide circle around Little Caldwell. He stepped carefully around fairy rings growing in the woods. He walked through a field of wheat, fully grown in the winter greyness, filled with the traces of crop circles. He made soothing noises to a pair of cows until they let him take a look at their legs. The small incisions weren't serious.

At last he came to an ancient, shattered cottage, huddled in the very corner of a field, just a cluster of walls like rotting teeth. A bitter wind was whipping the clouds through the sky.

It must have been over a century since the house had burnt down. The rows of wheat curved around it, giving a wide berth to the eroded walls, the fallen stones and the weeds.

Perhaps it had been the original farmhouse, unsalvageable, left to rot after the fire.

'A good place to look for ghosts,' he said, leaning over the wall.

The middle-aged woman started gratifyingly, nearly knocking over her tape deck. She turned around, half in a crouch, and glared up at him through her spectacles.

'I hope you've brought an umbrella,' said the Doctor. 'I don't like the look of that sky.'

The woman stood up, leant on the wall, as though they were neighbours chatting over a fence. 'Do you come here often?' she said dryly.

The Doctor smiled. 'It's the only landmark for miles. Do you know the history of the place? Any murders, suicides, that sort of thing?'

'Little Caldwell has a grey lady,' said the woman. 'She's supposed to appear here, at a crossroads near a bridge, and very occasionally in the town. Supposedly she's an Egyptian woman who married an English nobleman. The story is either that he strangled her and set this cottage on fire to hide the crime, or that she committed suicide and was buried at the crossroads.'

'Is there any historical basis for it?'

The woman shook her head and held out her hand. 'Ellen Woodworth.' The Doctor shook her hand. 'Are you a local, Mister . . .?'

'Doctor,' he said. 'I'm on holiday.'

'I'm staying in Newbury for a few days while I do a little fact-gathering. You must be in the business yourself.'

'Oh, no,' said the Doctor. 'There just aren't that many things you can do with a cassette deck and a jar of plaster of Paris in the middle of nowhere.' A raindrop splashed him on the nose, and he blinked. 'Are you planning to stay overnight?'

'Just me and the bees.'

'Bees?' said the Doctor. 'In December?'

Woodworth smiled mysteriously. 'Look around you.'

The Doctor glanced around – and saw a trickle of buzzing insects, racing through the rain. 'There's a small hive in the far room,' said the ghosthunter.

'Remarkable,' said the Doctor.

'Do you fancy helping me set up the tent fly?'

'Why not?' The Doctor followed the wall until he found a charred gap, the remains of a doorway. 'You can tell me more about your ghost,' he said.

She unzipped the heavy bag of equipment. 'Remind me to buy you a drink later.'

Joel sat on his bed, leafing through his 'zine collection. The little photocopied newsletters lived in a couple of big cardboard boxes, neatly organized into folders by year and topic. Well, they were neatly organized up until about the beginning of 1983, when Isaac had given Joel the job of archiving them.

He rummaged through the last year's worth. There were UFO bulletins, *Professor X* fanzines, some New Age and witchcraft 'zines, and – ah! That was the issue of *Who's Who and What's That?* he was after.

He turned the pages. There. A blurry, but recognizable photo of the TARDIS.

Or possibly of a police box. The trick of reading 'zines was working out which bits were made up, which bits were distorted versions of real events, and which were the real thing.

Joel peered into the box of 'zines. There were a lot of questions the Doctor could answer.

Someone knocked on the open door. The Doctor's companion Chris was there. 'Hi,' said Joel.

The man beamed at him. 'Hi,' he said. He wandered into the room, taking up rather a lot of the available space.

'Can I do something for you?' said Joel, putting down the fanzine.

'I just noticed your models,' said Chris. In fact, he'd had to duck under a *Millennium Falcon* to get into the room. Now his face was level with a Y-Wing. 'I used to build model spaceships when I was a kid.'

Joel blushed a little. 'Yeah, well, you can't get those kits any more where I'm from.' He pulled out a cigarette and his lighter.

'They're neat.' Chris looked around the room. It always looked like a complete mess, though everything was where it was supposed to be, including the piles on the floor. Joel wished he could convince the Admiral of that. There were shelves crammed with books, and the desk was hidden under the Commodore 64 and a bunch of stuff.

Joel pushed the window open an inch and blew out a stream of bluish smoke. 'What's it like, being a companion?'

Chris had his nose up to a noticeboard with a big green map pinned to it. He laughed. 'I never really thought about it before.' The map had a series of concentric circles drawn on it, with the middle labelled GROUND ZERO. 'Good fun,' he said, after some thought. Little Caldwell had a pin stuck in it, inside the ONE MILE radius. 'Most of the time.'

Go on, thought Joel, tell him.

Chris said, 'What's it like working for Admiral Summerfield?'

Joel shrugged. 'Good fun,' he said, grinning. 'It's a great way to meet people, so long as you don't mind how many eyes they've got.'

'Hey, what's this?' asked Chris.

Joel craned his neck around. Chris was pointing at a small cane hoop, strung with a web of fishing line, with three feathers hanging off the bottom. It was nailed to the wall over Joel's bed. 'Oh,' he said. 'That's a dreamcatcher. I get nightmares sometimes.'

'Me too,' said Chris.

'About Daleks, right?'

'No,' said Chris, 'Not real-world stuff, just weird things. There was one, once, with me and Roz trapped inside this giant hourglass. The sand poured down all over us, burying us together. What do you figure it means?'

'I think it means you watched the wrong *Batman* cliffhanger as a kid,' grinned Joel. 'I wasn't allowed to watch *Professor X* for years because of the nightmares. Missed lots of classic episodes. Still, I'm getting a chance to see them now.' Oops. No, it didn't mean anything to future boy.

Chris sat on the end of the bed and picked up the fanzine. 'Hey, that's the TARDIS,' he said.

'Yeah.'

'Wow.' Chris was scanning the 'zine. 'You guys really have been studying the Doctor, haven't you?'

'Yeah,' said Joel. 'You can't be in this business and not know about the Doctor. I really want to get a chance to talk to him.'

'He's really cool,' beamed Chris. 'Hey, do you feel like coming with us? For a while, anyway?'

'Are you kidding?' said Joel. 'I don't want my arse exterminated.'

After a hundred adventures, you start to know when you're being watched.

Benny hadn't been able to shake the feeling for an hour; the back of her neck prickling as she and her father counted books and typed titles into the PC. While he was waiting for the database program to update, she tiptoed over to the door opposite the staircase, and pushed it open.

'Aha!' she said. 'I thought so.'

There was an elderly cat sitting in the hallway, its single eye wide with surprise. It sniffed her proffered hand, decided she was acceptable, and rubbed itself on her legs.

'We inherited that cat,' said Isaac. 'Everyone has a different name for him.' Benny knelt, stroking the animal's tattered fur. 'And the Lacaillan is called Myn Jareshth.'

Benny froze in mid-pat. The blue humanoid was watching her from a doorway along the hall, slender fingers clasping the wall.

'Hello,' she said, standing up slowly. 'My name's Bernice.'

The Lacaillan stepped into the dimly lit hallway. He moved like a ballet dancer, fine white hair floating around his head. 'Hello.'

'Myn Jareshth and one other Lacaillan were caught breaking into the National Hurricane Center in Florida,' said Isaac. 'Or rather, they were almost caught. We managed to get them away before they ended up in the laps of the FBI.'

He switched off the PC. 'Myn, are you and Ia planning on coming downstairs this evening? It'll be your last chance before you go.'

The Lacaillan considered for a moment, then shook his delicate head, carefully imitating the human gesture. 'I cannot – I *can't* find Ia Jareshth,' he breathed. 'She is not in our room.'

Isaac was instantly on his feet. 'You didn't plan to split up?'

The Lacaillan shook his head again. 'She has left no message. I *don't* know where she has gone.'

'Damn,' said Isaac softly. He glanced at Benny with those cool grey eyes. 'Myn. Stay here. We'll search for her.'

'We didn't have anything to do with this,' said Benny.

'Of course not.' Her father pulled his communicator out of a pocket. His expression was unreadable. 'See if you can find the Doctor,' he said. 'We'll need everyone.'

8

One of our extraterrestrials

'Our timing's marvellous as usual,' said Roz, stomping through a puddle.

Chris looked down at his muttering partner, hidden beneath her brolly like an annoyed mushroom. It had started to rain in earnest an hour ago, just as they'd set out from the village. The TARDIS's ever-changing wardrobe had noticed the weather, it seemed; big waterproof coats and a couple of strong umbrellas had been waiting for them.

'We turn up,' grumbled Roz, 'and immediately, pow, there's a crisis.'

Chris peered through the rain. They were coming up to a crossroads. 'That's usually because we create one.'

'Not this time,' said Roz. 'Despite what Admiral Summerfield seems to think.'

'Does he really think we kidnapped the Lacaillan?'

Roz shrugged. At least, Chris assumed that she shrugged. Her umbrella moved up and down. 'Us, no. The Doctor, maybe. For all we know, he's gone mad and decided to collect blue humanoids.'

'What do you think about all of this? Little Caldwell, I mean.'

Roz's umbrella moved up and down again. 'They make up in experience what they lack in formal organization,' she said. 'And Isaac's crew trusts him implicitly.'

'But?' said Chris.

'But they're amateurs.'

'What are we, then?'

'Trained.' Roz harrumphed. 'You'd think that after all this time they could manage not to lose their aliens.'

Chris recalled the meeting they'd had at the Pyramid.

Benny had phoned them at the cottage. Five minutes later they were at the Pyramid, ignoring the CLOSED sign hanging on the door. The crew had already gathered around a table where Isaac had spread out a map of the area.

Isaac was marking an irregular shape around the town with a red pencil, following the roads that surrounded it. 'Roz and Chris, I want you to do a sweep right around this perimeter. We're expecting Albinex back from Aldermaston in the next hour. Joel, Tony, I want you to check out the church, the forest, anywhere close at hand where Ia might be hiding.'

'Do we know why she went?' asked Roz.

'Once or twice, guests have just wandered off in a fit of claustrophobia. Each time we found them nearby and calmed them down.'

'What if she's left the area altogether?' said Chris.

'Then that's her business,' said Isaac firmly. 'We can't help her if she doesn't want our help. But Myn thinks it's unlikely that she'd leave without letting him know. Which brings us to our third, least pleasant, possibility.'

'She was abducted,' quavered Tony.

The door bells jingled as Benny came back into the shop. 'Um. I can't find the Doctor,' she said. 'We'll have to start without him.'

Thunder cracked suddenly, and the lights flickered. 'I'll be staying here,' said Isaac. 'I want to do a head count of the guests. I'm not letting Myn out of my sight, and I need to coordinate the rest of you. Report *anything* out of the ordinary.'

Jason said, 'What, you mean aliens, time travellers, that sort of thing?'

'Anything,' said Isaac sternly. 'If Ia was picked up, she'll be the first alien we've ever lost. We'd have to bug out.'

That was an hour ago. They were still doing the perimeter sweep, with no sign of the Lacaillan. Chris frowned. If their coming here had triggered this somehow, it would be so . . . unjust.

'They must've had some amazing adventures,' he said.

Roz smiled involuntarily. 'Well, they must have. It would make a great sim series.'

'Yeah, but who wants to watch a bunch of aliens?'

'Oh yeah,' said Chris. 'Funny thing. In this century nobody likes aliens because they're supposed to be invaders, and in our century nobody likes aliens because they're supposed to be janitors.'

'Yeah, well don't let them hear you say that, or it'll be slime time.'

Chris returned her smile. 'I *like* aliens. The more tentacles the better.'

They stopped at the crossroads. Chris pulled out the communicator Joel had loaned them. 'This is Cwej calling the Pyramid,' he said. 'Cwej calling Pyramid. Come in!'

'Hello, Chris.' Isaac's voice was half hidden by a storm of static.

'We've reached the crossroads, sir,' he said. 'We haven't seen anything we recognize as being out of the ordinary.'

Roz hissed at him, suddenly, and he dropped the phone into his pocket almost before he knew what he was doing. A car was coming towards them, headlights slashing through the rain. It slowed down as the driver saw them. 'What do we do?' said Chris.

'Good question.'

The driver's window rolled down. The short man inside was in his twenties, with thick eyebrows and a pouting mouth. He wore a dark grey jacket over a white T-shirt. 'You must be Cwej and Forrester,' he said.

'Albinex,' said Roz.

He nodded. 'Any luck so far?'

Roz shook her head. Albinex frowned. 'Can I give you a lift back into town?'

'We need to finish our circuit of the boundary roads,' said Chris.

'I'll see you back there, then. Good luck.' He wound up his window and drove off slowly.

'Wherever the Doctor is,' said Roz, grimacing up at the sky, 'I'll bet he's dry.'

* * *

'Why do you look for ghosts?'

Woodworth took the kettle off the camp stove and poured the steaming water into their mugs. 'There are all sorts of reasons,' she said. 'Curiosity. The chance to look beyond the veil. Solving historical mysteries.'

'Ah,' said the Doctor, taking the mug of tea from her. 'But why do *you* look for ghosts?'

Woodworth sat back, listening to the rain hammering the tent fly. It was large enough to cover the remains of the room, keeping them dry if not exactly warm. 'Because they're dangerous,' she said.

'So it's the adventure.'

'No. I . . . was once in the military. And that was because I wanted to protect people. But there are plenty of police.'

'But not many ghosthunters.'

'Exactly. Oh, for the most part, the apparitions are harmless – bad dreams, or overactive imaginations, or a squeaking floorboard that the landlord likes to say is the footstep of a phantom.' Her eyes were hard in the yellow light of the lamps. 'But for centuries, people have been driven mad, or actually killed, by ghosts. We need to understand them so that we can protect ourselves from them.'

'So you see them primarily as hostile,' said the Doctor.

'Mm-hmm, yes.'

'Some people just collect stamps, you know,' he teased.

Woodworth gave him a sarcastic smile. 'What about you?' she said. 'How do you spend your spare time?'

'I travel.' He took a mouthful of the tea. 'What I'd really like to do is busk.'

'Busk!' said Woodworth.

'Don't you ever feel like putting aside all your responsibilities –'

'No.'

'– and just making people happy?'

'No.'

The Doctor made a glum face. 'You must have hated *The Muppet Movie*.'

Woodworth barked a laugh and hit him on the arm, nearly making him spill his tea. 'You're mad!'

'Mad as bees in December.'

'Tell me something,' she said. 'Are you –'

A face was peering at them from over the wall, lit in yellow patches. 'Bernice!' said the Doctor.

'There you are,' she said. 'We need you back at the shop.' She looked at Woodworth. 'There's been a spot of bother.'

The Doctor stood up. 'Will you still be here tomorrow?'

Woodworth grinned. 'That depends on the ghost.'

'Come on, Doctor,' said Benny. 'Water's seeping into my socks.' She waved at Woodworth. 'Sorry for the interruption.'

'Not at all,' said Woodworth. 'I still owe you that drink,' she told the Doctor.

The Doctor awkwardly handed her back his tea. 'Perhaps I'll catch up with you in Little Caldwell.' He doffed his hat. 'Good luck!'

As they walked away, Benny elbowed him in the ribs. 'Who's your girlfriend?'

The Doctor blinked at her, unfurling his umbrella. 'A ghosthunter. What's the matter?'

'One of our aliens is missing. And I think Dad is convinced it's your fault.'

Behind them, Woodworth frowned as her lamps flared blue. In the next room, the bees were buzzing in the rain.

9

Benny

They'd scoured the countryside. They'd counted the holo-gram projectors. Ia Jareshth was out there somewhere, alone, with a thin layer of illusion between her and humanity.

Isaac had assembled the rest of the guests in the Pyramid. Rather than make the aliens wear their hologram projectors, Isaac had Joel set up a single hologram inside the shop doorway, making it look as though the place was empty.

The two Ogrons were adamant that they hadn't eaten anyone for weeks. They were waiting for a passing trans-porter to get them back into the galactic mercenary market.

The Bannerman had been living in a cardboard box in London for the last five years. He had probably survived the 1959 incursion, but his memory wasn't working any more. He didn't know where the Lacaillan had gone. He just wanted to go home.

Benny hovered, not sure where she should sit. Isaac and Jason and the Doctor were sitting at different tables, studi-ously ignoring one another.

It had not been the best of beginnings.

'You know Heseltine's threat hasn't stopped them over at Greenham,' Ms Randrianasolo was telling Isaac. 'They've been going in, but thank God, no one really has been shot so far. Maybe this isn't the right time. I can talk to someone . . .'

The Admiral shook his head. 'It'll occupy the military's attention. I appreciate your staying with us. I know it's a difficult time.'

'Zak,' said the black woman, 'I may be determined to civilize this century, but this –' she gestured around at the shop '– is always my first concern.'

Isaac gave her one of his serious smiles. 'There's something I need you to do for me.' He stopped suddenly, glanced up at Benny. She frowned, pushing her hands into her pockets, and decided to see how the Doctor was doing.

Roz was giving the Time Lord a *sotto voce* sitrep. 'They've got no security to speak of. If the Lacaillan wanted to walk out under their noses, she could have – and I don't think it would have been hard to snatch her away, either.'

'They've been running this operation for twenty years,' said the Doctor. 'They know what they're doing.'

'Do they?'

'They've contacted a dozen of their associates, all over the country. They've got quite a grapevine. Academics, astronomers, journalists, a Local Group of the *Professor X* Appreciation Society.' He turned his cup around in his hands. 'Isaac,' he finished gloomily, 'was very careful not to mention any names.'

Chris said, 'The Admiral says the Lacaillan mothership is due here the night after tomorrow. They'll make the pickup with or without Ia Jareshth.'

Benny looked at Chris and Roz, sitting together across the booth.

'I'm worried about the timing,' said Roz. 'We turn up, and almost immediately they're missing an alien.'

No, thought Benny, trying not to smile at the pair of them. They couldn't be.

The Doctor frowned, looking into his cup as though trying to read the tea leaves. 'I rather think Isaac's worried about the timing as well.'

'Yeah, but what I mean is, have we done or changed anything that might've caused this?'

'We have to find her,' said Chris. 'Show them that we're on their side.'

'I've been thinking.' The Doctor pushed his tea to one side. 'Perhaps I should go away for a little while.'

'What?' said Chris. 'Where?'

'Isaac can't relax while I'm here,' he said. 'Perhaps I should give him and Benny a little time to get to know one another.'

Benny put her arms over his shoulders and hugged him from behind. 'Of course not. We have to help them now that we're here. Besides, I want you two to get along.'

Chris jabbed a finger at Jason in a not very subtle gesture. Benny looked over to where her husband was glumly pouring himself and Albinex another drink. She sighed, and changed tables again.

'I've been part of the operation since the beginning, I'm proud to say.' Albinex was diminutive and fashionable, his hair gel intact despite the rain. 'The *Tisiphone* caused a few interesting radar blips, but for the most part, their arrival went unnoticed. Except by me. I'd been watching for new arrivals ever since I crashed here in the fifties.'

Benny sat down and picked up the bottle, pouring some of the whisky into her empty coffee mug. 'They must have been in a state.'

'The Admiral was as cool as ice. The others were in shock. He still does that in an emergency, just switches it all off and gets on with the job.' Albinex took a mouthful of whisky. 'They ended up piling into my van, and I drove them back to my flat in Ammanford. Beilby died two days later, insisting they didn't take him to a hospital.'

'How did Little Caldwell begin?'

'At first it was a library in Llanelli. Then it was a centre for the homeless in London. Those were good years, the late sixties and early seventies. Busy years, too. While UNIT was mopping up the invasions, we were mopping up after UNIT.'

'Albinex,' called Isaac, from across the room.

'Sir.' Albinex got up. 'Excuse me.'

Jason and Benny sat opposite each other for a few moments, Jason toying with his glass.

'Wish you wouldn't do that,' he said.

'What?'

'You know what I mean. What does my body language tell you, then? That I'm jealous of your father?'

Benny sat back. If anyone had heard, they were politely

66

pretending they hadn't. 'I wasn't trying to read you,' she said. 'Actually, I was just thinking –'

'Can I just talk about it?' said Jason. 'Can I just talk and you listen?'

Benny swallowed hard and said, 'Let's go outside, then.'

Outside it was raining fiercely onto the awning, a wide puddle forming in the gutter. Jason stood with his hands in his pockets, staring into the near-darkness. Benny folded her arms and waited.

'I've been looking into myself. You know?' he said, eventually. 'And I think I've always been jealous of him, right from the start.'

'Jealous of my dad?'

'When you used to talk about him, I could hear this terrible . . . all your life you'd been walking around like a jigsaw puzzle missing one piece. I wanted to go and find him and bring him back for you, and make everything all right.'

Benny glanced back at the shop. The hologram made it look empty and dark. Jason said, 'It was bad enough having to hear about the Doctor all the time. But at least I could do stuff with you the Doctor couldn't do.' Benny smiled sadly and held Jason's coat lapel in her fingers. 'But how could I compete with this mythical other man? And now we actually find him, and he's doing –' he gestured around him '– this. He's a hero.'

Benny looked at him. 'I promised you I'd back you up, no matter what, and I meant it. But how can I compete with that?'

She walked up to him, grabbed hold of his ears, and angrily kissed him. Jason made a surprised noise.

'You get back in there,' she said, 'and you talk to him like a human being. That's all he is, a human being.'

'I thought you'd be furious,' he said.

'This isn't a competition.' She kissed him again. 'I want you to like one another. Go on, get in there.'

'What about you?'

Benny sighed. 'I need a bit of fresh air.'

Jacqui didn't like the Friday evenings. Usually she stayed at the peace camp, sitting around the fire with the others, playing her recorder. But this time she thought it would be a good idea to come back to Little Caldwell, help with searching or something.

She had spent a little bit of time tidying up in the cottage she shared with Ms Randrianasolo and the Bannerman. The poor alien left things all over the place, not because he meant to, but because he just forgot about them. He was stone deaf, too, so you couldn't ask him where he'd left things. When she was finally finished, she switched off all the lights and locked the front door.

It was raining steadily, making a soothing, drumming noise on her umbrella. She sloshed through the puddles in her wellies, humming to herself. It would be her thirty-fifth birthday in two days.

Someone was standing outside the Pyramid, watching the rain come down. As Jacqui got closer, she could see it was Bernice Summerfield. There was a hologram up, making the shop look empty. She didn't know why they bothered with that. Mr Sullivan the postman went home to Newbury at night, and it wasn't as if anyone was going to come here in weather like this.

Bernice had noticed her. 'Hello,' she said.

'You're getting wet,' said Jacqui. She thought her voice always sounded tiny and rusty, like a bit of machinery that hadn't been used for a while.

'I just needed to get outside for a bit,' said Bernice, scooping sodden hair out of her eyes. The shop's rolled-up awning didn't offer much protection.

Jacqui waited to see if she was going to say anything more. 'I'm caught between three men,' said the Admiral's daughter, at length. 'I don't believe this – we've only been here one day.'

Jacqui nodded seriously. 'Do you feel as though it's all going a bit fast for you?'

'It was always like this.'

'Travelling with him?'

Bernice looked down at her. 'We're lightning rods,' she said wearily. 'The Doctor and the Summerfields. Whatever's started here, it's not going to get easier: it's going to get harder. More complicated instead of simpler.'

'Lightning rods,' said Jacqui.

'I'm sorry,' said Bernice. 'You must be freezing down there. Let's go inside.'

Jacqui shook her head. 'I'm all right. It's my birthday in two days.'

'Well, happy birthday for Thursday.'

'Thank you.'

Jacqui turned around and went back down the street, the rain pouring from the rim of her umbrella. Perhaps the Admiral's daughter watched her go.

The clock over the sink chimed softly. Quarter to midnight. Isaac pulled the plug out, found himself watching the suds go down the drain.

The Doctor and Jason had moodily volunteered to do all the washing up, probably at Benny's insistence. But the final tidy-up was the Admiral's job – making sure everything was in its place. Even if one of the cups had been broken during the day, even if it couldn't be saved with a drop of glue, it made him feel right to *know*.

Cups broke without warning, of course. You didn't look at each cup and think about the day it must inevitably break.

There were other times, much worse times, when you could look back afterwards and see all the little warning signs you'd missed. Like when Beilby had started to sniffle. Ms Randrianasolo had laughed and said it was the ancient pollen, that he had hay fever.

A tiny cloud on the horizon in the morning, a storm at night. Now, sometimes, when they had a bit of bad luck, Isaac wondered if someday he would look back on this tiny caveat.

There was a footstep on the stairs. Isaac looked up from his reverie, realized he was holding a teacup, put it carefully back into the cupboard.

'What were you thinking about?' asked Bernice.

'A storm in a teacup,' he said, with a small smile. 'Couldn't you sleep?'

She leant on the counter. God, she looked like Claire. But in the warm light, her eyes were a hundred years old.

What had she been through? What had he done to her?

'Do you really think you're going to have to pack up and leave?' she said.

Isaac frowned. He got out a cloth and wiped down the counter again. Benny stood back.

'We can't know unless we find Ia Jareshth,' he said. 'Or something else happens. Rashly deciding to leave could be worse than staying put.'

'It would be terrible if you had to leave after all this time,' said Benny. Well, how could he reply to that? 'Listen . . .'

He yawned, loudly. 'That's enough for one night,' he said. 'We can't do anything until the morning, and we'll be no use to anyone if we're not rested.'

'You haven't asked me once about Mum,' she said.

Isaac closed his eyes. His fingers curled around the damp cloth. 'Your mother also had a very direct way of speaking.'

There was a long silence. He could hear the soft sound of the dishwasher, the drumming of the rain. Benny took a breath as though to say something more.

'There is a reason,' he said.

She was looking at him with big, frightened eyes, teeth pressed into her lower lip. Suddenly she was seven years old, afraid to tell him that she'd broken his favourite mug, not so much because she might be punished but because she couldn't stand the idea of his being upset.

But she had asked him point blank, and he was going to have to tell her.

'I haven't asked because I don't want to know. I don't want to know whether she's alive or dead, because if she is alive I'll want to go back to her and if she's dead I'll want to go back and save her.'

He continued before she could say anything. 'You might be thinking, "He doesn't want to damage the timelines," which would of course be very noble. No. Claire is not going to be a bargaining chip in this.'

Like the seven-year-old who had been so bright, so quick, she said, 'You don't want to have to ask the Doctor for anything.'

Isaac shook his head firmly.

He couldn't read her expression. Disgust, perhaps, that he still didn't trust the Doctor. Didn't trust her, by implication. There was so much he wanted to tell her, to fill up that silence. But he couldn't. It was too soon. It might always be too soon.

After a few moments, she said, 'Actually, I thought perhaps you and Ms Randrianasolo –'

He smiled again. 'No.'

'You worked it out a long time ago, didn't you?' she said. 'What you'd do if a time traveller came along – someone with the power to get you back to Mum?'

'The time travellers are dreadful, Bernice. They always offer to take you back to save a dead relative, or correct some terrible mistake. Which doesn't mean much when you know they're stranded because they forgot to bring spare batteries for their time machine.'

Benny laughed, just a small laugh, some of the tension leaving her face.

'Do you know what the Draconians call him, Benny?'

She shook her head.

'The Oncoming Storm.'

Above them, thunder crashed, making the crockery rattle in the cupboard. They both smiled at the timing.

'We can't help it,' she sighed. 'We're lightning rods.'

10

Knight on Earth

Chris snapped out of sleep. He'd been dreaming about Roz again, the same old dream, he –

Wait a minute. No, he hadn't.

He opened his eyes, focusing on the hard smoothness of the painted wooden ceiling, and waited for his heart to slow down.

He'd dreamt that he was following the Doctor up a hill. He'd been leading a grey mare, easily, as though he'd been handling horses all his life.

Chris sat up on the edge of the bed, closing his eyes. It had been like something out of a King Arthur sim. The hill was thick with grass and flowers, the air soft with summery smells. He had been wearing his uniform – no, some kind of old-fashioned armour, bulky and heavy but somehow familiar.

The Doctor had been dressed in his usual linen suit and white hat, but he didn't seem out of place in the medieval landscape. He glanced back at Chris, as though to make sure he was still following, and smiled at him.

At the top of the hill there was a woman in white. 'Is this your new steward?' she asked the Doctor, glancing at a pocketwatch. 'Or have you brought me a sacrifice?'

The Doctor turned around and looked at Chris again, an expression of surprise crossing his face.

Then his hand had gone to his shoulder. There was an arrow-head between his fingers, brilliant metal glinting in the sunlight.

The woman watched, impassive, as he stumbled down the hill to Chris.

But before Chris could catch the Time Lord, he had woken up . . . with the intense feeling that someone was watching him.

He froze on the edge of the bed. There was someone in the room with him, but he couldn't see them. Where? Where were they?

After a few seconds the eerie sensation ebbed away. He couldn't hear anything. He looked around, cautiously.

There wasn't anyone here. It had just been a leftover feeling from the nightmare.

The window exploded inwards.

He jumped up with a yell. No, it hadn't exploded, it had just blown open. The rain pounded into the room, drenching him as he struggled with the old-fashioned glass-and-wood structure, trying to work out how to make the two halves join up in the middle.

There was something else, as well. Not just the freezing water – bees! The room was suddenly full of the fat insects, droning as they looped through the air. What had they been doing out in the storm?

Chris fastened the window and shot out of the room, slamming the door behind him. He could still hear the insects through the door.

'Gee,' he said.

He'd better check that Roz was okay.

Except that his trousers were on the other side of the bedroom door.

The rest of the small cottage was quiet. He crept around, checking the windows and doors in the front room and kitchen, and tiptoed up the stairs.

Roz's door was shut. He hovered. Should he knock, or just push it open and peek inside?

He nearly fell backwards over the banister when it opened of its own accord.

Roz blinked at him. She was wearing a set of flannel pyjamas two sizes too big for her. 'What is it, Chris?'

'Um,' he said, wishing he was wearing something more than his socks and a pair of Daffy Duck boxer shorts. 'Something weird just happened in my room.'

'Yes?'

73

'Er, well, nothing much. Some insects got in. I just wanted to make sure you were all right.'

'I'm fine,' yawned Roz.

'Um, sorry . . .'

'No sweat.' She slapped his arm. 'I think we're all a bit on edge at the moment.'

Chris realized that his heart was thumping. She was less than a metre away, close enough for him to catch the soft scent of her skin and hair. Goddess, surely she knew, surely she could tell.

'Well, if you're sure you're okay . . .' he said, being casual.

'I promise I'll call you if a flying saucer comes to beam me away. Goodnight, Chris.'

She closed the door.

He went back downstairs, put an ear to the door of his bedroom. Was the buzzing sound still there? He wasn't sure.

He got a spare blanket out of a cupboard, curled up awkwardly on the sofa, and dreamt about Roz's pyjamas.

The Doctor seldom slept. Night on Earth was a good time to be up and doing things, while human beings were still and quiet and unlikely to interfere.

But, as he kept reminding himself, he was on holiday.

So he lay on top of the spare bed in the bungalow Joel and M'Kabel shared, his arms folded behind his head, and listened to the rain.

He thought about poor Woodworth huddled under her tent fly. He hoped she was wearing thick socks.

How could Little Caldwell have been here all this time, without his ever noticing it?

Part of the answer was UNIT. From what little he'd picked up, Isaac and his crew were adept at avoiding the military, even the United Nations Intelligence Taskforce, with its special interest in the extraterrestrial. And during the early seventies avoiding UNIT meant avoiding him too. He'd taken refuge with the taskforce during the long years of his exile, and it had blinded him to what was happening outside it.

But there was more to it than that. They'd been waiting for him to arrive, all this time. Expecting him to take one look and knock them down like a row of dominoes.

He frowned at the ceiling. They could run rings around MI5 or the CIA, but he was the threat they couldn't predict, couldn't prepare for. After everything he'd done to protect Earth, they saw him as their greatest danger.

He was stung.

He started as a flash of pain jumped across his temples and was gone.

He blinked in the dark. Ah, well, goodness, now wasn't that clumsy?

He slowed down one of his hearts, unpicked the tapestry of his mind until at least part of it was asleep. One set of threads was still vibrant with activity. Why had the Lacaillan run away? He had a nasty suspicion that he knew.

The sparkling, stabbing sensation came again. This time it wasn't painful, the bubbles of light and sound sinking softly into his brain. He let them move about the sleeping part of his mind, tentative and disorganized.

He wouldn't visit Lacaille 8760 until far in the objective future. No, Ia Jareshth had no reason of her own to fear him.

But what had Isaac and his crew told her about him?

He captured one of the bubbles, gently, altered it, sent it spinning back to the others. After a few seconds, the presence withdrew from his mind.

She hadn't even left a message for the other Lacaillan. She'd fled in panic, from the one place on Earth it might be safe for her to stay.

Oh, she'd be back, when she realized there was no other way off the planet. It might be for the best if he wasn't here when she arrived.

He let the rest of his mind shut down, softly.

Four hours later, he woke up with a violent start, and stumbled out of the cottage.

He ran through puddles in his bare feet, whirled around outside the post office, looking wildly up and down the main street.

The TARDIS was gone.

He sagged against the bicycle rail, water pouring down his face. 'It never rains,' he whispered.

PART TWO

LOOSE THREADS

Non-violence is a flop. The only bigger flop is violence.

Joan Baez, 1967

11

The morning after

Benny struggled out of sleep into the coldness of the morning. Her dreams had been full of glittering insects and desert sands.

Once so much touching would've made her uncomfortable, but now waking up alone, without Jason wrapped around her, felt wrong. The big bed was conspicuously devoid of husband. On the other hand, the overstuffed easy chair across the room was occupied by the Doctor.

The thought of the Time Lord quietly sitting and watching her sleep naked, even under the covers, was a bit much.

'Where's Jason?' she said, clutching the eiderdown.

'He wasn't here when I arrived.'

'Well,' said Benny. 'Er. What can I do for you?'

'The TARDIS is gone,' he said.

'What? Do you mean pinched gone or dematerialized gone?'

'I woke up in the middle of the night, and she was gone.' He shook his head, slowly. For someone who hardly ever slept, he looked as though he could use eight hours right about now. 'I don't think she dematerialized. I think someone has picked her up and carried her away.'

Benny was about to leap out of the bed and into action when she realized this would also mean leaping into conspicuous nudity. 'Right,' she said. 'What do we do?'

The Doctor didn't move, a shadowy shape in his chair. 'Benny,' he said, 'I think someone's trying to tell me something.'

'What do you mean?'

'I don't think I'm welcome here.'

'Of course you're welcome here. You and Dad have got to stop trying to second-guess one another. When are you going to realize you're on the same side?'

The Doctor just shook his head. 'I'm going to go and look for her, Benny.' He took the bleeping machine out of his pocket. The little black box's lights and noises were silent. 'I expect her to be somewhere in the area.'

'Hang on,' sighed Benny. 'I'll pull on some clothes and come with you.'

'No,' he said. 'I want you to stay here, with your father.' He put the machine away in his pocket and stood up. 'They're having breakfast downstairs,' he said. 'I've been talking to Myn Jareshth. He screamed when he saw me, Benny.'

Screamed! 'Why?'

'I want *you* to talk to your father, Benny.' He took her hand, suddenly, squeezed it tightly, standing beside the bed. 'You know me,' he said. 'Tell him what I'm like.'

Realization dawned. 'You think Dad took the TARDIS,' she breathed. 'Why would he do something like that?'

'I'm going to go into Newbury,' he said. 'Just for a day or so. Ia Jareshth was terrified of me. I want to give her a chance to come back.'

Benny pulled his hand until he leant down, and gave him a kiss on the forehead. He blinked. 'Trying to keep all these egos intact is wearing me out,' she said. 'I'll bet Jason is off somewhere having a good sulk.'

'I'll leave you to talk to Isaac, then . . .'

'I wish the two of you would talk to one another,' she said. 'At least come downstairs and have breakfast first.'

Joel was grinding his teeth on a chunk of gum which had long since lost its flavour. He was making mountains of toast and fried eggs (free-range, on Ms Randrianasolo's insistence). The Admiral, of course, was making coffee.

The Doctor's other companions were talking quietly over their breakfast. The big blond guy, Chris, caught Joel's eye and smiled. He abandoned his third helping of eggs and wandered over to the counter.

'Do you guys want a hand or anything?' he said, reading Joel's CAFFEIND T-shirt.

Joel scraped the accumulated burnt gunk off the griddle. 'No, that's okay,' he said, around the gum. 'This is my job, this and the gas station. What're you guys going to do today?'

Chris waved his hand. 'That depends,' he said. Joel matched his glum look.

'Joel,' said the Admiral, 'could you give me a hand with this?'

'Sure.' Joel picked up a dishcloth and went to the sink.

'Um,' said Chris.

Joel looked up. The tall man was pointing behind him, at the cooker, his mouth slightly open. Joel turned around, expecting to see the stove in flames.

The white plastic spatula was moving by itself, continuing to lift the fried eggs off the cooker and pile them onto a plate. As Cwej watched, the spatula flipped an egg out of the carton with its handle. It flicked the broken halves of the shell aside and hopped back to the counter, away from the heat.

'Oh,' said Joel, relieved, 'that's just Graeme.'

Chris looked at him. 'Graeme the spatula?'

The spatula gave a little bow.

'Right,' said Chris. He sat back down again.

Ms R and Albinex came in. They both looked like death warmed up. No one, thought Joel, had had a good night.

This morning Joel had been woken by a crash of thunder. He'd pulled the covers over his head and waited for his heartbeat to slow back down. At last he'd reached a hand out from under the covers, found the clock radio. He breathed out a sigh as a voice announced 'Synchronicity II.' Saved by DLT again.

When he'd emerged from his bedroom, he'd found the Admiral in crisis mode, making phone calls in the dim light of the coffee shop.

Isaac's daughter was coming down the stairs, followed by a grumpy-looking Doctor.

He didn't look like much, really. A short man of indeterminate age wearing slightly odd clothes. It must be camouflage,

Joel decided. The clothes looked ordinary until you got close enough to take a look. The man looked ordinary until your invasion fleet unexpectedly dropped into the sun.

He gave Bernice a smile. 'Eggs?'

'Yes,' said the Doctor, 'they are.'

Bernice smiled back at Joel. He handed her a plate. 'Have you seen Jason?' she asked. Joel shook his head.

The Doctor stood at the counter, one hand tapping out a preoccupied rhythm, looking up and down the café as though he was missing something. Joel glanced between him and the Admiral, feeling that uncomfortable feeling when you're sandwiched between two people who aren't talking.

Benny looked as though she was going to lean over the counter and kiss the Admiral, but instead she said, 'Morning, Daddy.'

Joel glanced at his fearless leader, who was taken aback, fighting down a smile. 'Has there been any news about Ia Jareshth?' Benny asked. The Admiral shook his head.

'I have only one thing to say,' said the Doctor.

Everyone turned to look at him. If there'd been a piano it would have stopped playing.

'Jasper,' he said.

Ms R said, 'Stewart.'

The Doctor stopped drumming.

'Oh,' said Ms Randrianasolo. 'What a giveaway.'

The Admiral was looking at Ms R, his face unreadable. Even though he'd been here only a few months, Joel could see the quiet anger in the slope of his shoulders. 'What's this?' he said.

'Last night,' said the Doctor, 'someone tried to read my mind while I was sleeping. I implanted a small post-hypnotic command so I could identify them. Every time they hear the name Jasper –'

'Stewart!' hiccuped Ms R.

The Doctor walked up to her. 'I gather you're the resident psychic.'

'What have you done to me?' she said softly.

'Nothing that can't easily be fixed.' He reached up suddenly and tweaked her earlobe. 'There.'

Ms Randrianasolo rubbed her ear. 'I'm sorry,' she said.

The Doctor walked to the door, plucking his hat from one of the hooks. 'You know,' he told Isaac, 'it's possible you haven't found your missing alien because you've been looking in the wrong place.'

He left.

Joel let out the breath he'd been holding. He and the Admiral exchanged glances. Isaac walked around the counter and peered at Ms R. 'Are you all right?'

'I'm fine,' she said shakily.

'Jasper and Stewart?' said Joel.

'Um,' said Chris. 'They're teddy bears. We won them at the Sprunge festival on Vashig.'

'I shouldn't have asked you to do that.' The Admiral looked up at his daughter. 'What did he mean, looking in the wrong place?'

'The Doctor thinks that Ia Jareshth might have run away because she was frightened of him,' said Benny reluctantly. 'He's going to stay away from Little Caldwell until the Lacaillan transport arrives.'

Roz Forrester spoke up. 'If he thinks the Lacaillan's going to come back, that would mean she's holed up somewhere nearby.'

'Somewhere,' said Chris suddenly, 'where a slightly odd woman travelling by herself wouldn't be noticed.'

'Oh, *hey*!' said Joel.

Ms R said, 'Oh my God. Why didn't we think of that before?'

'Perhaps,' said the Admiral, 'because we were too busy looking in the wrong direction.'

Jacqui was squished into the back of the car between Ms Randrianasolo and the Doctor, with his black lady companion in the front and Joel driving as usual.

Jacqui looked at the Doctor, who was staring out of the window as they drove along. The trees were big skinny black shapes against the dead white sky. It looked spooky.

The Doctor wasn't very spooky or weird-looking. Well, maybe a bit weird, but not scary. Actually he looked a bit like an uncle of hers. He did seem a bit cross, though, frowning from time to time as he thought of things that made him angry.

She said, 'Have you seen me somewhere before?'

He turned to look at her with his sad blue eyes. He thought about it, seriously. 'I don't think so,' he said. 'I'm sorry, should I remember?'

She shrugged, which was hard to do squashed like that.

Ms Randrianasolo scrunched herself down awkwardly to peer through the windscreen. 'Nearly there,' she said.

Jacqui craned her neck, looking out of the window past the Doctor's face. Suddenly the fence appeared from behind the greenery, and there was the main entrance into USAF Greenham Common.

There were women all over the place, pale faces peeking out of layers of winter clothing. Some were huddled around a big fire; others were washing up at a card table. A huge banner announced that this was GREENHAM COMMON WOMEN'S PEACE CAMP.

'Are you sure you don't want to come?' said Jacqui. 'Men are okay in the daytime.'

'I need to get on to Newbury,' said the Doctor. 'I'd love to visit, though. I hope I get the chance.'

Jacqui, Roz and Ms Randrianasolo watched as Joel carefully pulled back out onto the wet road, gave them a wave and headed off. The morning rain was slowing, becoming a constant frozen drizzle.

A woman almost hidden inside a bright orange parka came up to them, smiling broadly. As she got closer, Jacqui saw it was Bridget. 'Hi Jacqui! Hi Ms Randrianasolo!' She gave Jacqui a hug, and reached for their companion's hand. 'Hi! I'm Bridget Evans.'

'Roz Forrester. Oh, *shit*!'

Roz grabbed the short, dark-haired woman and dragged her out of the way as a car skidded onto the grass. Jacqui stumbled backwards, bumping into Ms Randrianasolo. They blinked at the car as it shot past and was gone.

Bridget looked up at Roz. 'Thanks. You okay?'

'The driving conditions aren't *that* bad,' said the companion, peering after the car.

Bridget shrugged, disentangling herself from Roz's fierce grip. 'You want a cup of tea?'

'How have you been, Bridget?' said Ms Randrianasolo, as they followed the short, dark-haired woman to the fire.

'Oh, I'm still high from the weekend before last,' said Bridget happily. 'The papers said we cut down about a thousand feet of fence, but I reckon it was closer to three or four miles.'

'That was good fun,' said Jacqui.

'It was brilliant! There were a couple of thousand women here.' Bridget looked up at Roz. 'Can you stay overnight? There's a bit of space in my bender, if you want.'

'We're looking for someone,' said Roz.

Bridget looked at Ms Randrianasolo. 'It's okay, Bridget,' she said smoothly. 'There was a Swedish backpacker staying with us, and we think she got lost. We were wondering if she might have ended up at the camp.'

'Oh, right,' said the diminutive woman. 'Swedish? Okay, well, we can ask around.'

They sat around the fire while Bridget made tea in a billy. Jacqui watched Roz watching the women, her cool eyes kind of sucking in all the details. One small group were making a shelter out of fallen tree limbs, bending them into a curved shape. A pair of women were joking as they dug up a patch of frozen earth, working on a garden. Military cars were driving in and out of the base, stopping at the gate. Beyond the fence she could see long, low buildings.

'So,' said Roz, 'exactly what do you do here?'

'Anything we can,' said Bridget, carefully pouring tea into a mug. 'Short of violence. We believe in non-violent direct action. Taking down the fence. It shouldn't be there anyway – this is common land. Blockading construction vehicles. Or getting into the base and painting the planes.'

'Painting the planes?' said Roz.

'Mmm-hmm.' Bridget gave Jacqui a smile and some tea. 'For a nuclear installation, the security is dead lax. Sometimes we can't even find someone to arrest us.'

Ms Randrianasolo was rummaging in her handbag, as though she was looking for a tissue. Roz looked as though she was trying not to say anything because she didn't want to be rude.

'Okay,' Bridget said, 'right now there are, um, five camps, all around the base. And there's probably about a hundred women, plus visitors. So if nobody at Yellow Gate has seen your friend, maybe we could go for a walk around the perimeter.'

The Doctor became aware that Joel kept sneaking peeks at him in the rear-view mirror. He glared at the mirror, making the young man jump. But he didn't seem frightened, just excited.

'Do you mind if I smoke?' said Joel.

'Infinitely,' said the Doctor.

'No problem. Wow. This is so cool.'

'I wish Admiral Summerfield shared your enthusiasm,' sighed the Doctor.

'Oh,' said Joel. 'So . . . what's it like?'

'What's what like?'

'You know.' When it became apparent that the Doctor didn't, Joel added, 'Travelling through space and time with your companions and fighting monsters. Saving the world.'

'Hours of tedium followed by moments of sheer terror.'

'Neat!'

The Doctor smiled, despite himself. 'You'll be asking for my autograph next.'

'Oh, cool!' beamed Joel. 'Hey, there are so many questions I want to ask you.'

'Oh, yes?' The Doctor sat up, wondering if Isaac had given Joel a list.

'Well, mostly stuff I've been trying to work out about UNIT dating,' said Joel. 'For instance, the time the Zygons attacked Parliament with their fleet of cybernetically enhanced plesiosaurs – was that nineteen seventy-five or nineteen eighty?'

'I'm not sure if I can remember . . .' The Doctor sat back with a sigh. 'You tell me something.'

'Okay.'

'What's it like working with Admiral Summerfield?'

'It's great.' Joel grinned in the mirror. 'I love *knowing*, you

86

know? I look up at the stars, and I know that there are people out there. I know there's a future.'

The Doctor said nothing, watching the white sky out of the window.

It had been, thought Woodworth, a generally lousy morning.

She had woken up long before her alarm had gone off, after another night full of half-remembered dreams and sudden awakenings. She checked in the cupboards and under the bed. Nothing but dust balls and the smell of wood polish.

She showered for twenty minutes, leaning her forehead on the steamy inside of the glass. Five hours' sleep after a night spent in a frozen field.

She wandered downstairs in search of coffee and the paper. The management was noisily throwing out a couple of dungareed wackos from the peace camp, who were just as noisily demanding to be served.

She sat in her room for a couple of hours, looking at maps and reading reports. She made a call home, and had to pull out her schedule for another look. Blast, she was going to miss lunch with her mystery man. And she hadn't even found out his last name yet.

Luckily, he was early. She found him in the bar at 11 a.m., looking morose. He was playing with a pocket calculator, which he put to one side when he spotted her. 'Hello again,' he said, waving his hat about.

She plonked herself into the seat opposite him. 'Morning.'

He regarded the bags under her eyes. 'Is everything all right?' he said.

'Oh, yes,' she said. 'But I've got to run off at twelve – my day's all muddled up.' He nodded. 'The truth is,' she added, 'I have a bit of a recurring nightmare.'

'Ghosts,' he smiled.

'Yes,' she said. Little white figures running about, prodding her with their slender fingers. 'Ghosts.'

'I'm sorry I had to run off like that,' he said. She still hadn't quite picked his accent. 'Family trouble.'

'Nothing serious, I hope.'

'Oh, no.' He pretended to be studying the menu. She had

just decided not to ask when he said, 'It's a longish story, but my . . . adopted daughter has just met her biological father for the first time.'

'Oh. Oh, I see. That must be very difficult.'

'I'm trying not to interfere, to give them a bit of space. I'm half tempted just to leave them together here for a while, except . . . I'm still not sure why she even wanted to meet him.'

'Couldn't comment,' said Woodworth. 'I had an adopted friend who never bothered to track down his original parents. He said they were just strangers and they might as well stay that way.'

'She's always wanted to meet him, ever since she was small.' The Doctor put down the menu. 'Not much in the way of vegetarian food,' he said. 'We're not getting on very well.'

'You and your daughter?'

'Her father and I.'

'Is he a bit of a villain, or do you just rub one another up the wrong way?'

He laughed. 'I think it's actually more professional rivalry than anything.'

'And what does your wife think about it all?'

He gave a strange smile. 'I'm not married. Currently,' he added hastily.

Woodworth glanced at her watch. She might not get a chance to do anything with that useful piece of information at this rate. 'Look, I've got to buzz off. But we must do this properly. Dinner?'

He folded his hands on the table. 'I'm all yours,' he said.

Isaac hung up the phone on the wall. 'Still nothing,' he said.

Benny stopped turning the handle on the coffee grinder. Her father came over to the counter and picked up some of the brown grains, rolling them between his fingers. 'That's enough,' he said.

'I'll never play the violin again,' said Benny, shaking her aching hand to get the circulation going. Her father picked up the little bowl of coarse coffee and moved to the cooker, where a saucepan of water was just coming to the boil.

He switched off the gas flame and measured six careful spoonfuls of the coffee into the boiling water. He was riveted by those tablespoons, smoothing the brown powder to make sure they were level. When was the last time she'd seen someone concentrate so utterly?

He repeated the process with the sugar. She watched, leaning on the counter, not daring to say anything. No problem, wait until he was ready, move the conversation around in gradual steps until she could ask a few carefully chosen questions. Mention her room in the TARDIS, that sort of thing.

He began to stir the dark fluid, slowly. 'Dad?' she hazarded.

'Yeh,' he said, without looking up.

'Do you think you're going to find Ia Jareshth?'

He didn't react. No, he did react, but on the inside. God, she thought, he's like one of those stiff-upper-lipped Academy teachers, never showing a flicker of humanity to any of their students.

But she couldn't imagine any of them trying for the thirty-eighth time to recapture a cup of coffee they'd had in Mexico three years ago. Not those cardboard cut-out lieutenants.

She still hadn't told him about Spacefleet.

Her father stopped stirring and stood back a little, contemplating the steeping coffee. He looked at the clock over the stove. 'Five minutes,' he said. 'I don't know. If she's not here tomorrow night, they're going to have to leave without her.'

'Do you think she ran?'

Isaac made a little waving gesture with the metal spoon. 'She'll be a damned fool if she doesn't run right back.'

'Dad,' blurted Benny, 'did you have anything to do with the TARDIS going missing?'

He raised a blond eyebrow at her. After a moment he said, 'He left you here to find out.'

'No he bloody didn't,' she said. 'Answer the question.'

'No,' said Isaac, 'I didn't have anything to do with it.'

'Had it occurred to you,' said Benny, hoping the relief didn't show in her voice, 'that you and the Doctor might have a mutual enemy? Someone who took Ia Jareshth *and* the TARDIS?'

He tapped the spoon against his chin. 'It doesn't make sense,' he said. 'If they knew about us, they'd raid the place. This is more like cat and mouse.'

'They who?'

'UNIT, or the British or American military. Or Department C19, or the secret service, or the CIA. Conceivably the KGB.'

'It would have to be someone who knew what they were looking for,' said Benny. 'Knew what the TARDIS was.'

'Exactly,' said her father. 'I tend to discount the military, who are kept very much in the dark about these things, and the KGB, whose information on extraterrestrial incursions outside the Soviet Union has never been very good.'

He took out two coffee mugs and a big silver tea-strainer, and put them on the counter. 'It is possible that they're trying to avoid upsetting the American military with an outright raid so close to their base. Though they could always use the usual "nuclear terrorists" claim to hush it up. I think it might be a good idea to send Albinex to see a few of our . . . friends.'

'What if it isn't any of them?' said Benny.

The Admiral poured coffee through the strainer until his mug was almost full. 'It would be very embarrassing if someone was abducting aliens from Little Caldwell,' he said.

It took her a moment to realize that he meant it as a joke.

'Listen,' said Benny. 'There are some things I need to tell you.'

He took a drink of the coffee. 'Close,' he said, and looked at her.

'Um,' she said. 'I don't know what you'll think about this.'

He waited, patiently. Not unconcerned, not pretending to be unconcerned, just open.

'Well,' she said, 'firstly, I'm not a professor. My twenty-sixth-century credentials are fake.'

He nodded, taking another mouthful of the coffee. 'Why is that?' he asked.

'Um,' said Benny again. 'All right, skipping over some important details, I ended up at Spacefleet Academy. But I

90

went AWOL and lived in a forest for a year.' The corner of his mouth tugged up. 'Well, they shouldn't have taught us wilderness survival in the first term. Anyway, skipping over more details, they caught me and drafted me.'

'And you went AWOL again, and became an archaeologist through experience.'

She nodded. 'Hang on,' she said. 'How did you know that?'

He put down his coffee cup. 'Dorothée told me.'

Benny's jaw dropped open. When she regained control of her faculties, she said, 'Ace was *here*?'

'In the seventies,' he said.

'Why didn't she tell me?' Benny said. She hung onto the counter. 'Did she know – did she know it was *you*? Why didn't she tell me?'

'She wanted to,' he said softly. 'She wanted to. Perhaps she just hasn't found you yet.'

'I should've realized she'd come here,' said Benny. 'A twentieth-century epicentre of weirdness like this. Ace. My God. And she told you all about me.'

'No.' Isaac put down the cooling cup of coffee. 'I stopped her. It was good to know you were alive, that you were all right. But I couldn't know too much. Not too much.'

'You're just full of surprises, you know that?' said Benny.

Bridget and Ms Randrianasolo were walking up ahead, talking about what the peace camp was going to do when the missiles arrived. Jacqui walked with Roz, her boots squelching in the cold mud. She was only a bit shorter than the black woman – actually, they were about as tall, because of the pompom on the top of Jacqui's woolly hat.

'What do you think about the camp?' asked Jacqui.

Forrester didn't look at her, concentrating on not slipping in the mud. 'I've seen hundreds of protests,' she said.

'You must be kind of an expert then.'

'I'd never really thought about it like that,' said Roz.

'Chris said you and he used to be police. In the future.'

'That's right.'

'So was it your job to stop protesters?'

'If it wasn't a legal protest.'

'Like painting the planes,' said Jacqui. 'Criminal damage.'

'I suppose so.'

Jacqui laughed. Roz glanced at her. 'Sorry,' she said. 'It's just funny how you get arrested for stopping nuclear bombs and not for blowing them up. We need police who arrest the people with the bombs.'

'Right, thanks for that,' said Roz. 'Now let me ask you something.'

'Mmm-hmm?'

'Why do you take part in the protests, when you know the future? You must know the base is going to be decommissioned eventually, and that World War Three never happens.'

'Oh yeah,' said Jacqui, 'but the Admiral says that the future could change if something happens. Anyway, I couldn't just do nothing.'

'Why not, since you know the outcome anyway?'

'Well, because, doing nothing is like saying it's okay,' said Jacqui. 'I hate it when people do that.' She stepped over a fallen tree limb. 'Here's the next camp.'

'Three down, two to go,' muttered Roz.

The Doctor had stayed in the pub to think. He ordered a lemonade and sat by himself in a booth, tapping his fingers on the table and scowling.

He'd told Benny he wasn't going to get involved here. That this was Isaac's territory. And yet merely arriving had precipitated so many events. He should have dropped her off and come back in a month!

A young man brought him his lemonade, smiling. The Doctor took a long drink. There were two basic possibilities regarding the TARDIS. One, that Isaac had decided to hide her away as a sort of hostage. Two, that that was a panicky move which didn't suit what they'd seen of the Admiral at all, and that someone else had taken the old girl. Someone who knew just what she was, and had been watching the village.

And if they'd been watching the village, they might have taken Ia Jareshth while they were about it.

They were facing a common enemy, and they were so busy mistrusting one another that they'd missed the chance to work together.

The Doctor kicked himself mentally. He'd promised himself not to make that same mistake again. He had to get back to the village, talk to Isaac – if the Admiral would accept his help.

The only thing was, he didn't seem to be able to get up.

He slumped against the wall. 'Oh, for goodness' sake,' he murmured.

A blurred face swam into view. 'Hello, granddad,' it said. 'Have you fallen off the wagon again?'

He tried to fend off two pairs of strong hands as they lifted him out of the booth. Someone clucked their tongue. 'And before lunchtime, too. Don't worry,' they told someone else, 'we'll get him up to our room. He can have a little lie down. Won't you, granddad?'

It wasn't far back to Little Caldwell from Greenham Common.

The problem was that Joel had panicked and driven the car down a side road, and now he had no idea which way he was going.

The helicopter buzzed him again. Joel yelled involuntarily at the sheer *noise* of the thing. He slammed the accelerator pedal down hard, skidded as a tyre went into the mud, dragged on the steering wheel.

He was so terrified that his brain felt like a superconductor, colder than ice and running at ten times normal speed.

This was what they wanted – to force him into some obscure spot so that they could grab him without witnesses. If they wanted to kill him, they'd be shooting at him right now.

He could radio for help. But even if he could take his hands off the wheel for a moment the chopper would only hear the message. He had to get back onto a main road, drive away from Little Caldwell.

Two minutes later he lost control and slammed sideways into a tree.

Luckily, it was the other side of the car.

'So much for that brilliant plan,' he gasped, his whole body resounding with the shock of impact. His ears rang in the sudden silence – and then the chopper was behind him, its blades booming as it slowly came down.

It would take them no more than thirty seconds to land, get out, and come and get him.

He kicked open the door and ran for the line of trees a hundred feet away. Some part of his hyperactive brain was waiting for the bullets. They never came.

He didn't look back as he reached the trees. There was no shouting, just the sound of running feet, the whine of the helicopter's engines as they slowed down.

He sprinted at random through the forest. The mist was still heavy on the ground. It wrapped itself around him, obscuring logs and rocks. He barked his shins, tripped, got up and kept running. It was deadly quiet.

There was a fallen tree, its leaves hanging down, heavy with moisture. He got on his hands and knees and crawled under it, turning instinctively to face back the way he'd come, flattening himself against the frozen ground.

He couldn't stop shaking. But it was the cold. The fear hadn't hit him yet, not in any way he could process. He pushed his head down against his arms and listened as the soldiers came through the forest towards him.

They had slowed down, which meant they'd lost sight of him and were trying to work out which way to go. Possibly they'd realized he'd hidden. By the sound of it, there were only two or three of them, crunching about in their heavy boots.

There was nothing for it but to lie very still and hope they didn't see him. Fear not, Ranger! he told himself.

The walking sounds came closer. He caught a glimpse of one of them, a big uniformed man. British Army. Shit. If this was just because of Greenham, he was going to strangle Ms Randrianasolo.

They walked around him and past him, deeper into the forest.

He waited ten minutes, counting the seconds in his head, and dying for a cigarette.

It was absolutely still. He was still shaking inside his anorak, wishing to God he'd worn something warmer.

It had always been summer when he and his role-playing friends had headed out into the park to play war games, 'shooting' one another by calling out one another's name. The aim of the game was to get back to the base without being seen.

Once, he'd hidden between a couple of bushes, wriggling into the leaves with his eyes closed to avoid a poke in the pupil. Instead of running around looking for people, he'd let them come to him, saying their names very quietly as they walked past his invisible hidey-hole.

In the end he'd 'shot' four of the other players. They'd all gone grumbling back to Morgue Rock to wait out the rest of the game.

After twenty minutes, he'd become bored waiting for the fifth player to stumble past. With only one other player still in the woods, it'd be easy to slip back to base without being seen.

And then he'd stood up.

And player number five, who'd been standing right behind him for ten minutes, said, 'Joel.'

There was a hard bulge in one of his anorak pockets, sticking into his ribs. He slid his hand carefully down and pulled out the communicator.

He could get up and run, but he was between the soldiers and their helicopter. He could wait for them to come back, on their way back to the chopper, but they might find him – or radio for more soldiers to help in the search.

There was only one thing for it. Slowly and carefully, he brought the communicator up to his frozen face, and hoped to God that player number five wasn't standing right behind him.

12

Interrogation Blues

'Come along, granddad,' said the Caxtarid.

He half-dragged the small man across the landing. Indigo gave an embarrassed smile to a couple heading for the stairs. They sniffed and pushed past the two young men and their inebriated grandfather.

Indigo unlocked the narrow wooden door. Roze pulled the small man up, then walked forward, pushing him through the door into their room. With a sigh of relief, Roze dropped him face first onto the bed.

'He's not that heavy,' said Indigo, locking the door.

'Yeah, but he's a dead weight.'

Indigo reached down and rolled the little man over. 'I don't see what all the fuss is about,' he said, looking down at their prisoner.

Roze sat on the bed. The embroidered cover was a strange texture under his fingers. No stranger than anything else here, he thought, shivering in the thin, cold air. He rubbed his eyes.

The little man blinked up at them, sleepily. 'Caxtarids,' he murmured.

Roze started back. 'How'd he know that?'

'He knows a lot of things,' said Indigo. He reached down beside the bed and picked up his rucksack.

'I've got to get these contact lenses out,' said Roze, as Indigo rummaged in the bag for his tape recorder. He wandered into the tiny bathroom, with its smell of lavender and mould. 'Can you hang on a minute?'

'We need to get on with it before he wakes up,' said Indigo. He blew into the microphone, puffs from his cheeks, watching the sound levels. 'Okay,' he said, sliding up next to their captive. 'What's your name?'

Dreamily, the Doctor told him.

Roze called out, 'Must be hard getting that on the front of an envelope.' He plucked out the second contact lens, trying not to flinch, and slipped it into its little wet container.

'Very funny,' Indigo was saying. 'And what's today's date?'

'The eleventh of December, nineteen eighty-three.'

Roze tilted his head, looking at himself in the mirror. Were his roots starting to show? Indigo might be able to get away with his metallic red hair, but two people with the same dye job . . . it was a shame about the contacts. The sparkling red and gold of his irises looked good with the black hair.

'How many fingers am I holding up?'

'Three.'

'All right. Looks as though it's working.' Indigo glanced up as Roze came back out of the bathroom. 'If we have to leave in a hurry, you're in trouble.'

Roze felt in his shirt pocket for a pair of sunglasses, just in case. 'It's not like he's a big threat . . .' He sat down on the bed, and started emptying the man's pockets in case there was anything useful there.

'Okay, Doctor,' said Indigo. The little man's eyelids fluttered, and Indigo gave him a shove to wake him up a bit. 'Let's move on to the harder questions. Where are we from?'

'Lalande 21185 in Ursa Major,' said the Doctor. 'At least, that's what they call it here.'

Keys, coins from a dozen different planets, bits of technology held together with gaffer tape. Roze picked up a little black box with flashing lights, turned it around in his hands. Didn't do anything. It was all just junk.

'When did you visit our planet?'

'Eight Lalandan years ago.'

'What did you do there?'

The Doctor's eyes grew cloudy with remembering. 'Stopped the virus.'

'Can you tell me more about that?'

Roze said, 'I thought you said we had to get on with it.' Indigo snapped his fingers at him, and Roze shut up.

'There was a virus,' said the Doctor. 'Killed everything with DNA. They were going to have a war . . .'

'No, we weren't,' said Indigo. 'We were trying to stop one. But the rebels couldn't understand that. They left us without any defences!'

Roze gave a little sigh. Indigo always had to bring politics into everything. He picked up his own bag, checking the vitamin supplements in their little brown bottle for the third time that day. There was still only a week's worth left. 'Will you stop fidgeting?' said Indigo. Roze grimaced and put the pills away.

'The virus was no defence,' the Doctor was muttering. 'One mistake and you . . .'

Indigo put a finger across the little man's mouth, silencing him. 'We had a mandate to create and deploy the virus,' he said. 'Who did you think you were, coming from outside and interfering in our democratic decisions?'

The little man looked shaken, even through the haze of the drug. Roze ventured, 'Indigo, you'd better get on with it.'

Indigo pulled a piece of paper out of his rucksack. He peered at it for a few seconds. 'True or false,' he said. 'You were on Earth in nineteen seventy-three.'

The Doctor frowned. 'True.'

'You were involved with UNIT at that time.'

'I –'

'True or false.'

'True.'

'You had access to top secret information about nuclear weaponry during that time.'

'True,' said the Doctor sleepily.

'All right,' said Indigo. 'This is your chance to make up for what you did to our planet.'

'I didn't save it,' murmured the Doctor. His eyes were closed now. 'I didn't save your planet.'

'No. You just messed around in our internal politics. A lot of people died in that rebellion. Roze and I just barely escaped. Look at him, Doctor.' The Time Lord rolled his head loosely to the side, frowned up at Roze. 'Look at him. He was just a junior clerk, but they would have torn him limb from limb.'

'I didn't save you,' muttered the Doctor. Roze was hooked on his eyes.

'And the rebels just deployed the viral weapons anyway. How can you sleep at night?'

'Don't,' said the Doctor. 'I don't sleep.'

'What do you mean, you don't sleep?'

'I try not to sleep . . . two years from now one of the viral caches is triggered by the government.'

'What?' said Roze.

'Two years from now,' repeated the Doctor. 'Another rebellion. The virus gets out and chews up everything living.'

'This won't work,' said Indigo. 'You can't lie to me.'

'I can't lie,' said the Doctor. 'I'm full of truth serum, remember?'

Roze breathed, 'How do you know?'

'I've been back to Lalande,' said the little man. 'But by then it was too late. History was locked in place. It had taken another five years for the virus to spread across the entire planet.'

'But the emergency evacuations,' said Roze. He realized he was standing up, hands pressed to his mouth. 'But they planned . . . they have the evacuations planned.'

'Everyone was infected,' said the Doctor. 'Everything was infected.' His pupils were so dilated, they looked like two dark holes in his face, holes into nothing. 'The virus chewed through the ships the way it was designed to.'

'But why didn't you just come up with a cure or something?' Roze breathed. 'Why didn't you just go back in time and warn them?'

'It was too late,' said the Doctor. 'It had happened.'

'Two years from now?'

'That's the truth.'

Roze looked at Indigo, his glittering eyes filling up with tears. He felt himself stumbling away, finding the door handle. Behind him, Indigo was shouting something, but he didn't care.

Alekto

One picosecond from now

You can't go through SOLID stuff. Where my fingers brush on the cinnamon bricks, they (the bricks) get older and younger, a few seconds, that's all. Maybe you could see my fingerprints in those sluggish atoms, if you looked close enough. But who's going to look?

So I have to go up, up, into the air, stepping on the spinning molecules. I can walk right around in a big SPIR-RRRALLLLL, see? My arms move through the nothingness between the liquid dancing of the particles, lifted, drifting, faint peppermint.

The glass is a liquid too, you see? I can shoulder my way through that slow cascade. The pane is already a little thicker at the bottom. I push my face into the stuff, thrusting my fingers into the waterfall. *There!* My hand is right through.

I look back as I wriggle and slide through the glass. Where I've touched it, there are tiny smudges and sparkling colours inside the window. More of my fingerprints. But who's going to look?

There's a couple of aliens in the room. One up, one down, lying on the bed. What're they up to?

Piece of METAL, that heavy electron soup a sharp fleck in the empty air of the room. The one up has got a pocket knife. He's talking – he's the man in charge. I have to tune in to those waves in the gas to find out what's going on.

100

'I said you couldn't lie to me,' he says. 'You know what I want.'

He's sitting down next to the alien on the bed. He's got that blade right up to his *eye*! 'I'm waiting.'

'There are only the two of you, aren't there?' says the man on the bed. Oh, he's sparkling with time, he's been all through time, its fingerprints are all over him! He's the one I've been looking for! I have to talk to this guy! 'What on earth do you think you're going to do?'

'Like,' says knife-man, 'I'm really going to tell you.'

He's going to do it, he's really going to do it!

He's got one hand up in the air, his free hand. I close my own hands around it, pressing my palms to the organic envelope of living skin.

A few months from now he gets a ride back to Lalande. It's only eight light years away, right? A passing flying saucer. The sharp tang of the strange gasses in the ship's air. The lurch in his belly as they touch down. Home.

And then he spends a couple of years trying to get back into the government. He eats some *real* food and talks to some *real* people. And then everybody dies.

He remembers that afternoon of complete panic, two years from now, him and the other civil servants trying to keep what has happened secret, but the corpses come stumbling out of the cordoned-off area in their hundreds of thousands, the grass disintegrating where they tread.

His own face peels off in chunks in a tiny government shuttle crammed so full that the living keep the dead standing up.

It hasn't happened yet. He drops the knife. He starts screaming and screaming. He runs out of the room.

The guy on the bed just lies there, sleepily turning his head to watch. His eyes are okay. 'Thanks,' he says softly.

Wow, this is the real thing. I peer into his face. Can he see me? How does he know I'm there? He reaches out to me, just a movement of the fingers of one hand. I curl my fingers around it.

We both get the shakes. It's like two radio stations jamming each other. Luckily he's tranked and I'm used to this

101

stuff anyway. After a few seconds the waves of jittering fade away and we're in contact.

I see what I look like to him. Yeah, I've got a human face, human hands, but the rest of me is tracks and trails of time and molecules, spreading and spiralling back and out like feathers. I look like I have wings.

'You're beautiful,' he breathes. 'What's your name?'

I'm running my other hand over his hair and face, I can't help it. His timelines are all tangled up. He's like a book I want to read, before he can wake up and run away.

'It's been a long time since I had a name,' I tell him. 'What's your name?'

'I'm the Doctor,' he says.

Doctor! 'Can you make me well again?'

There's a machine next to him on the bed, along with some bits of junk. It sends spiralling lines out into time, and when they brush against me, the machine's lights flicker and it beeps and twitters. I press my hand against it, and it squawks and squeals and dies.

'What happened to you?' he asks.

I wish I could remember what happened to me.

'I found something . . . I'm not supposed to be like this! I found a thing that did this to me.'

'You're slightly out of phase,' he says. 'That's all it is. You must have been this way for a long time.' I nod. He sees a thousand faces nodding, smearing like a rainbow. 'Your temporal tangent is blurring all over the place. But all we have to do is put you in stasis for a few seconds, and re-anchor you.'

'You mean you could do it?' WOW! 'You could fix me?'

He frowns. 'I need to find my TARDIS first. The equipment I'll need is inside. My space-time ship. She's gone . . .' He's blinking, trying to stay awake. 'Can you help me find her?'

'Yes,' I say. 'I know what to look for. Go to sleep.'

'No,' he says. Suddenly he makes a sound, a sort of moan, as my fingertips brush down over his left shoulder. Ghost pain. I take my hand away.

'Was that the past or the future?' he asks, breathlessly.

'You should sleep off that drug,' I tell him. 'When you wake up, you'll be fine.'

'No,' he says. He can't keep his eyes open. 'I don't want any dreams, no dreams.'

So I run the fingernail of my ring finger over his forehead, and the blackness and the silence wrap him up. No dreams.

13

Abduction Greys

Chris and Tony had been sent to ask at the police stations around the place, looking for their slightly odd 'foreign' friend, who might have lost her way while camping.

After three different lots of mildly bored police, they stumped glumly back to the car. The disguised Tzun sat in the passenger seat, hands primly folded in his lap, letting Chris drive.

'It's weird,' said the Adjudicator, as he pulled out onto the road with much more than his usual caution. 'You're better at faking the twentieth century than I am.'

'I still find the police intimidating,' admitted Tony. 'A bit hard to hurdle.'

'I didn't know whether to threaten violence or offer a bribe.'

'Sometimes I think it would be more straightforward if I switched off the hologram.' Tony's voice changed into a ridiculous buzz. 'Bow before me, Earthling scum, or I'll eat your heads!'

Chris broke up laughing. 'Don't do that in front of Roz,' he said. The Tzun made a muffled noise like a phone ringing. 'Hey, how'd you do that?'

Tony took out his communicator. 'Hello? Yes?'

The voice at the other end was so faint they could barely hear it. 'It's Joel. I think I have an emergency here.'

'Where are you?' said Tony, speaking softly. The answer was indistinct. Chris spun the wheel, pulling over. Cars flashed past them in the murky afternoon as they strained to hear.

'Woods near Greenham.' Joel was whispering. Tony was operating controls on the communicator to try to get a fix on him. 'Two soldiers. Helicopter. I'm hiding.'

'Stay there,' said Tony. 'We'll come and get you.'

'Should we get reinforcements?' said Chris.

Tony pulled the map out of the glovebox. 'He's right about *here*. We have to beat them to him.'

'Right you are,' said Chris, turning the key. Gravel sprayed out from the tyres as they pulled back out onto the road. The Adjudicator floored it.

'Oh dear,' said Tony.

Roz sat on a folding stool, irked.

There were a number of irksome things in her immediate vicinity. She kept herself amused by listing them. Firstly, there was the miserable weather. Secondly, there was the appalling cheerfulness of the women who were trying to live in a bunch of tents in said weather. Thirdly, there was said women's gruesome dedication to peace, non-violence, colourful artwork, a better world, and smiling when they were up to their ankles in freezing mud.

This was the third camp they'd visited. A woman and her young daughter were making a banner. They laughed, splashing paint over the long strip of cloth. Jacqui and Ms Randrianasolo were chatting with a couple of women. It was all women. Roz supposed there was a sort of strange balance there. Women outside the fence with the tents, men inside with the guns.

A car drove up to the camp. Two women emerged and sloshed through the mud to where Jacqui and Ms Randriana-solo were talking to the others. Roz hoped that in between the chit-chat they remembered to ask about Ia Jareshth.

Plus ça change. She'd arrested protesters at Subport Eight who had sat down around polaric VTOL craft so they couldn't take off without killing the crowd. She'd held back crowds of Undercity rabble who'd been protesting the genetic damage they said was done by the city's gravity beams.

Shame she couldn't tell the cheerful women that ten centuries from now it'd still be the same, with the state doing whatever it liked and nearly everyone going along with it. That ought to take the rosiness out of their cheeks.

'Hey, Roz,' said Ms Randrianasolo. 'You ought to hear this.'

Roz got up and walked carefully through the muddy grass. 'We just had a right scare,' said one of the newcomers, a little old lady with huge glasses, starting her anecdote over again. 'We were in the Cooked Goose, trying to get some service, when a couple of soldiers marched in and asked where the "troublemakers" were. We just about fainted. Anyway, it wasn't us they were after. It was a couple of punks who'd been running around yelling.'

'Punks,' said Roz.

'You should have seen one of them. He'd done something to his eyes. All sparkly they were, like red tinsel.' Ms Randrianasolo gave Roz a meaningful look. 'Anyway, the soldiers took them away, but they gave them a terrible knocking around first. I've never seen people panic like that in my seventy-two years.'

'I think I might make a phone call,' said Roz.

'There's no phone box,' said the old woman. 'Unless you want to pop round and borrow the phone in the sentry box.'

This made all of the cheerful women laugh, for some reason. Roz found herself silently praying for sleet.

Chris pulled over and switched off the engine. He looked at Tony. 'You're in charge,' he said.

The Tzun took Chris's communicator and fiddled with it for a moment. 'This will lead you to his tracking signal,' he said. 'The wood is only a kilometre thick, though it's about five kilometres long. Joel isn't more than a klick from here.'

'What do I do if I run into a soldier?'

'Pretend you got lost,' said the Tzun. 'Don't let them get hold of your communicator under any circumstances.'

Chris nodded. 'What will you do if you run into a soldier?'

Tony produced a long, silver wand with an oddly shaped,

flat piece of metal on the end. 'I haven't used one of these since the incursion.'

'What is it? Some kind of, um, probe?'

The Tzun's hologram smiled weirdly.

Benny shook the Doctor's shoulder. 'G'way,' he said, 'I'm sleeping.'

'No, you're not,' she said.

He blinked awake, looking up at her and Isaac. 'Oh,' he said. 'How did you find me?'

'The usual way – we just followed the trail of disturbances. The hotel owner let us in.'

'Mmm.'

'Are you all right?'

'Mmm-hmm.'

'Doctor?'

'Yes?'

'You and Isaac need to talk.'

'Mmm.'

'Doctor?'

'Five more minutes.'

There was no way to move silently through the forest. No way that Chris knew about, anyway. He settled for crunching along, listening hard with one ear while he held the communicator to the other.

There was some kind of tracking doohickey in Joel's communicator, sending out little quantum pulses that the other communicators could follow. Chris heard it as a soft pinging, Dopplering up as he moved in the right direction.

There was no sign of the soldiers. With luck, they'd already given up and gone home.

It wasn't more than ten minutes before the communicator started pinging wildly, indicating close proximity. Chris switched it off, looking around, puzzled. There was no sign of Joel. He hoped the boy (boy? – he wasn't much younger than Chris) hadn't just dropped his communicator.

'Over here,' someone whispered.

Chris spun around, and saw Joel peeking out from under a

fallen tree, his pale face framed by the leaves. 'Wow,' he whispered, hunkering down to help him out. 'You sure were hidden. Any sign of the soldiers?'

'I haven't heard the chopper take off.' The boy was shaking all over. His clothes were soaked. 'But I haven't heard them for maybe twenty minutes.'

'Let's get you back to the car.' Joel nodded stiffly. Chris took out his communicator. 'Tony?' he whispered.

'I'm afraid I can't talk right now!' spluttered the device.

There was a shot, not too far away.

'Oy gevalt,' said Joel.

'Run for the road,' said Chris. 'You'll see the car.'

Joel obediently wobbled off through the forest as quickly as he could manage. Chris ran towards the shot, wondering what he was going to do.

He almost ran right into one of the soldiers. The man was standing stock-still, his mouth hanging open, staring off into the trees. Chris waved a hand in front of the man's face. Nothing.

Tony nipped out from behind a tree and jiggled his wand about. 'He's just reliving some childhood experiences,' he said. 'He'll be fine. Where's Joel?'

'I sent him back to the car.'

'Let's go.'

Chris followed the Tzun through the tangled branches. Suddenly, there was another shot. He looked around wildly. The soldier was running at them from their left. He stopped to take another look.

'Tony,' said Chris. 'Go!'

There wasn't time to discuss it. The camouflaged Tzun glanced back once and ran on.

Chris dived for cover as the man fired again. 'Hey!' he shouted. 'Don't shoot! I give up!'

The man was less than twenty feet away, the rifle still raised. 'Stand up and put your hands on your head!' he shouted.

Chris peeked out from behind the log. There was another man working his way through the trees towards them. He put his hands up and stood up, carefully.

The soldier with the rifle came right up to him, careful to keep him covered as the other man pushed him up against the tree and patted him down. 'Why were you shooting at me?' Chris demanded. 'This isn't private property.'

'I reckon he's human,' said the man who was searching him.

'How the hell would you know?' said the other one. 'Go get the stretcher. I'll keep him covered.'

'Aren't you going to read me my rights?' said Chris. The man with the gun didn't answer.

Benny stood on tiptoe, trying to see between two planks that had been nailed over the broken window of the church. The tips of her boots sank into the soft ground, and she swore as she almost slipped.

'Careful,' said someone. She turned, hanging onto the wall. It was Albinex. 'Can I help?' he said.

'I'm looking for Jason,' she explained. 'He doesn't usually sulk past lunchtime.'

'Oh, well, let me show you the secret entrance,' said Albinex.

She followed him around to the side of the church. He was short – even shorter than the Doctor – wearing denim and a lot of hair gel. It made him look younger than he must be. 'What have you got in here?' she asked.

'Nothing,' smiled Albinex. 'It's a red herring.'

'Oh . . .'

'It's helped to distract awkward visitors on more than one occasion. Ghosthunters are particularly enamoured of it.' They had come to a boarded-up side doorway. Albinex reached up under the boards and undid a catch, and the whole criss-crossed mass of wood swung open. 'It's just an old flyscreen door with planks nailed into it,' he said.

Benny followed him into the church. It was designer-messy on the inside – a layer of dust coating carefully arranged fallen beams and skewed pews. There was no sign of Jason.

'We should just check the crypt,' said Albinex. 'I've been talking to our contacts in the military,' he continued, as they climbed over the rubble. 'Usually they have a few interesting things to tell us.' He opened a heavy door, letting out a puff of stale air. 'Usually there are all sorts of leaks. Not this time.'

'Dad said it was as though we were being teased,' said Benny. Albinex gave the lightswitch a few experimental flicks, then took out a pocket torch.

'Hmm. The military usually wouldn't be so subtle.' Albinex took a few steps down the old stone stairs, and shone his torch around. 'No one home,' he said. 'Have you told the Admiral he's missing?'

'Missing.' Benny pressed her teeth into her bottom lip. 'I don't like this,' she said.

'I don't blame you,' said Albinex. 'Come on, let's see what we can do about it.'

Woodworth's object de lust (and she *still* hadn't found out his last name) was messing about, like a mad scientist, with a bunch of electrical components, peering at them through a delicate pair of bifocals.

Woodworth glanced at her watch. The smell of solder was mixing with the smell of the coffee shop. She'd called in to take a look around the bookshop, and found him here, muttering to himself as he worked.

He yelped as he burned the tip of one of his fingers. 'What exactly is it you're doing?' she said.

'I'm making a ghost-detector,' he said, with the complete seriousness of someone who doesn't realize they're mad.

'I see.' Woodworth took a spoonful of fluff off the top of her cappuccino. 'How does it work?'

'The "ghost" is actually a sentient individual who has been shifted forwards in time by one picosecond,' said the Doctor. 'Producing some very strange effects. This –' he tapped the jumble of components '– will detect the characteristic ripples in local space-time as she moves through it.'

'She? You sound as if you've seen a ghost.'

'I have,' he muttered, joining two diodes with a paperclip. He looked up at her suddenly. 'She could explain the bees,' he said. 'And the out-of-season wheat. Small-scale temporal distortions.'

Woodworth breathed a silent sigh. Who was it who'd said, 'The story of my life – if they're handsome, they're nuts'?

'I would have thought you'd be fascinated,' he said.

'I am,' said Woodworth, 'but that doesn't mean abandoning my natural scepticism.'

He'd finished whatever it was he was doing. Now he wound gaffer tape around the thing to hold all the bits in.

'So what are you going to do with her when you find her?' Woodworth said.

He smiled at her. 'I could ask you the same question.'

14

Aliens R Us

'What's he like?' said Isaac.

Benny was sitting in the overstuffed chair in the middle of the upstairs guestroom. Myn Jareshth watched them both from the edge of the fold-down bed.

Benny said, 'He's like . . . he's like an uncle. An uncle who has a job you don't know much about.'

'How do you mean?'

'You know, something a bit nasty, which none of the grown-ups can tell you about because you're too little . . . so you know little bits about it, just things you've overheard or things you've glimpsed.'

'As though he's in the army.'

'I suppose so.'

'Why an uncle?'

'Well, because he takes you on trips. He's kindly and a bit odd.' She smiled as she drifted back through years of memories. 'He likes jazz and the Beatles, and cats, and dipping croissants in coffee. He's a vegetarian who doesn't like pears.'

'But he's not an uncle if you're an alien monster.'

'He once said that he's what monsters have nightmares about,' said Benny. Her smile faded. 'But everybody's a monster sometimes. I've seen him be callous, and dangerous . . . sometimes he just fails to understand. And then you realize that the friendly uncle is –'

'A façade?'

'No, that's not it. It's more like a mode he can drop into so that he can relate to you.'

'Is he . . . a good man, Benny?'

'Yes.' She nodded firmly. 'Yes, he is.'

'Even if sometimes he does terrible things?'

Benny considered. 'He never does anything because he's lazy or greedy, or for revenge.'

'Does motive make a difference if it's your planet that gets blown up?'

'Maybe not,' said Benny. 'But he really does the best he can.'

Downstairs, ten minutes later.

The Doctor was surrounded by empty coffee cups, his face a grimace of concentration. He held up the device he had built, close to one blue eye, and twiddled with the components.

Isaac watched from behind the counter. He wondered if it looked as though he was hiding there. Determinedly he put down the glasses he was polishing and walked up to the Time Lord.

The Doctor glanced up at him in mid-twiddle.

'I didn't take your TARDIS,' said Isaac.

'And I didn't take your Lacaillan,' said the Doctor wryly.

'We have a problem,' said Isaac.

'Yes. Sit down.'

Isaac sat down. 'What are you making?'

'It's a ghost-detector,' said the Time Lord.

Isaac nodded. 'The aliens who assaulted you were taken by the military,' he said. 'So far as we can tell. I've made a few enquiries, but they've vanished into thin air.'

'They were after information about nuclear warfare,' said the Doctor, 'though I don't know exactly what information, or why they thought I'd have it. It can't be a coincidence, though, that your base of operations is a neutron's throw from a major nuclear facility.'

'We've been here a lot longer than the USAF,' said Isaac. 'We did consider moving when it was first announced they'd be storing Cruise down the road from us.'

'It must have been a bit of a shock.'

113

'You could put it that way,' said Isaac. 'But in the end we discovered the base drew attention *away* from us. And up until now, there haven't actually been any missiles.' He started gathering up the empty cups.

'Ah,' said the Doctor.

'Ah, what?' said Isaac, putting the used cups on the counter.

'That's why they were so interested.' He breathed out a sigh. 'They had very specific information about me. A government source, perhaps. I'm starting to wonder how much they're involved in all of this.'

'You're nothing like the way you're described,' said Isaac.

The Doctor snapped the last component into place on his ghost-detector. 'That's because I'm not your mortal enemy.'

The doorbell jingled. Joel and Tony both tried to get in through the door at once, got jammed, and shot into the shop like corks out of a bottle.

'Doctor!'

'Chris!'

'Admiral!'

'The car is a write-off!'

'They took Chris! We can't track him by his communicator, he tossed it –'

They both yelled as Benny slammed through the door behind them. 'Doctor,' she said, 'there's still no sign of Jason. This has gone beyond sulk.'

'Chris is gone!' said Joel, waving his arms about.

'What!' said Benny. 'Is there a spatio-temporal anomaly around here that people are falling into?'

'They must have been waiting for us! They took him!'

'Who took him?' said Benny. 'What's happened?'

'We'll have to bug out – this is completely out of control now!'

Isaac and the Doctor looked at each other. Together, they shouted, 'Quiet!'

Benny, Joel and Tony fell silent.

'We have a customer upstairs,' said Isaac.

'A helicopter drove me off the road,' said Joel in a stage whisper. 'Two soldiers had me pinned down in the woods, and Tony and Chris came to get me out. The soldiers took Chris.'

114

'RAF?' said Isaac.

'Army,' said Joel.

They all whirled as Roz came into the shop. She looked at them. 'Ms Randrianasolo and Jacqui decided to keep looking. I took a taxi back.'

'Right,' said Isaac. 'Joel and Roz, I want you to evacuate the resident aliens.'

'Myn Jareshth will be safest waiting for his own people tonight,' said the Doctor.

'Someone should stay with him at all times,' said Isaac.

'I will,' said Benny. 'But Jason –'

'What did you say about his father?' said the Doctor.

Benny took a deep breath. 'That he might kill the man. To stop him from beating his children.'

'Jesus Christ,' said Joel.

'We can't let him do that,' said the Doctor, getting up.

'What's that?' said Joel.

'A ghost-detector,' said the Doctor.

'A ghost-detector?' said Benny.

'Hey cool,' said Joel. 'A PKE meter.'

'What?' said Benny.

'Quiet!' shouted the Doctor again. Everyone glanced at the ceiling. A board creaked as Woodworth stepped on it. 'Roz, Chris is missing.'

'What!' said Roz.

'The ghost!' said Benny. 'Oh my God! She must have followed us!'

'I wish I could contact UNIT,' said the Doctor. 'We might be able to get this cleared up.'

'We can't risk it,' said Isaac.

'I don't believe this!' Roz whispered, not very quietly. 'People are just *vanishing* around us, and we're just *sitting* here!' She glared at the Doctor. 'The holiday is over!' She rounded on Isaac. 'And so's the turf war! It's not coincidence that this has all happened since we arrived. Maybe Ia Jareshth did run off, but where is she now? Who took the TARDIS? Where the hell are Jason and Chris? We have a *situation* here.' She planted her hands on her hips. 'What are you two going to do about it?'

115

'Are we bugging out, sir?' said Tony, in the awkward silence that followed.

'I'll let you know,' said Isaac.

There was nothing in the storeroom but more books. No files, nothing obviously unusual.

Woodworth figured she had at least another few minutes before they stopped arguing about whatever it was. She pushed open the other door and found herself on a narrow, carpeted landing. Three other doors led off it.

She opened the nearest door. It was a bedroom – spick and span, no clutter at all. She slipped in, leaving the door open an inch.

When the odd radio signals had first been detected by the USAF, they'd passed them on to the British Army for identification. But the signals had stopped after a day, and anyway no-one knew what they were, so the matter was forgotten.

One of Woodworth's contacts had brought her a copy of the signals, and, more importantly, the triangulation that had placed the source in Little Caldwell. She'd spent a shivering night with an army radio in the hope that whoever was sending the signals might transmit again.

It had been worth it, even though there'd been nothing more. That kind of transmission had been recorded only half a dozen times. Oh yes, indeed, it had been worth it.

There was a safe. She ignored it. She found what she was looking for in the sock drawer.

She picked up the black sphere, turned it around in her hand. It was light and heavy at once, as though there was some dense object inside the thin shell, slightly off-centre. She'd seen enough nonhuman technology to recognize it when she saw it.

So why was there a red stencil on the side saying EMER-GENCY TRANSPONDER?

She put the device back in amongst the socks and pushed the drawer shut.

In the cupboard, in a plastic bag, there was a strange uniform. She unzipped the bag a little, felt the strange fabric

116

between her fingertips, caught a distant smell of aftershave and smoke.

She slipped back into the bookshop moments before the proprietor appeared at the top of the stairs.

A few more minutes, and she'd drive back to the base and see how they were getting on. She'd have to organize a raid on this place, and soon, before they worked out what was going on and took off. There was plenty of room at the base. Room enough for everyone.

15

Interlude, With Tabby

'You know, Wolsey,' said Jason, 'I don't think we're in
Kansas any more.'

16

Belling the cat

Roz caught up with the Doctor as he was about to get into Albinex's car. She put her hand on the door before he could close it. 'Right,' she said. 'Exactly what are you up to?'

The Time Lord looked up at her from the driver's seat. 'I'm borrowing Albinex's car to look for Chris,' he said.

'Then I'll come with you,' she said, starting to walk to the passenger side.

The Doctor got out and waved his hands at her over the roof. 'Wait a moment, Roz,' he said. She gave him one of her best glares.

'Listen,' he said. 'You were right. Everything that's happened hasn't been coincidence. Someone noticed my arrival. And now they're trying to get my attention.'

'By stealing people.'

'And the TARDIS.'

'I hope,' said Roz, leaning on the roof, 'that this isn't one of your brilliant let-the-baddie-bash-me-up schemes.'

The Doctor couldn't help but smile. 'No, it's more of an if-they-want-me-let-them-come-and-get-me scheme.'

'I'm not sure I can see the difference.' Roz swung herself into the passenger seat. The Doctor ducked his head and blinked at her across the driver's seat.

'You know, there was a story they told us once at the Academy. Something for the cadets to think about. Once upon a time the mice decided they'd have to put a bell on the local cat, so they'd hear her coming.'

119

'Yes,' said the Doctor. 'I've met the author.'

'So you know the ending. None of the mice would volunteer to confront the cat and put the bell on its collar. Because who wants to get eaten? None of this is your fault.'

'I should have got involved,' he said, 'instead of going off in a huff.'

'Well, you're involved now,' she said. 'For Goddess' sake, get in the damned car.'

'You're kind . . .' said Myn Jareshth.

Benny smiled at him from the big chair, looking up from the magazine she was totally failing to read.

The alien had simply sat there for ages, not looking at anything in particular. Politely, patiently, waiting.

'You and your father are brave,' he said softly.

'Believe me,' said Benny, 'it doesn't take a lot of courage to handle the babysitting end of the job.'

Myn Jareshth tipped his head, not understanding. 'You're brave,' he repeated. 'To stay here with me. When the alien hunters are hunting me.' His delicate fingers traced shapes in front of him, as though looking to pluck the English words from the air. 'We come in pairs,' he said. 'The hunters will know that, if there's a Ia Jareshth Kto, there's a Myn Jareshth Kto.'

'It won't matter after tonight,' Benny said. 'After we get you home.'

He lowered his head, the fine white hair obscuring his eyes. 'There's not a Ia Jareshth any more,' he said.

'You don't know that,' said Benny.

'Your father is brave,' he said again. 'He came to the *National Hurricane Center*.' The words had a strange flavour, like a memorized phrase. 'Ia Jareshth and I were looking at one of the computers at the *National Hurricane Center*. The police caught us, and kept us in a room until *Colonel Kramer* could arrive.'

The Lacaillan blinked slowly, remembering. 'But *Mister Beven* communicated with your father. He pretended there was an emergency, and helped us run away. Then your father came for us. We were hiding in another room. *Admiral*

Summerfield and *Mister Beven* helped us run away to a car. Then your father drove us to an aeroplane while the soldiers were shooting at us.' He folded his hands back into his lap. 'I wish I could use your language more precisely.'

Benny said hoarsely, 'That's all right. Sometimes telling a story simply makes it more effective.'

Myn Jareshth said, 'You are also half of a pair.'

Benny bit her lip. 'Yes. I am.'

'Then we are having a similar experience,' concluded the Lacaillan.

'You mean, you know how I feel?' Benny plonked back down in the overstuffed chair. 'Jason does this from time to time. He's usually so . . . clingy. But sometimes we just need to get a bit of air between us.' She cupped her chin in her hands. 'At least, I hope that's what he's doing. What if the people who took Chris have got him? Oh shit, I'm crying.'

Myn Jareshth raised his hands, wanting to do something, not sure of the etiquette.

'I'm okay,' said Benny. 'I'm all right. You're right, Myn Jareshth, we are having the same experience.'

He watched her, quietly. 'You are very brave,' he said again.

Graeme poked his tip around the corner. Woodworth was browsing the shelves. She had left her rucksack leaning up against the counter.

The spatula hopped across the floor, heading for the bag. Woodworth turned around, pushing the book she'd been looking at back onto the shelf. Graeme threw himself flat on the floor, and started inching across the wood like a worm.

He wasn't going to make it. Woodworth was reaching for the bag. She'd even see him when she picked it up.

'On your way?' said Isaac's voice.

Graeme hunched up and peeked around the bag. Woodworth had straightened up. 'I've got to get back to Newbury. There's someone I have to meet.'

'Let me give you one of our catalogues,' said Isaac, rummaging in the fliers on the counter.

Graeme sprang up and dived into the rucksack. Moments

later, Woodworth shoved the photocopied catalogue into the bag beside him and zipped it closed.

Roz was holding the Doctor's ghost-detector in her lap. 'Exactly how is this thing going to help us find Chris?' she said.

'It seems a little unlikely,' said the Doctor, 'that the kidnappings and the ghost don't have something to do with one another.'

'Fair enough,' said Roz. She poked at one of the wires hanging out of the lash-up. 'What's its range?'

'About four miles, reliably,' said the Doctor. 'Anything further than that is luck.'

Fifty miles away

They didn't ask him any questions.

Three soldiers – two men and a woman – literally dragged him out of the jeep and into the building. He got glimpses of a high metal fence, more soldiers crunching along a gravel drive, cars parked beside the cold brick house. It was hard to make out the details of where he was when the woman insisted on keeping him in a headlock.

'I can walk, you know,' he said.

They slammed open a door and dropped him headfirst on the floor with a *crunch*.

He lay very still on the floor, the bone and concrete sound echoing through his whole body. He didn't want to move, because his head felt as though it might roll away into a corner.

They grabbed at him, and he tried to protest, pushing them away with hands that had become as soft and useless as marshmallows. They pulled off his clothes, stuffing them into labelled plastic bags.

'Right,' someone ordered. 'Tiller, Heer, Weatherford, out of here.'

Chris pulled himself into a hunched sitting position and looked up. He was in some kind of clinic. The light seemed to go right through his face and bounce off the back of his skull.

The door slammed behind a middle-aged woman in street clothes and a man in a white coat, like a cartoon scientist. The woman was holding a gun. She wasn't pointing it at him, just holding it, the way the scientist was holding his clipboard.

'Who are you people?' exploded Cwej. He wanted to get to his feet, but a combination of dizziness and modesty kept him on the floor. 'If I'm under arrest, you've got to tell me what the charge is, and where I am.'

The woman said, 'I want a full medical. Blood and tissue samples, X-rays, the lot. If you find anything out of the ordinary, no matter how trivial, I want to know about it. And get his fingerprints checked out.'

'Right,' said the scientist. 'Get on the scales.'

It took Chris a moment to realize the man was talking to him. 'Like fun I will,' he said.

'I'll get you some assistants,' said the woman, going to the door. 'And for God's sake, if you kill him, get him to dissection straight away this time, will you?'

17

Rescue

Tony was sitting at one of the tables, drinking Tzun food supplement through a straw. Joel was fidgeting behind the counter, Nelson the cat circling round his ankle. Albinex stood at the window, watching the Admiral overseeing the evacuation. The volunteers had started arriving a few hours after the call had gone out.

Isaac was going over their routes once again, making sure the aliens were carefully hidden under blankets and bundles. The volunteers had done this a few times now. But this time there were lines of worry on foreheads. One couple had even packed up and gone home once they'd learnt the situation.

'This is awful,' said Joel. 'I hate waiting like this. If only we had a clue. Just any kind of lead at all.'

Tony sat bolt upright. 'Where's Graeme?'

Albinex looked behind the counter. 'I don't see him.'

'I'm getting a message,' said Tony. He tilted his head in an almost human gesture, as though listening to a faint voice.

Albinex sat down opposite the disguised Tzun. 'What is it?' he said. 'What's the message?'

'He's . . . he's in a bag. At a house. He got inside someone's bag.' Tony's hologram eyes widened. 'It's that woman who came to visit the Doctor this afternoon.'

'The one who was in the bookshop?'

Tony nodded. 'The house is far away. It's full of soldiers. It's – that's Chris! That's the Doctor's companion!'

'Rock and roll!' said Joel. 'Smarter than the average spatula!'

Albinex said, 'Can he guide us there?'

Tony nodded. 'I can follow his telepathic transmission.'

'I'll get the Admiral,' said Albinex.

'Hang on,' said Joel. 'My car's a write-off, and we can't all fit into yours.'

They looked at one another.

'There's only one thing for it,' said Joel.

The Doctor drove on the way back, his mouth drawn into a tight line. Roz cradled the ghost-detector in her lap. There hadn't been a peep out of it.

'We'll find him,' she said. 'We'll find all of them.'

He glanced at her, sideways. 'I was counting on you to be the pessimist I could disagree with.'

Roz didn't smile. 'The truth is, wherever they are, they're probably causing as much trouble as they can manage. Chris can take care of himself. And from everything I've heard about Jason, so can he.'

'If we just had one proper lead,' said the Doctor. 'To tell you the truth, I feel . . . I feel unrehearsed. I didn't know about any of this. There wasn't time to prepare.'

'It's not the first time we've walked into a new and dangerous situation without a map,' said Roz. 'And it won't be the last.'

'I don't want to lose one of you because I didn't see it coming,' said the Doctor, with difficulty. Roz decided she didn't like the implications of that, and didn't say anything.

The Doctor slowed as they were coming up to the petrol station just outside Little Caldwell. Isaac, Joel, Albinex and Tony were gathered at the entrance to the garage. The Time Lord pulled up to one of the petrol pumps. 'What are they up to?' said Roz, craning her neck to see.

There was a roar from inside the garage, the sound of an engine that hadn't been used for a long time. Isaac and Tony stood back.

Out of the garage rolled a van. Its many-coloured paint was faded, and one of its windows had been smashed, a big piece of cobwebbed plastic taped in place over the frame.

Joel rolled down the driver's side window and said, 'It

needs gas. And we'd better bring the toolkit along.'

Albinex came out of the garage, clutching a big metal box as the Doctor and Roz walked up. 'Got it.'

'What's up?' said Roz, as Joel rolled the van down to the petrol pumps.

Isaac glanced at the Doctor. 'Graeme stowed away in Ms Woodworth's bag,' he said. 'She took him to some sort of military base, fifty or sixty miles from here. Chris is being held there.'

'Ellen?' said the Doctor.

'Graeme?' said Roz.

'The spatula,' said the Doctor. 'He's an Auton, isn't he?'

'Just a shred of Auton matter,' said Isaac. 'He was left behind after the last invasion. He and Tony have a sort of rapport. We can follow Graeme's signal to the base.'

'Outwitted by a spatula,' said Roz.

'What about Myn Jareshth?' said the Doctor.

'I've got one of our volunteer hosts to take him on until tonight,' said Isaac. 'We've evacuated all of our guests. It's entirely possible we won't be able to come back here.'

'What's the plan?' said the Doctor, clasping his hands behind his back.

Joel said, 'Simple. Schlep over to the base, bust in, and rescue Chris and anyone else who needs rescuing.'

The Doctor smiled at Isaac. 'Will you be wanting any help?'

'All hands on deck,' said the Admiral.

Benny stood outside the Pyramid, hands in the pockets of her denim jacket. The sun was just going down.

It was possible they wouldn't be able to come back here. Ever. Her father had asked her to lock up the shop, and bring a big cardboard box downstairs that contained their important records.

Little Caldwell stood sad and quiet in the sunset, evacuated.

Suddenly, a psychedelically painted van drove up the main street.

Benny grinned madly at the Doctor, who was leaning out of the driver's window, waving at her. 'What's this?' she said.

'A relic of the seventies!' said Joel, slamming open the side door. 'I always wanted to see this thing come out of mothballs!'

Benny hefted the cardboard box and jumped in. 'So we're going incognito, are we?'

The Doctor drove the van along the M4 about twice as fast as a human being could safely manage. Roz sat in the passenger seat, gaping out of the window, as they passed yet another police car too quickly for them to read the van's plates.

And she'd thought Chris's driving was a nightmare.

Roz half turned in her seat. In the back, Isaac's crew were sitting cross-legged on the floor, quietly preparing themselves.

'Hologram projector,' said Isaac. Albinex, Joel, Jacqui and Ms Randrianasolo all made the same gesture, tapping themselves on the shoulder to check their projector was in place. 'Handscan.' Attached to their belts. 'Communicator.' In jacket or jean pockets.

Benny was sitting at the back of the van. She glanced at Roz over the top of the ritual preparations. 'Glasses.' Joel and Isaac both had a pair, looking like ordinary sunglasses, but with heads-up displays and X-ray and IR scanners built in. 'We probably won't need these, but keep them handy.'

Only Tony wasn't taking part in the equipment check, sitting very still. He had switched off his hologram generator to conserve power. His big, slanted black eyes were blank with concentration as he 'listened' for messages from Graeme.

Roz hefted the bag they'd brought from Greenham Common. Jacqui and Ms Randrianasolo had borrowed three pairs of bolt-cutters, strong enough to snip through the fence that surrounded the USAF base.

There were no guns. They were going in without weapons of any kind.

They were going to get their butts kicked.

The group had finished their check. Isaac was following their progress in a big, skinny book of roadmaps, talking to Albinex. Ms R and Jacqui were joking about something. Ms Randrianasolo reached up and tapped her hologram generator, and suddenly wasn't there. Jacqui laughed and thumped her on the invisible arm.

On the other hand, thought Roz, this bunch of amateurs knew what they were doing.

The van hadn't even broken down once.

It was very dark by the time Tony announced they were nearing the base. The Doctor had slowed down as they negotiated the smaller roads. Benny had changed places with Roz, peering out of the window with a frown on her face.

'I've been here before,' she said.

The Doctor didn't take his eyes off the road. 'Yes,' he said softly.

In the back, Jacqui was dozing, leaning on Roz. Joel was fidgeting with his seatbelt. Her father's eyes were closed, as though he was trying to sense their surroundings, build up a diagram of danger and opportunity, a tactical map inside his head.

The Doctor pulled over to the side of the road and switched off the engine. The sudden silence rang in Benny's ears. Jacqui came awake, blinking.

'It's about half a mile down the road,' said Tony. He switched his hologram back on, changing from Casper the Friendly Ghost back into the bearded cook from the Pyramid.

'Two teams,' said Isaac. 'Doctor, take Roz and Jacqui to the main gate. Joel, Albinex, Tony, Ms Randrianasolo, Benny and I will cut the fence and search for Graeme. Once we're in, we'll split up into pairs.'

'What's our cover?' said Ms R.

'Peace protesters,' said Isaac. 'Don't fight, just make a lot of fuss. We'll need all the distractions we can get.'

The Doctor had been rummaging in his pockets. He brought out a couple of passes in plastic wallets. 'These are reasonably up to date . . .' he muttered, examining them. 'If nothing else, we can take up some of their time arguing the point.'

Benny looked at him. 'You're sure about this.'

'Oh yes,' said the Doctor.

'Let's do it,' said Isaac.

Woodworth was running an eye down the clipboard, looking for anything interesting. She glanced at the man in the dentist's chair. He had started to cry, and the tears were running up his temples.

Jacobus was waiting impatiently for her approval, fiddling with the buttons of his lab coat. He always wore that spotless white thing, for some reason. If you really had to do quarantine work, Woodworth knew, you had to wear a lot more than a white coat. Thankfully, the path work was all negative. Very negative.

'He's a little *too* healthy,' said Jacobus, trying to peer over the top of the clipboard. 'Don't you think?'

'Maybe he was born without an appendix,' she commented, without looking up. 'It happens.'

'It's not only the appendix. It's a lot of little things.' Jacobus tried to reach over the top of the clipboard. 'He's never had chickenpox, for instance. We can't find any scar tissue on him that's more than a few years old. His only health problem at the moment is the concussion your clumsy troopers managed to give him.'

Woodworth looked down at the man again. He was blinking in the violent light of the dentist's chair, eyes cloudy with tears and confusion. He pulled at the straps holding him down, fitfully, and the dentist swore as his probe poked into the gum.

'Is he human?' Woodworth asked.

'There are some genetic questions I want cleared up before I decide that,' said Jacobus. 'And then there's his teeth and nails . . .'

Woodworth put down the clipboard, crouching beside the man, and snapped on a latex glove. She took one of his hands. The skin was cold and clammy. The nails were – like a woman's nails, she thought. No, thick like a man's, but sharp. Shaped wrong.

The dentist caught her eye. 'I want these,' he said, tapping a probe against the man's teeth. 'If you're not planning on keeping him.'

Woodworth consulted her clipboard again. 'They were sharpened?'

The dentist shook his head. 'They grew that way,' he said.

He plucked cotton wool from the man's mouth. 'Can I please have a drink of water?' said the 'patient' woozily.

'He'd better rest up,' said Jacobus, 'if you are keeping him . . .'

Woodworth handed the dentist his clipboard.

'I haven't decided yet,' she said.

Benny and Isaac were running across the grounds of the big, old house. They dropped behind a bush, squinting into the lights that surrounded the building.

'I thought the place would be crawling with guards,' she whispered.

'Only at strategic points,' he said. 'And sometimes not even then.'

'This isn't the first time you've done this.'

Isaac shook his head. 'You said you'd been here before.'

'In nineteen sixty-eight,' whispered Benny. 'The Doctor was held here for three weeks. They were supposed to have closed the place down. I'm worried about him.'

'Will he let us down?' asked Isaac.

'No!'

'Then you let me worry about him.'

They both ducked down as someone appeared from a side door. It was a white-coated lab worker, a man in his thirties. He lit up a cigarette, peering into the darkness beyond the brilliant lights.

'Right,' said Isaac. He touched the hologram generator on his shoulder, and suddenly he was gone.

White Coat looked up at the rustling noise. Benny expected to see him jerk suddenly and crumple, punched by the Invisible Man. But instead Isaac used a nerve pinch, catching the man as he fell silently. Probably like one of the pinches she'd been taught at the Academy.

He blipped back into existence and waved at her. She climbed out from behind the bush. He was examining the man's ID badge. 'He's a dentist,' he said, surprised.

Benny glanced up at the house. 'I hope we're raiding the right place.'

Sergeant Lidz grimaced up at the pair of idiots who were making his life difficult. 'Look,' he said, 'like I told you, sir,

130

your pass is valid, but you can't bring your assistants onto the premises unless they have prearranged passes too.'

The little man made an exasperated noise. The black woman glared down at Lidz. The other woman looked around in a vague fashion.

'I want to speak to your commanding officer,' said the little man.

'I've already explained, sir, he's not available.'

The little man shoved the phone across the desk at him. 'Then call someone who is available.'

The main doors banged open, and suddenly the foyer of the building was full of troops. Lidz stood up to see past the three nuisances.

It was another black woman and a short man, being dragged roughly in by four soldiers.

'Smith?' said Lidz.

Private Smith saluted. 'We caught these two in the grounds, sergeant.'

'You're breaking my arm!' shouted the woman.

Lidz glanced back at the three pests, suddenly worried. The little man caught his eye.

Held it.

Lidz turned back to the trespassers. 'What are you doing here?'

The man said, 'We're protesting the military's use of this house as a base. It ought to be with the National Trust.'

Lidz glanced back at the little man, who nodded. 'How did you get in?'

'We climbed over the fence,' said the woman.

'Right,' said Lidz. 'Since you haven't done any criminal damage, I'm going to have you thrown off the premises. If you come back into the grounds, it'll be much worse, all right?'

The two protesters scowled, but said nothing.

Lidz jerked his head, and the soldiers hauled them out the door.

'In a good mood tonight, sarge?' grinned Private Smith.

'Watch it,' growled Lidz. Smith saluted again and scurried out after the others.

'Excuse me,' said the little man.

Lidz turned around.

The short black woman punched his lights out.

Gillikin was sure he'd heard a noise.

He put down his newspaper and came out of his office, switching on the lights in the main lab. It took a moment for the thick fluorescent tubes to buzz into action.

Nothing but space corpses. He grunted to himself.

Yesterday the colonel had been very seriously telling them to keep an eye out, in case any of the subjects showed signs of change or even resuscitation. They were alien life forms, she had reminded them. Anything might be possible.

As far as Gillikin was concerned, it was like Elvis's coroner had said, right. If they weren't dead before the post-mortem, they sure as hell were now.

Shit, there it was again!

Gillikin narrowed his eyes, turning, checking every shadow and every shape. He ducked down, hands on his thighs. Nothing was hiding under the trolleys, heavy with their plastic-bagged burdens. Nothing he could see, anyway.

Wait a minute. The cupboard. What if someone was hiding in the cupboard?

He mentally counted corpses, just in case one of them had got up and started to walk around. Nope, there was the blue one, and the two from today. And the three from last week, bagged, waiting for disposal orders.

Gillikin drew his pistol. In every horror movie, right, you were shouting 'Don't open the cupboard!' when some idiot went to open the cupboard. But they didn't have a gun, right.

He grinned and pulled open the cupboard door.

There was an alien inside with a huge white head and big slanted black eyes and a little smiley mouth.

There was a red-headed kid standing behind the alien, squished into the cupboard. 'Um,' said the kid.

Gillikin opened his mouth to scream at the alien. It reached up and tapped him between the eyes with its silver wand.

At least, that's what Gillikin's hypnotherapy tapes said happened.

* * *

Jacqui knelt down next to the unconscious soldier. There was a bit of blood on his mouth.

'Roz,' said the Doctor, looking at his companion, 'was that entirely necessary?'

'No,' she answered, with relish.

Jacqui helped them pick the soldier up and put him on the floor behind the desk. The Doctor rolled him onto his side to make sure he could breathe properly.

Someone came around the corner, making them all flinch, but it was only the Admiral's daughter. A moment later, the Admiral himself appeared out of thin air.

'There are only twelve people in the building,' said the little blond guy.

Ms Randrianasolo closed her eyes for a moment. 'Two are asleep,' she said.

'Closed for the night,' said Roz.

Jacqui sat on the corner of the desk. Nothing looked familiar, but she remembered the smell of the place, underneath the smells of fresh paint and winter.

'Almost all of them are downstairs.' The Admiral was reading the screen on his handscan. 'If we –'

He stopped short, staring at the Doctor. Jacqui followed his gaze.

The little man's eyes had grown huge, the pupils shrinking away to nothing. He pressed a hand to the centre of his chest and stumbled forward, eyes closing in a strange, intense expression.

Jacqui gasped and leapt back, nearly falling over the desk.

But nothing awful happened. The Admiral grabbed the Doctor before he could fall, supporting him awkwardly. Bernice took the scanner, and he helped the little man stand up.

The Doctor was shaking his head at Bernice. 'She's found the TARDIS,' he said hoarsely. 'She's found it.'

'Who's she?' asked Roz.

'Are you in pain?' asked Isaac.

'No,' said the Doctor. He straightened up. 'I'm all right now. Let's get a move on.'

He turned to go, but not before he saw the way that

Jacqui was looking at him. He frowned at her, not under-standing.

Jacqui trailed after the group, hands in her pockets.

Woodworth had dismissed the medical staff. She was sitting on an orange plastic seat, regarding the man in the dentist's chair. He was still upside-down – well, tilted back, anyway. He seemed to be fading in and out of consciousness, his eyelids flickering from time to time.

He made her stomach churn. They could at least have covered him up, decently, so she didn't have to look at him. But he was her responsibility, now. She had to decide whether to let the lab boys have him.

It was cold in the room, cold and bright. She was wearing her overcoat, despite the fitful efforts of a heater in the corner.

He rolled his head towards her, as though noticing her for the first time. 'Can I have my clothes back?' he said. His voice was raw and shaky. There was a nasty bruise on his forehead.

Woodworth reached into one of her files and brought out a photograph. 'Have you seen this man?' she said.

The boy looked at the picture, squinting. She held it closer. 'No,' he said faintly.

Woodworth turned the picture around. It showed a young man with long blond hair, caught by an amateur photo-grapher. Heathrow, 1982. Another snap showed the same man talking to Lethbridge-bloody-Stewart earlier this year. He was supposed to appear in disguise sometimes, too, but these were the only photos Woodworth had been able to get her hands on.

'That's a shame,' she said, tucking the pictures away. 'Tell me something, just between us, all right?'

He nodded.

'What are you? An alien? Some kind of mutant?'

'I'm human,' he murmured.

'Don't you dare say that,' she snapped. 'I don't know what kind of weird mutation or experiment you are, but don't you ever dare claim you're a human being.'

He looked at her, uncomprehending. 'Not to me,' she said. 'Never to me.'

She sat down again. 'I've been doing this job for a long time. A long time. Almost nobody knows the whole story about any of this stuff. UNIT keeps things from C19. C19 keeps things from MI5. MI5 keeps things from Parliament. And they all keep things from the public. You know who has to know all of it?'

'The Doctor,' he murmured.

Woodworth vibrated like a well-struck gong.

'Good,' she said. 'Ia Jareshth told us a lot, you know, but she hadn't actually seen him.' The boy looked at her, but didn't say anything. 'Never hitchhike,' she told him. 'You never know who might pick you up. Right, my lad. If you can tell us something about the Doctor, I might be able to keep you out of the hands of the dissection team.'

'You dissected her?'

Woodworth shrugged. 'She didn't know anything.'

'You killed her? But what about –'

'Her human rights?' smiled Woodworth.

His eyes focused, suddenly, just for a moment. 'You're going to have to cut me up,' he said, 'because I'm not going to help you.'

'Now, son,' she said gently. 'You think about what you just said for a moment.'

She looked around at the white plaster walls. 'This is an old house, you know,' she said. 'You might feel heroic, but you're just another one of the hundreds who've ended up here. You're not unique. Do you know how long I've had this job?' He didn't answer, but she wasn't really talking to him anyway. 'I was one of the few they didn't purge in the seventies. That's the gratitude you get for keeping the country safe, for keeping the *planet* safe all these years. So you see, son, I've seen dozens like you. It means nothing to me to send you down to the basement.'

He pulled against the straps. 'I haven't done anything,' he said. 'You don't want to keep the planet safe, you don't even care why I'm here.'

'Don't you try to put the blame on me!' snapped Woodworth. 'How dare you come here, and let diseases loose, and terrorize people in their beds!'

135

She shook her head. 'I don't know why you aliens can never get it through your skulls. This is what human beings *do*. You push us, and we push back.' She picked up one of the dentist's probes, tapping it against a fingernail. 'There's no Amnesty International for you. No human rights. You can come upstairs with me and answer some questions, or you can go down to the basement.'

'Go to hell,' breathed the boy. His eyes were closed.

'Anybody can die,' said Woodworth. 'Any amateur can manage it. But it's one thing to make your heroic decision, and another thing to have to live through the next few hours.'

He didn't say anything. Perhaps he was unconscious.

She picked up the clipboard and checked a box in red pen.

'Does this mean dinner is off?'

Woodworth whirled. 'What the hell are *you* doing here?'

'Doctor!' said the boy.

'Jesus Christ up a flagpole!' said Woodworth.

18

Chris Chris bang bang

Chris wandered back into consciousness. His first thought was that he had a nasty flu. His head pounded, his mouth was dry, he was a little giddy, and his bedroom light was unbearably bright.

He squeezed his eyes open. 'Mom?' he said to the blurred human shape above him.

'Shh,' she said. 'Lie still. You've got a bastard of an untreated concussion.'

'Roz?' he muttered.

'Yes.'

'Oh Goddess,' he said, suddenly realizing where he was. 'Am I okay? Are you okay?'

'Don't try to sit up, you idiot!' She pushed him back down, the heel of her hand pushing into his naked chest, but he grabbed hold of her and hung onto her.

'Oh Goddess,' he said again. 'I'm sorry, I can't think properly. Oh, Roz, they were going to cut me up!'

'It's okay,' she grumbled. 'You're all right now. Hey? You're all right.'

'I'm sorry,' he said. He was starting to cry, the panic he'd been forcing down coming out of nowhere. Bright lights flashed inside his head when he moved. 'I'm sorry,' he gasped. She was so strong that he could feel the steel of her muscles as she held onto him, awkwardly. 'I'm so sorry.'

'Quit that.' She took his face between her hands. 'You'll be all right. Just calm down.'

'Thank you,' he babbled. 'Thank you for coming and rescuing me.'

'Just stop it, Chris. You're okay now, for Christ's sake!'

He couldn't help it. He grabbed hold of her and kissed her.

She made a muffled, outraged sound, and kissed him right back.

She tasted like rosemary and gunpowder.

Somewhere in the middle of it, he lost consciousness again.

'I was here in sixty-eight,' said the Doctor.

Woodworth was sitting on the edge of the dentist's chair, her arms folded tightly. Her eyes were still blank, puzzled, as though she hadn't got over the shock of realizing who he was. She looked . . . embarrassed.

'They kept me cuffed hand and foot for three weeks,' he said. He looked around at the examination room, the tools and instruments on their metal trays, the sink, the lights. 'I really thought we'd closed down this place. I suppose it was another of those loose threads that I never got around to ravelling up.'

'I really don't give a shit,' said Woodworth.

'Oh, come now,' said the Doctor. 'This is the end of your career. You must be feeling a little bit of excitement. No more aliens to interrogate. No more interesting extraterrestrial bodies to slice up.'

'Don't try to make me feel guilty,' she said. 'Everything I've done has been for the good of Great Britain. For the good of the planet.'

The Doctor leant close, his eyes flashing with rage. Woodworth found herself flinching back. He was nothing like the man in her photos. 'The end never justifies the means,' he said, in a terrifyingly soft voice. 'Because the means used determine the kind of end produced. If I can grasp that, then so can you.'

'We need information,' said Woodworth. 'We have to have information to keep the country safe.'

'You've interrogated them,' said the Doctor. 'But did you ever try just talking to them? You don't do this because you're curious. You do it because you're frightened.'

'How dare you?' hissed Woodworth. 'The number of times I have risked my life –'

The Doctor reached out and poked her on the arm. She jumped back.

'Look out,' said the little man, with a wicked grin. 'An alien is going to touch you!'

Woodworth scrambled off the chair, backing away. 'For God's sake!' she said, as he wiggled his fingers at her like a manic magician. She bumped against the wall, found herself in the corner. 'God,' she said, 'I wish I had my gun.'

'There's something even worse in your handbag.'

Woodworth looked down at her bag in sudden horror. It was right at her feet, now, as though the Doctor had wanted her to back into it. *It was moving!*

She jumped away from it as something small and white and alive wriggled out of it. The creature hopped across the floor and jumped into the Doctor's hands while she cringed against the wall, hating herself.

'Ask me what I'm going to do with you,' said the Doctor, examining the little white thing. 'You tortured a friend of mine. You've kidnapped and murdered any number of people.'

'What are you going to do with me?' she choked.

'I'm going to take you back to *our* base,' said the Doctor. 'And then I'm going to lock you in a room with an extra-terrestrial and let *him* interrogate *you*.'

'You can't. It's a matter of national security. You can't let British secrets fall into the hands of extraterrestrials.'

'All that secrecy isn't good for you,' said the Doctor. 'Department C19 had become a positive cabal by the time the government decided to clean its house. I don't know how they managed to miss you. But you're the only one of the old school left. Substituting *Star Wars* for the Cold War.' He tucked the white thing into his jacket pocket. 'Well, there won't be any more secrets for you.'

He turned his back on her and went to the door.

She punched him in the shoulder, hard.

He turned to look at her in disgust. She backed away from

the glare, looking surprised, and finally had to bow her head.

He closed the door behind him.

'We're finished here,' said Isaac.

'No,' said the Doctor. 'We're not.'

'Reports, please,' said the Admiral.

Joel was checking his handscan. 'There are still four people in the building,' he reported. 'We've searched every room. There are no living aliens.'

'We found Ia Jareshth in the morgue,' said Tony, 'along with the two Caxtarids who assaulted the Doctor, and three other extraterrestrials.'

Roz looked up from Chris, who was dozing on a stretcher, covered by a fire blanket. She had a bewildered look. 'I think he'll be all right,' she said, 'but we need to get him the hell out of here.'

'Right,' said Isaac. 'Albinex and Ms Randrianasolo have brought the van up to the main gate. We'll make a dash for it.'

Roz and Joel lifted the stretcher. 'Oy,' puffed Joel.

Benny was peering at the Doctor in concern. 'Are you sure you're all right?'

'There was an intercom at the front desk, wasn't there?' he said.

Benny nodded. The Doctor marched off. She glanced at Isaac, and followed the Time Lord.

The Doctor knelt down behind the desk, where the sergeant was still lying on his side, snoring. He ran a finger along the man's eyebrow, and he came to with a start.

The Doctor said, 'There's an unconscious man in the morgue. Go and get him, and then leave the building right away.'

The sergeant bounced to his feet, wild-eyed. 'Yes, sir!' he yelped, and ran off down the corridor, past the strange crowd who were heading for the main door.

Woodworth gave the Doctor a puzzled look as Jacqui pushed her along, clinging to her arm.

The Doctor picked up the intercom and flicked a switch. His voice boomed out of a dozen speakers throughout the building. 'I'm going to burn the house down,' he said. 'Get out.'

He looked down in surprise as he switched the intercom off. There was a spiderweb of blood on the back of his hand. He sat down suddenly, in the sergeant's chair.

Benny helped him tug off his jacket. 'There's a shallow stab wound in your shoulder,' she said, ripping the thin silk of his shirt to get a better look. 'It's not serious.'

'I can't feel anything,' he whispered.

19

Jacqui

It wasn't raining tonight, though the clouds were thick and the mist was wet enough to dampen the cloth of Benny's coat.

She trudged down Little Caldwell's main road, boots crunching in the wet gravel. All the lights were on in the cottage Roz and Chris were sharing, as though they wanted everyone to be very sure that nothing was going on in there, nothing at all.

Benny pushed open the gate and went up to the door. It opened before she knocked. Roz peered out into the mist. 'He's fine,' she said.

'Can I come in?'

Roz pulled the door open. It was warm and bright inside. Benny followed Roz to the downstairs bedroom.

Chris was tucked into the bed, arms clasped on his chest above the covers. He was wearing a pair of stripey pyjamas. In the dim light, his face seemed lined.

He turned from the window as Benny hovered in the doorway, looked away again as he saw Roz behind her. The older Adjudicator walked back down the hallway.

'How's your head?' Benny said softly.

'Lots better,' he said. He didn't sit up. 'How are you? Are you okay?'

'Fine,' smiled Benny. She sat down on the end of the bed. 'I'm just happy we got you back.'

Chris didn't say anything. Benny's chest ached. Stuff like that shouldn't happen to him. Not Chris. He should be sheltered, taken care of, preserved.

'I can't imagine it,' he said.

Benny looked up, wishing she could make out his expression in the darkness. 'Imagine what?' she said.

'Being Woodworth.'

She smiled and patted the bump that was his feet. 'You'll be all right.'

The Doctor had protested lengthily when Benny had insisted he lie down for a bit. When she got back to Joel's and Tony's cottage, she expected to have to chase him back to bed.

She was surprised when she found him in the spare bedroom, wearing an old cardigan that smelt faintly of mothballs, and reading a copy of *Lakota Woman*. 'See,' he said, waving the paperback. 'I'm taking it easy. How's Chris?'

'He'll be all right. The question is, will Roz?' She planted a kiss on the top of his head. 'Why do we always have to get hurt?'

The Doctor took off his wire-framed glasses and slipped them inside the book to mark his page. 'We frighten people like Woodworth,' he said. 'They get confused when they've got the guns, and we still stand up to them.'

'I remembered something Dad told me when I first went to school,' she said. 'Bullies are just cowards, and if you stand up to them they'll run away.'

The Doctor nodded sagely. 'Did you try it?'

'I got the stuffing knocked out of me.' She fiddled with a corner of the cardigan, where the grey wool was unravelling. 'I was so frightened at the house when you had that bad moment. I thought –'

'Huitzilin is three years dead,' he said. 'We have nothing to fear from him. No, that was a very different ghost.' He reached for the bedside table, where his cobbled-together machine was sitting.

Benny watched as he unwound a roll of paper from the inside of the device. 'Here,' he said. He pointed to a long line drawn by a pen that meandered over the paper, like an ECG

143

reading. The pen had gone wild and wiggly at one point. 'That's the precise moment that I felt . . .'

Benny prompted him, 'You said, "She's found the TARDIS." '

'Yes. I told her I'd need the TARDIS in order to bring her back into this timeframe.'

'So if you find the ghost you'll find the TARDIS.'

'Hopefully before she gets curious again.' He absently rubbed his breastbone. 'I'm sorry, Benny. I assumed we'd find Jason, and the TARDIS, when we found Chris.'

'But I thought Woodworth must have the TARDIS.'

The Doctor shook his head. 'She doesn't know where it is. Leave her to M'Kabel. She's dangerous, Benny. A caged animal.'

'Yes, she ought to know all about that,' said Benny. 'What are we going to do with her?'

'You forgave Macbeth,' said the Doctor.

'Macbeth was a seventeen-year-old idiot when he dragged you to that house.' Benny shivered, despite the room's warmth. 'I don't like this. Bad memories. Too many ghosts.'

Isaac was coming down the wooden stairs when Benny reached the Pyramid. He looked grim. 'I've just broken the news to Myn Jareshth,' he said softly.

Benny grimaced. She put her hands on his shoulders, an abortive hug. 'I'm sorry,' she said.

'We shut them down,' said Isaac. 'Just in time, I suspect.' Benny took her hands away, awkwardly.

Isaac went behind the counter and filled a jug with water. 'Does the Doctor often go about burning buildings down?'

'Grief, no,' said Benny. 'But I think even Time Lords reach the end of their tether from time to time.'

'Something you'll be pleased to know,' said Isaac. 'I had a phone call from one of our friends a little while ago. They drove past Jason's family's home this evening, and everything seemed quiet.'

Benny leant on the counter. 'I'm afraid that's what it'll be like when that bastard starts bashing his kids, as well. Peaceful and quiet. On the outside, anyway.'

144

Isaac said, 'Sometimes I wonder if we're fighting the right villains . . .'

'You can't fight every monster,' sighed Benny. 'No one can.'

Joel was watching TV in the lounge when Jacqui knocked on the door. 'Hello,' she said, as he peered at her through his big glasses.

'Come on in,' he said. 'What can I do you for?'

'I just came to talk to the Doctor,' said Jacqui. She held onto her handbag for support. 'Is he still awake?'

'I think so. He's in the first room at the top of the landing.'

'Thanks.'

Joel smiled at her, awkwardly, and waited until she was on the steps before he went back into the lounge. He was a nice kid.

She knocked on the door at the top of the stairs. 'Come in!' called the Doctor. She pushed open the door and carefully shut it behind her.

He was reading, wearing a pair of little spectacles, as if he was an old man. He put down the book. 'Jacqui,' he said. 'What can I do for you?'

She took Woodworth's gun out of her handbag. The Doctor froze.

She pointed the gun at him. It was heavy, and cool after sitting in her bag.

He didn't say anything stupid, which was good. He just sat there, waiting to see what she was going to do.

She had to check one more time. 'Do you remember me?' she asked.

He peered at her above the glasses. Slowly, he shook his head. 'I'm sorry. I really don't.' He looked at the gun. 'Obviously, I ought to.'

'You killed my baby.'

He stared at her.

'I was at that house,' she said. 'Where we went today. Some kind of big telepathic explosion came out of you. And it killed my baby, inside my stomach.'

His mouth opened in an expression of horror. 'I don't – I didn't –'

145

The gun had drifted down a little in her grip. She straightened it back up again. 'Do you remember killing my baby?'

He closed his eyes. 'I can't,' he whispered. 'I'm sorry.'

'Why can't you remember?'

'It wasn't me,' he said. 'I was possessed. Fighting for my life.'

'You told me to get out.'

'Were you one of the experimental subjects?'

Jacqui nodded. 'They wouldn't let me leave.'

'Have you been looking for me for all these years?' he said softly.

'Yes,' she said. 'When I found out about Little Caldwell, I came to live here, because I knew one day you'd show up.'

He opened his eyes. They were so sad. It was a big sadness, as though he had seen everything sad that had ever happened, and was remembering it all.

It was even bigger than hers.

'Do you want to kill me?' he said.

'No,' she said. 'I wanted you to remember.'

She put the gun down on the end of the bed.

He held out a hand to her. But she picked up her handbag and went back down the stairs to call a taxi.

If he wept, she didn't see it.

Benny had been crying for a quarter of an hour when Albinex found her. She had been sitting in the coffee shop with only a big box of tissues for company. She had been sobbing silently, the way children can, partly hoping that no one can hear them and partly hoping that someone will come and see what the matter is.

'I'm all right,' she said nasally.

'Of course you're not all right.' He sat down opposite her, careful not to intrude into her space. 'Your husband is missing. You've found your long-lost father, only to have everything turn sour.'

She smiled ruefully. 'It's just like the old days.'

'When you travelled with the Doctor?' She nodded. 'But it wasn't always bad, was it?'

'Oh, no,' said Benny. 'We had such fun. When we weren't being shot or tortured.' He returned her smile. 'It was never boring. I loved it. We did a lot of good.'

'It's just the same living here,' said Albinex. 'We've had some harrowing times. We've lost friends. But we've saved a lot of lives. It's very serious work, Benny. It's important. We're lucky, because we have a chance to change the world.'

Benny sniffled. 'I just hope Jason isn't trying to change his world. If he kills his father, he'll never be born. Even if he just frightens the bastard into never beating his kids, Jason will never leave home, and I'll never meet him.' She looked up at Albinex. 'Am I being selfish?'

'Of course not. Jason mustn't change the timelines. Don't worry, Ms Summerfield.'

'Please,' she said. 'Call me Benny.'

He smiled. 'We'll find Jason, Benny. And the TARDIS too.'

His watch started beeping. 'It's a quarter to one,' he said. 'Almost time for the pick-up.'

Benny stood up and collected her used tissues. 'Let's go and save another life,' she said.

He was sleeping, breathing softly, his head turned so that his hair fell against the pillow.

Roz hovered in the doorway, telling herself to go to bed. Telling herself she just wanted to double-check he was okay, after his weird dream or whatever the other night, after everything he'd been through. Remembering his serious eyes, his frightened eyes.

Shit. He couldn't get serious on her now. She needed someone to be more cynical than.

'I'm sorry,' he said.

She started, palm slapping against the doorframe. 'Didn't mean to wake you up,' she said.

'It's all right.' He sat up. 'Is everything okay?'

'They've gone to send the Lacaillan home.' She picked at a splinter in the wood. 'I tried watching the television, but the jokes don't make any sense.'

'That's not surprising. Like, they're a millennium old.'

She wandered over to the window. 'No more bees?' she said.

'No.' She could feel his eyes on her back. 'Nothing like that. I don't know what that was all about. Roz?'

'Yes?'

'Nothing.'

She looked at him over her shoulder. 'You'd better get some sleep.'

'Yeah.'

She went back to the doorway. 'Um . . .' said Chris.

She waited. But he didn't say anything more.

Benny was holding the Doctor's divining rod, turning it around in her hands. It didn't move, she didn't feel any tingling. It was just a stick.

The Doctor came out onto the verandah. He smiled at her, taking the rod away. 'More sensitive than the ghost-detector,' he murmured, 'in the right hands. Benny . . .'

'Yes?' She looked up at the sky, at the few stars peeping through the clouds.

'Why did Chris kiss Roz?'

She looked at him in surprise. He was serious, puzzled.

'Don't you remember?' she began, but he shook his head sharply.

'I remember it all. Being human. But I don't understand it.'

It struck her how much he was being left out. What she and Jason had, what Roz and Chris were beginning to feel, even what she felt for her father . . . all of it, so simple, so alien to him. The things she took for granted were beyond his comprehension.

Maybe that was why he'd fight so hard to save those things – being alive, being free, being in love.

She gathered him up into a hug, feeling suddenly very protective. 'Don't you disappear as well,' she whispered.

20

Watch the Skies

The wheat field was like the ocean in the dark. Benny felt her brain freezing in the wind, and fumbled with her scarf, trying to tie it around her face.

Myn Jareshth was a lonely, elfin figure, waiting patiently at the edge of the crops. As Benny watched, he reached out a slender hand, touching one of the stalks. Strange, alien plants, growing in a strange season, on a strange, hostile planet. What would he have to say about Earth when he reached his home, alone?

Joel and Ms Randrianasolo came crunching out of the winter wheat, walking carefully between the rows. They were carrying boards and a big ball of string. 'The circle looks fine,' Joel told Isaac. 'We touched up the edges a bit.' The Admiral absently rumpled Joel's hair.

The Doctor was standing a little distance away, holding his divining stick, looking up into the sky. Benny wondered if he could see anything through the thickness of the clouds.

He seemed so quiet and sad after the day's events. It made her feel slightly off-centre. How much did she need him to be the all-powerful, all-knowing hero? Was that why it shook her so much to see him injured, or even just confused?

The first lights erupted inside the clouds, silent lightning. Joel shouted something out, his voice lost in the wind, pointing up at the sky as the ship descended.

It hovered high above them for long seconds, its shape indistinct in the darkness. Globes or smears of pearly luminescence moved around it. Benny strained to make out whether they were windows or external lights.

'Ready to go home?' Isaac said to Myn Jareshth, putting his hand on the alien's arm.

The Doctor was holding up his divining rod. At first, Benny thought the stick was moving in the wind.

With a yell, he ran into the wheat.

Something made her run after him, stumbling through the grain. 'Doctor!' she shouted, but suddenly everything was glaring light and rushing sound.

She arrived at the crop circle to see him standing in the middle, gazing up into the burning, green-tinged light.

Benny fell to her knees in the chaff and mud. There was a flash of light above her, and suddenly darkness so thick that for a moment she thought she'd gone blind.

When she could see again, the Doctor had vanished.

'Oh, bugger,' she said.

PART THREE

THE PLOTS THICKEN

My means are sane, my motive and my object mad.

Herman Melville, *Moby Dick*

In Joel's dream

It's always night-time, for some reason.

In Little Caldwell, the single road is dimly lit by a couple of old streetlamps, by the pale yellow glow from the Pyramid.

This being a dream, he can see Newbury as well. The narrow streets are crammed with cars and people, pushing through the cold and wet. But inside the houses, it's warm in front of the *Street*.

As far away as Calais, people turn away, blinded.

In ten seconds, the fireball has already eaten Newbury and Thatcham. The peace camp and Little Caldwell are puffs of gas, exploding into the sky.

The winds and the flame howl outwards, hurling trees into the air, smashing cottages into the soil, gouging a burnt hole where Berkshire used to be.

In Basingstoke, buildings catch alight as cars tumble across the ground.

In Reading and Hungerford, people's skin burns off where they stand.

In London, a boy switches on the radio. Static. He twiddles the dial. Static. Where are the radio stations? Static. What's happened? Static. What's happened to the world?

He draws a breath.

As far away as Paris, people turn away, blinded.

21

Albinex . . .

. . . looked at himself in the mirror.

He'd turned the illumination in Suite 6 way down, but there was a striplight at the bottom of the mirror. It shone up into his face, doing strange things to the lines and curves.

Albinex turned his head from side to side. The face was familiar now, after all these years. He knew fourteen different smiles and six different frowns, as well as perhaps a dozen sundry expressions. Not that he used them much.

It was the opposite of the way the Admiral used his face, he reflected. Isaac was careful never to let anything show unintentionally.

He turned on the overpadded seat. The Doctor appeared to be sleeping peacefully.

You didn't get a choice of faces, of course. That was randomly selected for you. So it was a little like having a real human face.

His was in its twenties, with pale skin and a few light freckles, dark eyes and dark eyebrows and a small mouth with a tendency to pout.

His face never changed, of course, so he was careful to keep it in fashion. This year he'd dyed his hair, but let the dark roots grow out under the blond. It was swept up away from his face and gelled in position.

Albinex glanced at his wristwatch. It had been four hours. He wondered whether the Time Lord might be faking it. Oh well, he'd get bored eventually.

He'd had the servitors go over the room, even though it had been sealed for years. The tiny robots had gathered up the few specks of dust and had freshened the musty air. They'd had a go at the bloodstain on the carpet, but it was a bit late for that.

The Doctor was lying on the double bed. He'd stopped snoring when he'd rolled onto his side, shrugging his injured shoulder irritably. Albinex's simulated heart had beaten faster when he'd thought the little man was about to wake up. But that had been an hour ago.

'You haven't had a lot of practice at this, have you?'

Albinex sat up, absolutely rigid, to keep himself from falling off the chair.

The Doctor was watching him from the bed, head resting on his arms. He hadn't changed position, he'd just opened his eyes. There was something slightly amused in them, and something slightly bored.

'How do you feel?' asked Albinex, automatically.

The Doctor sat up and stretched, taking no notice of the weapon his captor was holding. 'Well rested,' he said. 'Lights up.'

Nothing happened. Albinex said, 'The ship's computer is keyed to my voice.'

The Doctor nodded, rotating his shoulder a few times. He yawned, hugely. 'Now what?'

'Now you're going to do a few things for me, and tell me a few things I need to know,' said Albinex.

'I doubt it,' said the Doctor. He was looking around the cabin, mildly interested. 'Can we have some lights? It's a bit glum in here.'

Albinex sighed. 'Lights up,' he said.

The Time Lord took in the plush carpet, the neon tubing, the soft furniture. 'Well, this makes a change,' he said. 'Five-star accommodation. Torturing me in here is a terrible idea. The carpet will get all sticky.'

'I think you're getting a bit ahead of both of us,' said Albinex. He moved the weapon in a small circle. 'Let's go to the engine room.'

'Why not?' The Doctor hopped up off the bed. Short as he

was, he was still two inches taller than Albinex. 'I didn't have anything else to do this morning.'

Isaac was sitting at the bookshop counter, writing in his journal. He was using a fountain pen – a gift from Ms Randrianasolo – scratching out the events of the last couple of days in his careful handwriting.

Benny had been pacing the shop since breakfast, flipping through the occasional book, as though a page might fall open on the answers to all their problems.

The real Lacaillan craft had shown up fifteen minutes later, and they'd seen Myn Jareshth safely on his way. Benny had insisted on waiting for two hours in the bitter cold. There had been no sign of the Doctor.

'None of this should have happened,' she said. Isaac looked up from his writing. 'None of this was supposed to happen. We should have swapped anecdotes over coffee for a couple of weeks. It should have been like an exceptionally dull slice-of-life novel.'

'Perhaps you're drawing an unwarranted conclusion,' said her father. '*Post hoc ergo propter hoc* and all that.'

'Wherever we go there's trouble,' she said glumly. 'The Oncoming Storm, remember?'

'Is it really true, though?' He put down his fountain pen. 'Surely you didn't spend all your time with him battling monsters.'

Benny picked up a copy of Macbeth's *Look! Up in the Sky!* 'Interludes,' she said.

'Woodworth didn't even know who he was.'

'Woodworth didn't kidnap the Doctor in a flying saucer!' Benny shouted. She put a hand to her mouth. 'Woodworth didn't kidnap Jason,' she said, more quietly. 'There's someone else out there. We have to do something. I don't understand how you can just sit there!'

'What do you want me to do?' he said.

'I'm sorry. What the hell are *we* going to do, Dad?'

'Get whatever we can out of Woodworth,' he said. 'Make sure she and C19 don't have anything to do with this.'

'What about Jason? And the Doctor?'

'The Doctor can take care of himself,' said Isaac. 'He obviously knew what he was doing when he ran into that field.' He raised a blond eyebrow at her.

'*I* don't know what he was up to!' she said, exasperated. 'He was waving a divining rod around, for goodness' sake!' She'd brought the stick back with her, tucked it away in the spare bedroom, as though it was something precious.

'Listen,' she said. 'I want to go to Jason's family's house. I want to see if he's done something to his father.'

'Why don't you just phone?'

Benny blinked at him.

He pushed the phone across the desk at her. When she reached for it, he took her hand.

'Bernice,' he said. 'We'll do whatever we can to help the Doctor and Jason. But sometimes waiting is all we can do.'

'I obviously didn't get your patience gene,' she said, biting her lip.

She was about to pick up the phone when she saw what the book had fallen open on.

She turned the book around so he could see the illustration. It was a large sailing ship floating in mid-air, a seagull caught in mid-flap in front of the hull. The caption said 'Sky Yacht, artist's rendition'. Isaac looked at her, puzzled.

'It's the ship that took the Doctor,' said Isaac.

'More than that,' said Benny. 'It was there when the *Tisiphone* fell into the wormhole.'

Alekto

It was almost noon when Chris woke up. Dull winter light was leaking into the empty bedroom. The air was sharp and cold, his breath curling in white puffs above him. The window was open, just a little.

He sat up. The pain in his head had subsided to a distant buzzing, and the dizziness was gone. 'All right!' he said. 'Back in action.'

He got up and shut the window. The buzzing grew louder. He rubbed the back of his head where it had thumped the floor, squinting in the white light of the sky.

There were bees on the windowsill.

Chris jumped back as they lazily droned into the air. He ducked his head, tucking his arms instinctively under his armpits so the insects didn't go into his sleeves. 'Hey, um, Roz?' he called.

There was a face at the window.

No, it was *in* the window, in the glass itself. As though a face-shaped ripple was moving through the stuff towards him.

There was a sudden, rushing movement, into the room. Chris had the momentary impression of a hundred wings, a million feathers, exploding past him, whirling around him.

He felt himself uncurl, as though his life were a long, long line, spiralling backwards into the past, a silver cord that stretched back to his mother.

And the rushing motion was along the line of his life now,

from his birth to his first kiss to the time he burnt to the time he could hear Roz's thoughts to the last person he had killed to his last kiss.

Into the future.

Where Roz smiled at him and they were together in some dark place, with wet, soft grass against the skin of his back and the feel of her scars under his fingers.

And he was standing alone in the frozen air of the bedroom, hands flung out as though to ward off whatever was storming in through his closed window.

The bees settled onto the bedclothes, buzzing with satisfaction.

22

The name of the Roz

'If all you needed was a sort of galactic road repair service,' said the Doctor, 'you could have just asked.'

Albinex was sitting on a counter in the laboratory, a toolkit and some spare parts pushed to one side to accommodate him. He held the gun in his lap.

'You know,' he said, 'you're right: I am new at this. But I can already see why you always defeat the villains. You must annoy them to death.'

'I'm quite serious.' The Doctor took the jeweller's lens out of his eye and rolled his sleeves back down. 'If all you wanted was to get back home, I'd have been pleased to help. No fees, no questions asked.'

'But that's not all I want,' said Albinex.

The engine was a glittering mass six feet wide, with a central core like a massive salt crystal surrounded by extrusions and barbs. It looked as though it ought to crumble into powder at a touch, but the Doctor had been prodding and poking at it with a ballpoint pen for twenty minutes, making some sections light up and others chime.

'What do you think?' said Albinex.

'Well,' said the Doctor, 'the entire dimensional interfacing array has collapsed, which isn't surprising, given that it was stuck back on with model aeroplane glue.' He traced the fracture across the crystal with his pen. 'It must have been a nasty accident.'

'The ship was lucky to survive,' said his captor. 'And so

was I. Can you make it work?'

'Possibly,' said the Doctor. 'But what if I refuse to help you?'

'What? Then I'll shoot you.'

'While I'm standing behind your time engine?'

'It's not a projectile weapon,' said Albinex. 'It won't damage the engine.'

The Doctor stepped out from behind the crystal. 'There's one thing I would like to know.'

'Yes?' grated Albinex.

'This is a Navarino time engine,' said the Time Lord. 'So where did you get it?'

'I'm a Navarino,' said Albinex.

'They have a saying on this world: pull the other one, it's got bells on.'

Albinex got down from the bench. 'I am a Navarino,' he repeated, slowly, hoping it would sink in this time.

The Doctor grinned. 'A Navarino with a gun and an evil plan?'

'If you like.'

'The whole Navarino culture is based on frivolity and recreation,' said the Doctor, as though he was lecturing a dull pupil. 'They're so harmless the Time Lords even let them have limited time travel so that they can go on holidays.'

'And you tax us mercilessly for it,' said Albinex.

'Good grief,' said the Doctor. 'And I thought Navarinos just wanted to have fun.'

'I'm the exception,' said Albinex dryly. 'You've been to Navarro, then?'

'A while ago,' said the Doctor. 'For some much needed R and R. It was all we could do to get Chris back into the TARDIS. I think Benny still had the hangover three weeks later.'

'That's what they do,' said Albinex. 'That's all they do. The only people who ever do anything constructive are the children, and all they do is fix the machines that run the planet and let the adults get on with partying.'

'But what about your artists? And your writers? Navarino literature and art are all the rage in this sector.'

161

'Adventure stories and comic books,' said Albinex. 'There's no art on my world. You can't have art without suffering. There's no conflict. There's no striving. The Navarinos are soft, fluffy, empty things.' He set his jaw. 'We weren't meant to live like that.'

'I seem to recall,' said the Doctor, 'that the Navarinos were the only nation who survived the war on your planet, precisely because they couldn't be bothered to join in the fighting.'

'And they let the other nations tear one another apart,' said Albinex. He almost smiled, realizing. The Time Lord had got him talking, just as the stories said. 'Will you fix my engine?'

'Well,' said the Doctor, 'no.'

'It's not much to ask,' said the Navarino. 'Especially in exchange for your life.'

'The Caxtarids were your agents, weren't they?'

'Yes, they were.'

'You see,' said the Doctor, 'they asked me some very worrying questions.' He took a step towards Albinex, who raised the gun. 'Now, if you're after the sort of information I think you're after, it's the sort of information I don't want you to have, and that means that, whatever the rest of your plan is, it's probably the sort of thing I'm not going to be too keen on either. If you see what I mean.'

Albinex blinked. 'What?'

The Doctor came another step closer. His eyes were open, honest, vast and bluer than the sky. 'If you ask me,' he said, 'you ought to just tell me what you have in mind. I want to help you. Why don't you put down the gun, and we'll see what we can work out?'

Albinex shot him.

Ms Randrianasolo found herself at a loose end.

Jacqui was gone, but presumably she was back at the peace camp, not spirited away like Chris or the Doctor.

She wondered if Zak was right to wait, if they'd be safer clearing out. It was very seldom that he misjudged a situation – which was why they were still here, in Little Caldwell, after all these years. There had been a dozen times when they'd almost bugged out, and only his determination had saved them. And kept them here. Home.

If you couldn't get home, you had to make a home.

She'd been standing outside this door for fifteen minutes.

The Admiral and his daughter were deep in discussion in the bookshop – heated discussion, by the sound of it. Joel was down at the garage, 'pumping gas' and working over the exhausted van after its return appearance last night. Forrester was still looking after Cwej, but by all accounts he'd pull through without difficulty.

And both the Doctor and Jason were still missing. Not to mention the Doctor's time machine. They were under attack from some unknown direction.

Or was it unknown? The Doctor had seemed to know what he was doing when he let himself be captured by that spacecraft. And he'd known all about the house Woodworth and her agents had been using.

It was strange, given the stories, but the Doctor hadn't struck her as a manipulative or cunning sort of person. More of an improviser – someone who came up with brilliant things when in a state of panic. Or perhaps that was just one aspect of his personality.

She put her hand on the doorknob, took it away again.

Her mother hadn't wanted her to join Spacefleet. She had memories of her mother only as an old woman; it had taken her most of her adult life to get out of the Fleet.

She remembered her mother at work in the rainforest, part of the Reclamation Project. Reaching out into the soil with her wiry mind, finding seedlings and landmines with equal ease, directing the workers. She never used the mental powers at home. But now she wanted her daughter to see what they had done to her, forced her to become, with their pills and injections.

'But mother,' she had said, 'what you do is wonderful. No one could do this with implants or AIs.'

'This is not what I did when I was in Spacefleet,' the old woman had said.

Madagascar was half a millennium away.

She pushed open the door.

The room was a study, most of the time. There were bookshelves, a painting, a big wooden desk and chair.

There were books all over the floor, and the painting had been smashed, a web of lines radiating from a circular hole in the glass. M'Kabel sat on the chair on the right side of the room, hologram off, holding his wand in his lap.

Woodworth was sitting as far away from him as she could manage, which meant on the desk, in the corner, knees drawn up to her chest and arms wrapped around them. Her hair and eyes were wild. 'You're human, aren't you?' she stammered. 'Get me the hell out of here!'

'How's it going?' Ms Randrianasolo asked.

'Slowly,' said M'Kabel.

'You're human – you're not one of this army of monsters!'

'Army?' laughed Ms R. 'You can count us on the fingers of your hands.'

'An army,' repeated Woodworth, 'covering the country-side. How can you leave me in here with that thing?'

'Don't mind M'Kabel,' said Ms Randrianasolo. 'He's a big softy.'

'He's been doing things to my mind!' Woodworth scratched at her forehead, compulsively. 'I've told him everything I can, everything I can think of. He made me. He made me.'

'So you want to get out?' asked Ms Randrianasolo.

'Yes!'

'I don't know. I think maybe we should cut you up when we're finished.'

Woodworth just stared at her, the scraped stare of someone who's been panicking for hours.

'It was people like you who forced my mother to become a psychokinetic,' said Ms Randrianasolo. 'The drugs were still in her system twenty years later when she conceived me.'

'What are you talking about?'

'I joined the military because I thought I could do some good. But it was all about making money. For the weapons companies, or the drug companies. And I was an asset. With a credit value. They weren't going to let me leave any more than they were going to let Mum leave. Except when her powers started failing. Then they threw her out, threw her all the way back home.'

Woodworth just shook her head.

'So I think we should cut you up. When we're finished with you, and you're not worth anything any more.'

M'Kabel stopped her in the doorway. 'Now do you see why the Admiral didn't ask you to do the mind-reading?' he said gently.

'Yeah.' She glanced back at Woodworth, who had buried her face in her arms. 'It wouldn't have been a good idea,' she said.

Roz was making lunch in the cottage's kitchen. She'd had enough twentieth-century experience now to recognize the different foods and appliances. She was slicing mushrooms when Chris came into the room.

He looked faintly bewildered. The top button of his pyjamas had come undone, revealing the fine golden hairs on his chest.

'Morning,' he said. 'What's up?'

'You are, at last,' she said. 'Nothing much is going on. If there's any news or they need us, they'll telephone.'

'We ought to be out looking for the Doctor,' said Chris. 'And Jason.'

'Yeah,' said Roz, 'well, you've got concussion, I'm baby-sitting you, and Isaac's in charge and he says we're not going anywhere. Ow, *frag*!'

'You okay?' He reached automatically for the hand she'd managed to slice instead of a mushroom.

She snatched it away from him. 'Sit down or something, okay?' she said.

'Look,' said Chris. 'It was an accident. I'd been hit on the head. Not that I'd have to be hit on the head before I'd kiss you, right, but I didn't mean to.' Roz was staring at him, pressing a tissue against her cut thumb. 'It was just a kiss, anyway. I mean, you're old enough to be my mother. Not that you're that old. We're friends. It didn't mean anything, right? We could kiss again right now and it wouldn't matter.'

They stared at one another, aghast, for about thirty seconds.

165

'Um,' said Chris.

'If you ever do it again,' said Roz, 'I'll rip your head off. Understood?'

'Yes,' Chris squeaked.

She grabbed hold of the front of his pyjama top and yanked, pulling him down over the counter. Their mouths met in the centre.

'Good,' said Roz indistinctly, a few minutes later. 'Now that we've gotten that out of the way, how about lunch?'

The gun's kick had surprised him. It was a small electric pistol, used for stunning rodents, part of the ship's odd stock of emergency equipment.

Albinex gingerly tucked it into the pocket of his jacket. The Doctor was sitting on the floor of the engine room, blinking rapidly.

'Don't try to hypnotize me,' he told the Time Lord.

'No,' said the Doctor. He stood up, with the help of one of the benches.

'That wasn't torture,' said Albinex. 'It was self-defence. Don't try to hypnotize me.'

'Can I ask you a question?'

'All right,' said Albinex, warily.

'How long have you been planning this? How have you kept it from Isaac?'

'That's two questions,' said the Navarino. 'Isaac's just a stepping stone. When I was stranded here, he was my best bet to find someone who could help me. I've been waiting a long time.'

He tilted his head, trying to read the Time Lord's expression. 'You still don't trust him. I'm surprised. *He* trusts. He's not always looking for ulterior motives. Which makes you the more intelligent one.' He waved the gun. 'Fix the engine. I'll be back in an hour.'

The Doctor folded his arms and raised an eyebrow.

'Don't you want to see your TARDIS again?'

'I was wondering when you'd get to that.'

'You knew I had her?'

'I knew she was on board the ship that was arriving above

166

the crop circle. And I knew it wasn't a Lacaillan ship. Only a handful of species had, have or will have time technology.' He tapped a fingernail on the bench. 'Why don't you let me see her? To show me she's all right?'

'She's not aboard. Not any more. But I know where she is. Fix the engine.'

'Albinex,' said the Doctor, as the Navarino backed towards the door. 'I'm not going to give you the destructor codes.'

Albinex stared at him.

'That's a fact. Alter your plans accordingly.'

'We'll see.' He stepped carefully out through the door, keeping his gun trained on the Doctor, and shut and locked it.

Albinex slumped against the wall, realizing he was shivering all over. This was hard. This was the hardest thing he'd ever done. Killing the crew and passengers had been a doddle compared with this. Eater Of All Flesh! It was as though the man could see into his head!

The stories. The stories were all true.

He looked at his watch. There was no way the Doctor was going to help him – the man just couldn't be frightened. In the next hour, he was going to have to come up with something else.

23

Jason

One of the first things Jason Kane had learnt, when he'd been sucked through space and time into Alien Wonderland, was that it's almost impossible to escape from anywhere through the ventilation shafts.

This, Jason would explain to you if you had a moment, was because air doesn't need much space. If you need to ventilate something – an underground complex, a huge building, a luxury spacecraft – you can do it quite adequately through ducts too narrow for a cat. There might be one or two shafts or access areas big enough for humans, but there won't, as a rule, be a convenient network scattered through the structure.

If you want to creep about unnoticed, your best bet is either a friend in security or a talent for disabling bits of technology, such as locks and cameras.

Unfortunately, Jason had almost no talent whatsoever in this department.

Fortunately, there weren't any security cameras, and none of the doors were locked.

He'd been wandering around the yacht for an hour. It had taken him forever to work out how to open the TARDIS door, kicking himself mentally that he hadn't paid more attention.

He'd thought it was a ghost ship at first. He'd cupped both hands around his mouth to shout out, see if anybody was aboard, but some instinct stopped him. Later, thinking about it as he skulked through the scullery and peered into musty

He was hunched in front of his computer, shoulders bowed, neck pushed forward. His glasses were a couple of inches from the screen, lit up with the flickering letters he was typing. There was a frown of intense thought on his young face.

She knocked on the open door. He didn't even look up. 'Yeah?' he said. 'Come in.'

The room smelt intensely of old cigarettes and boy. She sat down on the end of his bed, and waited until his brain finally registered her presence. 'Oh, Bernice, hi,' he said, turning around from the computer screen. He was wearing a T-shirt which said 'Kzin Diplomatic Corps – Let's Do Lunch'. ' 'Scuse me, I was in full technogeek mode.'

'Don't mind me,' said Benny. 'I'm just wandering about.'

'You okay?' he said.

'All this waiting,' said Benny.

'Yeah,' said Joel. 'You know, this much stuff doesn't usually happen at once.'

'What are you doing?' she asked.

'I'm on a BBS,' he said. 'There's a bunch of fanboys arguing about the Doctor.' He tapped the list of E-mail messages on the screen. 'They figure it's a code name, and they're having this big flame war about whether he could ever be a woman. Same old debates.'

'You must really miss the Internet.'

'Hell, yes,' sighed Joel. He took off his glasses and bowed his head.

'When were you born?' said Benny.

'Nineteen seventy-three,' said Joel. 'I'm ten.'

'You're old for your age.'

'What gave me away?'

'The twentieth century is a kind of hobby of mine,' said Benny. 'You kept dropping references to films and TV which haven't been made yet.'

'Bad fanboy habit,' he sighed. 'I guess I didn't figure any of you would know the difference.'

'Cheer up. The first time I saw *Star Trek*, I thought it was a documentary.'

Joel laughed. 'Really? Which ep?'

171

'The one where Captain Picard meets the alien whose language is made up of metaphors and references.'

'*Darmok*,' said Joel. 'A total classic. Or it will be, in nineteen ninety-one. You really thought it was a documentary? I would have thought *Trek* would be kind of a big twentieth-century cultural icon.'

Benny smiled. 'Ah well,' she said, 'there's a good reason, but I can't tell you without giving something away about the future.'

'Yeah,' said Joel, 'I keep having to do that with TV shows. It's like Marty McFly and the reruns: I've seen everything before.'

'I don't understand why you needed to keep it a secret, though,' said Benny. 'Was it something to do with how you ended up back in nineteen eighty-three, or . . .'

He was shaking his head. 'Nothing like that.' He took a deep breath. 'It's for the same reason the Admiral won't let you tell him about your mom.'

'Because we might offer to take you home,' said Benny. And bitterly, 'And that would put him at a strategic disadvantage.'

'He doesn't really understand this,' said Joel, fiddling with a ballpoint pen. 'But I don't *want* to go home. I was kind of homesick at first. I missed my videos and my computer and my dog.'

'What about your family?' said Benny gently.

'We don't get on too well,' said Joel. 'Me and my dad, anyway. It's like . . . When I first got here, I was in the States. In New York, same place I was in in nineteen ninety-three. But my parents don't move there until nineteen eighty-seven. Even if I found them, like, they're really going to believe me that I'm their son from the future.'

'Couldn't you prove it with a DNA test?' she said.

'DNA fingerprinting won't be around for a few years. And besides, how would I convince them to have a test in the first place? Believe me, I thought through all of that stuff. I was all by myself. I was homeless. I thought I would probably be dead inside a year.'

'I know a little of what it must have been like,' said Benny.

'I lived in a forest myself for years. And Dorothée –'

'Yeah, she told me a bit about being stranded on Svartos. I guess I was lucky I was still on Earth.'

'How did Dad find you?'

'I got screaming drunk one night on the last of my money. I just had what was in my pockets, and most of it had dates after eighty-three. I ended up in a homeless shelter, ranting and raving and demanding cigarettes. I told everyone there that I was from the future. A few days later, I'm under some bridge, half frozen to death, and this little blond guy comes up and asks me where I was when the *Challenger* blew up.'

Joel stuck the pen in his mouth, took it out again. 'He saved my life, Bernice. But it's more than that. He's cool, he cares about us, he cares about everything. He's real serious, but he still has a sense of humour. And he knows how to ask you to do something without making it sound like an order. And he's so *brave*. I kind of want to be him when I grow up. It's like . . . he's my dad now.'

'Well,' said Benny softly, 'I guess that makes you my little brother.'

She reached out and embarrassed him terribly by hugging him.

'Don't cry,' he muttered. 'Hey, don't cry. You know what? I bet that Mr Summerfield, I mean Jason, is up on that ship. The Doctor knew he was there and went to rescue him. I'll bet they both turn up safe and sound.'

Benny released the boy. 'I hope . . .'

'Yeah,' grinned Joel. 'I've read the stories. The Doctor can do anything.'

Jason had taken off his jacket and rolled up his sleeves. He was leaning over the vast, complex crystal that was lying on the workbench, holding it tightly while the Doctor did things to it.

'So what's this bloke Albinex's plan?' he asked.

The Doctor was peering deep into the crystal through a jeweller's eyepiece. 'Back in the seventies,' he said, 'the nuclear superpowers had a deal whereby a neutral country was given the secret launching codes for their weapons. The

173

idea was that if a launch was imminent, they could make all of the codes public, and force a cooling-off period.'

Jason frowned. 'That doesn't make a whole lot of sense.'

'As much sense as a strategy of killing your opponent's entire civilian population,' said the Doctor, mildly. 'Anyway, back then, the only superpowers were China, the USSR and the USA. So they gave the codes to Britain.'

'But wouldn't terrorists just get hold of them and use them?' said Jason, still trying to work out the point.

'The system was abandoned shortly after exactly that happened. But Albinex wants to know the codes.'

'Oh,' said Jason. 'And you know them.'

The Doctor nodded his head, slowly, as though it was heavy with the knowledge.

'But if the system was chucked, what good are the codes?'

'I presume Albinex's plan is to travel back in time to a period when they were still valid,' said the Doctor. 'He's probably going to do something tedious like hold the world to nuclear ransom.'

'Christ!' said Jason. 'Look, can't you just erase the codes from your mind, or something?'

'I might need them,' said the Doctor simply. Jason felt a chill trickle down his spine. 'Besides, I'd need the TARDIS to do the job properly. But I've buried them deep, deep down. It'll take a lot more than the basic mind-probe technology Albinex would have to get at them.'

'Christ,' said Jason again. 'You can't let him do it. Benny would never be born. Hell, I'd never be born.'

'I must have a long chat with Albinex about the web of time,' said the Doctor absently. 'In the meantime, I think that better than presence of mind would be absence of body.'

A set of coloured lines flared inside the stricken crystal. The Doctor stood back, satisfied. 'Six of one,' he said.

Jason hadn't noticed the tall archway standing against a wall of the engine room. The Doctor started moving it towards the bench. Jason gave him a hand. It was heavier than it looked, made out of some kind of dense red-black plastic, covered in printed circuitry patterns. 'And half a dozen of the other,' said the Doctor.

'What's this, then?' he said.

'Transformation archway,' said the Doctor. 'It's how Albinex appears human.'

Jason jumped back as the thing started to glow. It was as though there was a flat wall of the stuff bubbles were made of, stretched across the archway, softly glowing in rainbow colours.

The crystal engine was glistening with the same slick of colours, like oil on a wet road. 'It's some kind of feedback loop,' he said.

The Doctor was pressing the tips of his fingers against the stuff of the archway. The space inside glowed blue, silver, green. 'This is a bit difficult to do,' he said, 'given that I don't know where we are, and we're in flight. But —'

The archway gave a final flicker, and turned into the inside of the Pyramid.

'— it's amazing what you can accomplish with a bit of patience.'

Jason blinked. 'Oh great. You've invented television.'

The Doctor took off his hat, smiled his best magician's smile, and stepped through the archway.

Jason gaped at him.

'I'd come through right now if I were you,' said the Time Lord. 'I don't think that loop is going to survive for more than another —'

Jason hurled himself through the archway, colliding with the counter and winding himself.

'— twenty seconds,' said the Doctor.

Jason turned. There was a hole in the air looking back into Albinex's engine room. As he watched, it folded itself up and slammed away into nothing.

'Or less,' added the Doctor.

Alekto

And in the end Roz got fed up with chess and with waiting for the phone to ring, and had pulled on her coat and gone out into the freezing morning, leaving him in the lounge.

Chris had got hold of the Doctor's ghost-detector. The Time Lord had dropped it in the mud when the spaceship's beam had caught him; he must have been trying to take some kind of reading. Bit more precise than a divining rod.

Chris had dampened a tea towel and wiped off the worst of the mud and bits of wheat. The thing was making little humming noises, so it must still be working a bit. He could see a couple of batteries taped into the mechanism just behind the tea-strainer.

There was a roll with times printed on it and a long, slow line drawn by a needle. Mostly the line was flat. He gently lifted the needle and wound the roll back.

At about noon that day, the needle had gone berserk.

As he was staring at the roll, the pen jumped in his hand. He quickly pulled his hand out of the machine, and the needle started hopping and scratching all over the paper, faster and faster.

'Oh frag,' he said.

He bolted out of the cottage. She was just about to go inside the coffee shop. 'Roz!' he shouted. 'Wait!'

She turned, as he ran up the road towards her, the rough surface biting his feet and *he could see that feathered horror descending on her, rushing from all sides like a hurricane*

176

with her in its eye –

Roz batted at the thing as it battered at her, waving her hands wildly and shouting. Chris knew that no one else could see it. She could see it because it was attacking her, and he could see it because he'd already seen it twice.

He saw her mouth open as he sprinted the last few metres between them. He knew she was being taken back to the beginning, that her life was being read like a book that someone was flipping through, fast, uncaring, looking for a particular paragraph or picture.

He grabbed hold of her as she was catapulted into her own future.

And suddenly they were married, living on a lush green world where he surfed and fought villains and she danced and wrote laser-sharp political commentary. And from time to time the Doctor visited them, sometimes wearing a different face, but always with that conjurer's twinkle in his eye.

And suddenly they were lying on a road in 1983, free of the ghost storm, and it was so cold that he could feel his bare toes turning blue.

Roz was shaking in his grip, outraged, still struggling. He jerked backwards, letting her go, giving her space. 'Did you see it?' he asked her, as they sat up. 'Did you see it?'

'I didn't see anything!' she shouted wildly. 'Christ! I didn't see *anything*, all right?'

24

Plan B

Albinex pressed his palm against the engine room lock. The door slid open.

Inside, his time engine was lying in disrepair, little puffs of burnt stuff scattered over its surface like black flowers. His transformation arch had been dragged away from the wall, and was lying flat on the floor, sizzling softly.

The Doctor, not surprisingly, was gone.

'Never mind,' said Albinex. 'Never you mind.'

He turned on his heel and walked the short distance to his larder. The door slid open at his touch. He stepped into the room, found the canisters he wanted, brushing away the condensation to read the labels.

'I knew you would come in handy,' he breathed. 'The both of you.'

It's surprising what you can think of in an hour.

25

Conference

Someone was helping Roz up, flapping his hat at the bees that were still bumbling around her. Chris scrambled to his feet.

It wasn't the Doctor. It was Tom Sullivan, the old guy from the post office. 'Are you all right, missus?' he said. 'Is this fellow annoying you?'

Roz dusted herself down. 'No more than usual,' she muttered. 'No, I'm fine, thanks very much.'

Tom gave Cwej a suspicious glance, but pushed his hat back down on his head and wandered off down the road towards the graveyard. Roz watched him go, thoughtfully.

'It was the ghost,' said Chris. 'The Doctor's ghost. Well, not *his* ghost, but the one he was talking about before. That little machine started going nuts.'

'Oh, great,' said Roz. 'Government conspiracies, UFOs, and now ghosts.'

'It recorded stuff when I was having that dream this morning,' said Chris. He plucked a dead bee from his joggers. 'And the bees were there again.'

'Okay, well, we'd better let Isaac know.' Roz headed for the coffee shop door.

'It showed me the future,' said Chris.

Roz hesitated at the door. She didn't look back at him.

'At least, I think it was the future,' he said.

He wanted to go to her, put his arms around her again. Touch her. He wanted to touch her.

He stood where he was, still in the road, awkward.

'At least, I hope it was the future,' he said quietly.

Roz glanced at him with eyes like black glass. She pushed open the door, and followed the sound of bells into the shop.

On the staircase, Benny screamed, 'JASON!'

'The same,' he said, opening his arms.

Benny hurled herself down the stairs and shot across the floor. They ended up in an awkward embrace, with her arms and legs wrapped around him. He stumbled back under her weight.

Roz came up and stood next to the Doctor. 'You've been busy,' she said.

He glanced at her. 'What's yellow, black and fuzzy?'

'A bee,' said Roz.

'I don't know either,' said the Doctor, 'but there's one crawling up your arm.' He reached up his hand, and the lone insect hopped onto his index finger.

'Doctor!' Chris exploded into the shop. 'Jason!' He caused a moment's chaos by trying to shake Jason's and the Time Lord's hands, especially since Benny was still firmly fastened around her husband, trying to kiss him to death. 'What was that spaceship? Why did it look like a boat? Are you both okay?'

The Time Lord looked past Benny and Jason, to where Isaac was coming down the stairs. Their eyes met for a moment.

'Conference,' said the Doctor.

'What's all the shouting about?' muttered Joel.

He logged off the bulletin board and switched off the brand-new ancient computer. He gripped his cigarette in his mouth as he pulled on his trainers.

It wasn't until he raised his head that he saw the window. There was something wrong with it.

It was covered in bees.

Joel took a couple of steps towards the window. The insects were all on the outside, their furry bodies pressed up against the glass. They wanted *in*.

Joel's mouth opened, and the cigarette dangled from his bottom lip.

There was something in the room with him.

'Oh shit,' said Joel. *'Incoming!'*

His whole life flashed before his eyes in a flurry of beating wings. It was like being inside a bird, inside that furious heat and movement, all those feathers. It was as though his life was a ribbon of landscape below him and a roc (Frequency: Very Rare) had plucked him up and was flying over it, faster and faster.

There was the first time he saw *Star Trek VI* at the cinema, with a crowd of cheering fans, and the flow of happiness and excitement had been almost overwhelming.

There was his *Professor X* script, all carefully plotted out and typed up at the age of fifteen, ready to send off to London. Thrown out the door into the mud by his father because the pages were littering the floor of his room.

And *there* was the moment when the time rift had grabbed him –

There was a sudden jar, a grinding sensation that shook the insides of his bones. For a moment he thought it was going to kill him, smash him between its movement and the wall of time.

The beating wings grew louder, then faster, then frantic, and suddenly he was over that bump, that twist in the landscape.

The years seared past at blipvert speed.

He tried to protest as the bird dragged him onwards, into his future.

It was five minutes before it let him go, with a terrible tearing sound. He found himself on the floor of his room, breathing hard. The bees whirled away from his window with a lazy sound, tracing patterns of dots in the air.

Joel held onto his bed and kept breathing, taking slow, deep lungfuls, until the dizziness and the iron grip in his chest subsided. He pulled himself to his feet.

He plucked the cigarette from his mouth with both shaking hands and stubbed it out in the ashtray. Then he went downstairs.

They pulled chairs from under the tables, arranged them

181

in a tight circle at the back of the shop. Isaac and Ms Randrianasolo, Joel and Chris, Jason and Benny, Roz and the Doctor.

Graeme hopped up onto the counter. Chris held out a hand, and the spatula jumped down to join the circle. 'My hero,' said the Adjudicator.

The Time Lord said, 'I'm afraid that our problems haven't ended with stopping Woodworth's operation. I'm sorry to tell you this, Admiral, but I'm afraid Albinex is up to something. Something nuclear.'

Isaac nodded slowly. 'He's been gone since last night,' he said.

'He kidnapped me because he wants a set of government codes he believes will enable him to launch a nuclear missile.'

'Those Caxtarids,' said Benny. She was still hanging onto Jason, one hand on his shoulder and another on his arm, as though a beam of light might come through the roof and snatch him away.

'Indeed,' said the Doctor. 'He's holding the TARDIS hostage. He can't do anything to hurt her, though, not with the level of technology he has access to.'

'But why take Jason hostage and then not make any demands?' said Benny.

'I was just along for the ride,' said Jason. 'I was in the TARDIS having a think when Albinex took it. He probably just beamed it up into his ship, or something. The next time I looked out the door I was on board his yacht.'

'Why is it a yacht?' Ms Randrianasolo wanted to know.

'It's a conversion job,' said the Doctor. 'Navarino tourist spacecraft are always disguised. I expect he stole it.'

'Well, he's not running a travel agency,' said Isaac dryly. 'Do you know what he plans to do?'

'Not exactly,' said the Doctor. 'But if it involves throwing nuclear missiles about –'

'Greenham Common,' gasped Ms Randrianasolo.

'Exactly,' said the Doctor.

'Are you the only one who knows these codes?' said Joel.

The Doctor said, 'My guess is that he's tried to get them

from more mundane sources than the back of my mind. And then I arrived. Just at the right time.'

There was a moment's silence.

'What do we do?' said Benny.

'Wait for him to give himself away,' said the Doctor. 'The only bargaining chip he has is the TARDIS. He'll contact us and offer a swap.'

'Do you think he and Woodworth had anything to do with one another?' said Jason.

'I doubt it,' said the Doctor. 'Though I wonder if Albinex didn't do something that attracted her attention, contacted the wrong person or peeked into the wrong file . . .'

'And then there's the ghost,' said Roz stiffly.

'Ah yes,' said the Doctor. 'She's looking for someone to help her.' He suddenly ran both hands through his hair, as though exasperated. 'I can't do anything for her until I get the TARDIS back.'

Half an hour later Benny was still wrapped around her husband. He was snoring and he needed a shave. She hugged him tighter, prompting a series of comfortable muttering noises.

'I never had a chance to miss you before,' she whispered.

She hoped Dad and the Doctor were okay. Oh, the Doctor looked fine – he could breeze through almost anything. And Roz and Chris would look after him. She felt an odd pang of jealousy. She didn't occupy the privileged position of *companion* any more.

Or perhaps you never stopped being a companion.

She closed her eyes.

The flames had jumped into the night, searing colours against the blackness. The Doctor had insisted on staying, even after the fire engines had arrived, much too late. He'd been holding one of the handscans, supposedly double and triple checking that no one was endangered by the fire. But she knew he wanted to see that building *burn*.

And it wasn't because he'd been hurt there. It was because someone he loved had been hurt there.

What must it be like to be so old? To keep on living, and

see the people around you hurt and killed, over and over?

'*I'm* getting old,' she murmured to Jason. Being a companion meant risking things. Sometimes your sanity, sometimes your life. She didn't want to risk *him*.

Dad had been holding in a lot of emotions when he'd learnt the truth about Albinex. It was awful. They'd been working together for two decades. And now her father would be wondering whether Albinex had always been planning this. Whether they had ever really been friends.

Jason. Dad. The Doctor. She was still juggling the three of them.

For a moment something cold in her insides said that one of them was going to have to die. And, whichever one it was, it would be because of her.

She held onto Jason for a few more minutes. Then she carefully slid out of bed and rummaged for her clothes.

The Doctor had disappeared almost entirely into the van's engine. He was nearly upside down, with his legs sticking up, revealing one navy-blue sock and one *Rocky and Bullwinkle* Christmas sock.

Joel had never actually seen someone work on a car by climbing into its innards before. He just hoped nothing started up accidentally. Mind you, by this stage, something like half of the engine was scattered over the garage floor.

'So,' he said, 'about this ghost.'

The Doctor said something, his voice muffled. He hauled himself backwards out of the engine. Somehow, there wasn't a speck of grease on him.

He planted his feet on the ground and leant on the van. 'She's stranded,' he repeated. 'Trapped in the future. Just a tiny fraction of a second, but enough to have severe effects. It's only through a sort of temporal paradox that she's still alive.'

He stooped down and started picking over the engine parts he'd removed, turning them around in his hands as though they were geometric puzzles. 'So what's she doing?' said Joel. 'Why does she keep attacking us?'

'I don't think she sees it as an attack,' said the Doctor.

'She's trying to make contact, to communicate. That's why she's been concentrating her efforts on time travellers.'

'Benny told you,' said Joel.

The Doctor glanced up at him. 'So I was right,' he said, and grinned.

'D'oh!' said Joel.

The Doctor selected a piece of van and stood up, gazing down into the engine as though he was working on a particularly tricky jigsaw puzzle and was holding a piece of sky.

'Before you disappear back down there,' said Joel, 'there's something I want to ask you.'

'All right,' said the Time Lord.

'Okay,' said Joel. 'When I was growing up, my family had a nuclear shelter in the backyard. It was built in the fifties, long before we moved in. When I was a little kid I used to play around in it. Then Reagan got elected, and my dad decided it was time to fix the shelter up for real.'

The Doctor waited, patiently. By now Joel's dad would've been asking whether this was a question or a speech. 'He used to make Mom and me do drills, getting into the shelter in under a minute from anywhere in the house. If we blew it, we had to do it again. And again.

'I kept asking him if we could stop, because the drills used to scare me to death. I used to lie awake at night, if there was a storm, waiting for the thunder after every flash of lightning. I used to turn on the radio just to hear that the stations were still broadcasting and the world was still there.

'But listen . . . the ghost showed me . . . I saw the future, and I saw myself dying. And it wasn't from nukes.'

'You saw yourself die?'

Joel nodded. His eyes were almost as round as his glasses.

'The future isn't fixed,' said the Doctor gently. 'Whatever the ghost showed you is just one possible future. So if, say, you saw yourself die in a plane crash tomorrow, you might avoid taking that flight now . . .'

'Yeah, so, anyway, the point of all of this is that I'm bloody terrified about Albinex. What if he starts a nuclear war? Could he change history like that?'

'I'm afraid he could,' said the Doctor. 'Doing irreparable

damage to the entire universe, let alone the planet Earth. Just as your future isn't immutable, neither is the world's.'

'Great,' quavered Joel. 'I already had to grow up underneath the radar. I don't want to have to do it again.'

'Are you okay?' said Benny.

Isaac looked up from the sheaf of mail. He had spread it over one of the tables in the coffee shop, and was sorting it into piles. Bills, magazines, letters from contacts, a couple of packages.

'Yeh,' he told her. 'I'm keeping busy while we wait for Albinex to contact us.'

She sat down opposite him. 'I feel as though this is my fault,' she said. 'If we hadn't come here, Albinex would never have started on his evil plan.'

Isaac opened an envelope and took out the invoice inside. 'It can't be helped,' he said.

'I wonder how long he's been planning this,' said Benny.

'I've known him for a long time,' said Isaac. 'I thought I knew him. He saved our lives when we were stranded here.'

'It's not an easy thing, to be stranded,' said his daughter. 'After I escaped from the ship I'd been shanghaied onto, my pod crash-landed on Olundrun Seven. If it hadn't been for the monks . . . poor Joel had it worse, though. And Ace.'

'She told us a little about Iceworld,' he said. 'It's a good thing she was already angry when she arrived. I don't think she would have survived otherwise.'

'Um,' said Benny. 'Actually, about Dorothée. I was wondering something.'

He picked up another envelope. 'Yes?'

'You said she'd visited here a couple of times.'

'That's right. Twice.'

'I don't want to pry. But bearing in mind her reputation, and the fact that as a man more or less single, in practice at least, you would have motive, means and presumably opportunity, and considering the fact that if she were inclined to do so, she would . . .'

She threw up her hands. 'Oh, hell. You didn't shag her, did you?'

186

Isaac put the invoice into the right pile. 'Why?'

Her mouth opened and closed a few times. 'Why what?' she asked, at length. 'Why would you want to? Why do I want to know? Why do I –'

'Why do you want to know?' he said dryly. 'I think I could work the rest out for myself.'

'Er,' said Benny. 'I'm sorry. I suppose I was just curious.'

'You're fidgeting,' he told her. 'Your eyes are jumping around all over the place. It's more than just curiosity about a friend. Why?'

Benny leant forward and rested her head on her arms. 'Because then she'd be two out of three with the men in my life. Minimum. And I really don't want to think about the third.'

'I *see*,' said Isaac. He sorted the sales letters into a manila folder and stacked them on the seat beside him.

She tilted her head to look at him. 'The suspense is killing me.'

'The answer is no,' he said.

Benny puffed out her cheeks. 'Whew,' she said.

Isaac allowed himself a smile.

Joel breezed past. 'Oh cool,' he said, picking up one of the packages. 'A videotape. That's one of mine.' He tucked it under his arm and went upstairs.

'Allow me to change the subject completely,' Isaac said. 'What do you expect the Doctor will do about Albinex?'

Benny sat up again. 'Whatever needs to be done,' she said.

'That sounds very grim.'

'You haven't seen him at work,' she said. 'For him, the solution isn't blowing away the bad guy. He'll talk Albinex out of it. And if he can't talk him out of it, he'll throw a wrench into his plans. And if he can't throw a wrench in, he'll improvise madly at the last possible moment.'

She reached out, put a hand on his sleeve. 'I hope Albinex can be talked out of it,' she said. 'It's so hard, going up against someone who used to be your friend.'

'Yes . . .' he said.

'I understand,' said Benny.

'Do you?'

187

Simon Kyle

'I haven't told you how I ended up in Spacefleet,' said Benny.

Isaac folded away the last of the letters. 'You said you were sent to the Academy as an orphan.'

'There's more to it than that. A lot more. I want to tell you about Simon Kyle.'

Isaac listened.

'The first time I saw Simon I was asleep between two of his tortoises,' said Benny. 'That was his form of rebellion, keeping animals. The Academy was strictly no pets. So he sneaked out of bounds and built himself a tortoise hutch in the forest.

'They were reconstituted Galapagos tortoises, three of them, and they were beautiful. You probably saw them on *Life on Earth*.' Isaac nodded, smiling slightly. 'The hutch was over the hill from where I was living, in a lean-to made out of tree branches, right near a river. The funny thing was, I thought I knew every inch of the forest, but I never even noticed the hutch. It was that well hidden. Simon was even better at sneaking around in the greenery than I was.

'So I guess I might never have met him at all if it hadn't been for the storm. It rained for two days, solidly. I had wet weather gear that a couple of friends had smuggled out to me, but the shelter I'd built was bashed to bits, and the river flooded. I ended up wandering around in the dark, in rain so thick I couldn't see anything, and I literally stumbled across the hutch.

'Simon found me there the next morning when he skipped a class to check if his tortoises were still alive. He got a hell of a fright – there was this plastic-wrapped, soaked, half-frozen woman lying in the corner of his hutch, dead to the world or possibly just dead, wedged in between two annoyed-looking reptiles.

'He'd heard about me, of course – I had a bit of a reputation. The Academy had sent out sort of half-hearted search parties looking for me, but half the time they were people I knew who pretended not to notice me, and the other half of the time they were so bad at Wilderness 101 they couldn't find me anyway.

'He helped me put my shelter back together. I remember . . . he wasn't handsome, really, but he had one of those faces you'd never forget. He had freckles and a wicked laugh. He was always cracking jokes, terrible puns. I'd be laughing so hard I'd stuff my fist in my mouth in case there was a search party nearby.

'He was completely unafraid of being caught. This was opposed to me, who was obsessed about covering her tracks and moving her camp regularly. I don't know what the heck I planned to do with myself, but I knew I wasn't going back to the Academy.

'I was sixteen years old.

'Simon was eighteen. He ... . we fell in love. Or at least I did. He used to smuggle me news and supplies all the time, and then one night he stole this whole roll of bedding, dragged it up the hill to my shelter while I was trying to sleep on the pile of leaves I'd collected.

'Anyway . . .'

'Did he tell them where to find you?' said Isaac, softly.

'It was a bit more complicated than that,' said Benny. 'We both got caught, while we were down at the river one day, fishing. A bunch of troopers in uniform came out of the bushes and we both ran like hell. Smack into another bunch of troopers.

'I don't know whether Simon planned that, or whether he accidentally gave himself away when he was sneaking out one day, or whether it was just that our luck had run out. My luck.

189

'I thought they were going to shoot us. I thought the troopers in the forest would shoot us, and then when they just dragged us back to the Academy I thought they'd court martial us and *then* shoot us. In the end they just separated us and knocked us around a little bit.

'They chucked us into a holding cell together for about half an hour when they were done. We pledged eternal love and swore that we'd never give any evidence about one another, not even if they tortured us.

'They offered me leniency if I'd testify against Simon. I was so proud of myself when I said no.'

'The Prisoner's Dilemma,' said Isaac.

Benny said levelly, 'It turned out Simon had been keeping a journal of everything we'd been doing. Everything. They didn't find it: he'd hidden it too well. He handed it over to them in exchange for reduced discipline.'

Isaac closed his eyes.

'I didn't even tell them about his tortoises. I wish I had, because he didn't either, and the poor things eventually starved to death.

'I checked a few years ago, just before I met the Doctor. Cadet Kyle is a Captain now.

'All the things I wanted to say to his face still bubble up in my mind, sometimes, if I wake up at night, or when I sit down on grass or leaves . . . I never got the chance to say any of it, of course. I never will. For months afterwards it was like I had this constant inner dialogue where I was scripting what I'd say to him if we ever met again. I wanted to put it behind me, but I couldn't get it out of my head.

'The monks helped a bit, after I crash-landed on their planet. They did this strange meditation, where one of them pretended to be him, and I could call him a liar and a traitor and tell him how I would never trust him again and didn't love him any more because he'd shown me that he didn't love me. And that he'd just used me to have fun, because enjoying himself was all he cared about. And that I didn't want to hear his rationalizations. And that we'd obviously never really been friends at all.'

Benny stopped and ran a hand over her forehead. 'Anyway,'

she said, 'that's what happened with Simon Kyle, who was my best friend and my first lover. So yeah, Daddy. I understand. A little bit.'

She realized that Joel was standing on the staircase, hovering uncertainly.

'Oh,' he said, realizing he'd been spotted. 'Look. Um. Admiral, there's something you'd better see.'

The tape begins with a blast of unfocused movement, as though the camera was switched on before its operator was quite ready.

Suddenly it cuts to a figure, looming close to the camera, a dark blotch against a lighter background. The figure does something to the camera, and the brightness increases.

The figure steps back into shot. It's Albinex. He backs up and sits down, so that his head and shoulders appear in the frame.

'Hello, Admiral,' he says. 'Firstly, I want to apologize for this. It's not the sort of thing I usually get up to.'

He folds his arms, a little awkwardly, as though he's a bit embarrassed about the whole thing. 'But I'm very determined. I warn you, don't get involved. This is between the Doctor and me. Don't try to interfere.'

He sits back, and the automatic focus on the camera adjusts to follow him. 'This message is really for the Doctor. You already know what I want. I can assure you that I'm not going to use the destructor codes for any destructive purpose.'

('Suuuuure,' says Joel.)

He pauses for a moment, as though realizing the contradiction he's just presented. 'I can't tell you my actual plan, of course,' he goes on. 'But I can tell you that I'm not going to stop at anything. I need those codes.'

('Cut to the chase,' says Benny.)

'I've got your TARDIS, of course, but that didn't seem to be enough to persuade you. So now I've got something else to bargain with. Come with me.'

He gets up from the chair, obscures the camera as he picks it up. A blast of static as he switches it off. Then:

A shaky close-up of something – someone. The camera

191

zooms out, wobbling from side to side.

A hand-held shot of a young woman, unconscious, lying on a concrete floor. She's dressed all in black. She's half curled, as though sleeping uncomfortably. Her breathing is slow, but obvious.

(*'Oh my God,' says Benny.*)

She looks as though she's in her late teens. She looks terribly vulnerable, lying there on the floor.

The shot goes wild. After a moment, we see Albinex, who's presumably holding the camera at arm's length, with some effort. 'I'm going to add a location at the end of this tape,' he says, his voice echoing off concrete walls. 'Doctor, come alone. Let me emphasize that. Come here by yourself. I've got scanning equipment – I'll know if you bring any of the Admiral's crew or your companions.

'I won't hurt you. I won't hurt her. All I want are those codes.'

(*'But she's too young!'*)

The camera swings again. A final shot of the sleeping girl.

(*'But she's too old. She'd only be thirteen this year.'*)

The image cuts out, to be replaced by a miniature map, with a longitude and latitude.

(*'Maybe he's managed to get his time engine to work, just a little.'*)

The map cuts out in turn. It's been dubbed over the top of that last image of the young woman.

'Dorothée,' breathed Jason.

'Ace,' said Benny.

26

Demons

Joel climbed out of the van and aimed his boot at the side of the engine. 'Why won't the stupid thing start!'

'Because I removed the rotor arm,' said the Doctor, strolling into the garage.

They were about the same height, but, as the Doctor shot a glare at the van and its inhabitants, Joel suddenly had the impression of being looked down on from a great height.

The Doctor opened the sliding door in the side of the van. 'Everyone out,' he said.

Isaac's voice silenced the cries of protest. 'We can't let you go alone,' he said. 'It's too much of a security risk.'

'A security risk?' said Benny.

'If Albinex captures you, he might be able to learn the destructor codes,' said Isaac.

'I very much doubt it,' said the Doctor.

'Nonetheless,' said Isaac. 'At the same time, we can't let Dorothée become a casualty. So we'll rescue her, protect you, and capture Albinex.'

'No more troubles,' said Joel.

'At least, very few,' sighed the Doctor. He took his handkerchief out of his pocket and unwrapped the purloined rotor arm. 'I expect I can modify your hologram projectors to mask your biosignals.'

'All right!' said Joel, pulling the bonnet open.

Albinex hadn't gone far. The Doctor's hand-drawn copy of

the video map led them to a nearby small town. They parked the van at the back of a shop and walked the last couple of kilometres.

'What is it?' said Roz.

'A community centre, according to the map,' said Ms Randrianasolo.

'Hell,' said Roz.

'Albinex won't have chosen somewhere with a lot of witnesses,' said the Doctor, frowning.

'See the scaffolding?' said Roz. 'It looks as though the place is under repair.'

Isaac was consulting a handscan. 'I'm reading two humanoids, in different parts of the building. It must be them.'

'Either that,' said Benny, 'or a couple of builders are about to get the fright of their lives.'

Albinex had been waiting in the main hall. It was bitterly cold inside the building; if he had been human, his breath would be steaming in the air.

He looked up at the sound of approaching footsteps. Just one set of footsteps. He double-checked his handscan. Yes, just one. He stood up on the stage.

A small figure appeared in the doorway at the other end of the hall. 'You're late,' he told it.

'Traffic,' said the Doctor. He walked down the centre of the hall, steadily.

'Stop there,' said Albinex, raising the Tokarev he was holding. 'And take your hands out of your pockets.'

The Doctor did neither. 'You're going to shoot me,' he said. He hopped up onto the stage.

'That's close enough,' said Albinex. 'Believe me, if I think you're a threat, I will shoot you.'

'I'm no threat,' said the Doctor. 'How's Ace?'

'She's fine, she's just drugged,' said Albinex. 'It'll wear off shortly. She's not locked in, so she'll simply leave when she wakes up.'

The Doctor took his hands out of his pockets and spread them wide. 'I'm your prisoner now. You can tell me. Are you planning to destroy Earth, or just threaten to destroy it?'

'Threaten,' said Albinex. 'Once I've accumulated the power and technology I need, I'm going back to Navarro.'

'Ah,' said the Doctor. 'The barbarian who shakes the corrupt empire from its decadence.'

'We were a military power before,' said Albinex. 'And we'll be one again. The fun will stop when the first few bombs fall. The party is over.'

'You know,' said the Doctor, 'it's bad enough incinerating children to win a war. But vaporizing people because you don't like their lifestyle?' He sighed. His breath didn't steam in the air either. 'I think you've been on Earth too long, Albinex.'

'Whatever you say,' said the Navarino. He turned around and shot Joel.

Roz and Chris were following a handscan through the narrow hallways of the centre. It was a big, empty building, full of half-painted walls and exposed wiring. They walked past noticeboards covered in posters and fliers. The cold air smelt of sweat and plaster.

They followed the silent signal down to the gym, treading softly across the echoing wooden floor, until they came to a door.

Roz's left hand curled into the Adjudicator symbol for *right here*. Chris nodded and positioned himself to the side of the door. Roz put the handscan into the big pockets of her jacket and counted down *three, two, one, go!*

Chris booted the door. It wasn't locked. He ran into the room ahead of Roz, nearly knocking over a pile of hockey sticks.

There was nothing in the room but sports equipment and Dorothée.

Well, Ace, really. She'd been in her late twenties when she'd dropped the nickname. Roz crouched down beside the sleeping girl, pulling out the handscan. 'She's about eighteen,' she said. 'She's full of chlorpromazine. Enough to knock out four people.' She pulled the medikit out of her jacket.

'Wow,' said Chris. 'She looks completely different.'

195

'How do you mean?' said Roz, taking out a derm.

'At the wedding she was kind of tense and relaxed at the same time. Like a hunting animal.'

'I guess this is before her life started to go haywire,' said Roz, pushing the derm onto the skin behind Ace's ear.

'Hey, wait a minute,' said Chris. 'Did you say she was eighteen?'

Roz nodded, watching the young woman stir as the derm wiped the tranquillizer from her system.

'Well, didn't she leave Earth when she was sixteen? If she's eighteen, she ought to be off with the Doctor somewhere. So where did Albinex get her from?'

'Why don't you ask her?' said Roz, a moment before Ace jumped on her and tried to rip out her eyes.

Benny and Jason ought to have been following a handscan through the narrow hallways of the centre. Instead, they were having a stage-whispered row about who should go first.

'Look,' said Jason for the third time. 'If there's anything here, I want it to go through me first, right?'

'Will you please drop the macho thing?' said Benny. 'I've had about a billion times more experience at this sort of thing than you.'

'If you think you're the only one who's faced down hostile aliens –'

'*I* didn't *shag* them into submission!'

'*Look*,' said Jason. 'We're supposed to be on a *mission* here.'

'That's right! *We* are!'

They glared at each other.

The handscan screen started to flash. They both glanced down at it.

'Let's do this in alphabetical order,' said Jason.

'First name or last name?'

The point abruptly became academic. A door exploded outwards, knocked right off its hinges.

'Doctor!' said Jason.

'What the cruk!' said Benny.

The Doctor climbed over the door, fingernails pressing into

196

the wood of the doorframe. He was wearing an ill-fitting black uniform. His hair was too long, tied back out of his face.

He bared his teeth at them. His eyes were red instead of blue, as though he was a flash photograph.

'Oh shit,' said Benny and Jason together.

They dropped the handscan and legged it.

Slow motion:

Joel drops and rolls, frantically pushing himself out of the line of fire.

The Doctor grabs Albinex's gun arm as the Navarino tracks to take another shot. He pulls back, hard, knowing to expect the alien strength. Another shot bursts in the ceiling.

Isaac, coming up the stairs behind Joel, has flung himself to one side, landing hard on the wooden floor of the hall. 'What the *hell* do you think you're *doing*?' he explodes.

Ms Randrianasolo is racing up the steps from stage left. Upstage, Joel is yelping 'Shit! Shit! Shit! *Medic!*'

Albinex wrenches his gun arm out of the Doctor's grip and elbows the Time Lord in the ribs, hard enough to send him stumbling back across the stage. The Doctor collides with Ms Randrianasolo.

Isaac, halfway off the hall floor, sees the terrible moment in which Albinex could swing his hips back and forth and put a bullet into every single one of them.

The Navarino bolts, leaping down from the stage and sprinting for the doors. The Doctor follows, moving past Isaac even as the Admiral gets up off the floor.

The hall doors explode inwards as Benny and Jason run in, right for Albinex.

The Navarino does a cartoon skid, nearly losing his balance on the polished floor. He brings his gun to bear. 'No!' shouts the Doctor.

Something follows Benny and Jason into the hall.

Albinex is distracted for the moment it takes Jason to grab Benny and wrench her to one side. He looks at the monster bearing down on him. He puts all the bullets he has left into it and bolts from the hall, jumping over the body.

* * *

197

Roz yelled and leapt backwards, smashing into a rubbish bin full of plastic balls. They went everywhere as Ace went for her throat – with her *teeth* for Christ's sake!

Chris, reacting fast, thank the Goddess, landed a heavy double-handed blow between the girl's shoulders. Roz pulled at Ace's hands, trying to get her fingernails away from her eyes. God, she was strong. Roz's face was bleeding. She pushed hard, to get some distance between the girl's mouth and her carotid.

Chris wrenched Ace off Roz and threw her at the wall, hard. Bats and balls and stumps flew everywhere as she rolled hard down to the floor. When she got up, he picked her up and threw her again, harder this time.

It didn't stop her. She snaked out from under his grip and snagged his leg in her teeth, shearing through cloth and skin. He kicked her loose, his trainer crunching in her ribs. She shot up off the floor at Roz again.

Roz broke a hockey stick across the monster's face. It didn't stop her. She grabbed Roz's shoulders with both hands and sank her teeth into the woman's neck. The pain pierced straight to her heart, shocking the breath out of her, trying to rip her life loose.

Roz screamed.

Chris reached down and twisted Ace's neck until it broke with a resounding snap.

'Christ!' said Roz, trying to clamber out from under the body. The ripped flesh of her throat and shoulders was bleeding copiously.

Chris pulled the corpse off her and tossed it aside. He knelt down. 'You all right?' he said, and the tenderness in his voice broke her heart.

Benny looked between the body of the demon Doctor and the real Doctor. Jason was still holding her off the floor.

The real Doctor turned and ran back to the stage. Isaac had already jumped up there, and Ms Randrianasolo was picking herself up.

'Jason,' said Benny, 'put me down.'

He dropped her. They both ran to the stage.

Joel was lying awkwardly on his side, where he'd stopped rolling. The Doctor had already sliced open the arm of the boy's T-shirt with his Swiss Army knife. Blood was spattered across the stage. 'It doesn't hurt,' Joel said panickily. 'That's a bad sign, right? Am I okay?'

'You'll be fine,' said the Doctor firmly. 'You're in shock now. Don't worry, it'll hurt later.'

'Great,' said the boy shakily.

'Medikit,' said Ms Randrianasolo, passing it to the Time Lord.

'That son of a bitch,' said Joel, his eyes filling up with tears.

'Where are Chris and Roz?' said the Doctor, not looking up from where he was bandaging Joel's arm.

Isaac flipped out his handscan. 'Downstairs in a large room. Probably the gym. I'll go.'

'You stay right here,' said the Doctor. 'Benny, Jason, go and see if they're all right. Be careful. Albinex's signal was masked, so there's one more person in the building besides us.'

Benny looked between Isaac and Joel. The boy was looking up at the Admiral, trying not to cry.

'Right,' she said. Her father passed her the handscan. Jason followed her down from the stage.

Behind her, Isaac said, 'Good lad,' and reached down to tousle Joel's hair.

Benny picked up the handscan from where they'd dropped it. Jason stepped over the felled door and looked into the room. It had been torn to pieces, broken furniture everywhere, pictures ripped down from the walls. Only the security bars on the shattered windows had kept the monster in.

'What the hell was that thing?' he said.

Benny shook her head. 'We'll get the exposition later,' she said. 'Come on.'

Jason picked up a severed chair leg. He fell into step behind her, trying to keep an eye out in all directions at once.

The gym was silent, their footsteps echoing like tiny gunshots. 'Here,' said Benny, her whisper carrying loudly. Jason nodded and followed her to the open door.

Benny leant on the doorway. 'What have we here?' she said, loudly.

Jason looked over her shoulder. Chris and Roz were in a clinch on the floor, leaning up against a pile of mats. They jumped and looked up, guiltily, like a couple of teenagers caught by their parents.

Teenagers from a horror film. They were both smeared with blood. 'I'm not even going to *start* on the Freudian implications of this,' said Benny.

Jason put a hand on her shoulder. 'Are they the real ones?'

'Your average monster clone,' said Benny, 'isn't capable of simulating human embarrassment so accurately.'

A bright-red Chris helped Roz to her feet, wiping her blood from his mouth and throat. 'Let me have a look at that,' said Benny, serious now. 'What happened?'

'I think this did,' said Jason. He nodded down at the corpse in the corner. Benny looked, and bit her bottom lip so hard it bruised.

Ms Randrianasolo had fetched a couple of black plastic body bags from the van. Isaac had liberated a stretcher from a first-aid locker. 'I'm not dead yet,' murmured Joel. 'I feel happy . . .'

The Doctor was kneeling beside his double. A pool of blood was leaking out of it, black-purple, like ink from a broken pen.

The thing's face was fixed in a lethal snarl. He hoped *he* looked a bit more peaceful when he died.

He reached down and turned the thing's head, pushing the rough ponytail out of the way. Its skin was already stone-cold.

There was a triangular symbol etched into the skin over the collarbone. 'Bingo,' he said to himself.

He looked up at the sound of approaching footsteps. Benny and Jason were back, and Chris, helping Roz. The Doctor jumped up.

'It's not bad,' said the Adjudicator. 'Everyone stop making such a *fuss*.'

Ms Randrianasolo and Isaac had gently lifted Joel onto the stretcher. 'How is he?' said Jason.

200

'He'll be fine. Doctor, you and I will take Roz, Joel, and Ms Randrianasolo, and get to the hospital. Everyone else will clean up the mess and be ready to meet us when we get back.'

Benny looked down at the body bags. 'Euw,' she said.

Roz refused to have anything to do with twentieth-century medical treatment. She sat in the van, letting Chris work on her with a medikit. 'We can't all crowd into Casualty,' said Isaac, as they pulled up. 'Doctor, Benny, you come with me. The rest, stay here.'

They carried Joel in on the stretcher, despite his weak protests that he could walk. Isaac overrode the nurse who told him he couldn't follow the boy into the treatment room and marched in after him.

Benny and the Doctor sat in the waiting room, surrounded by kids with asthma, sprained ankles, and an author who'd managed to stick herself in the eye with a copy of her own book.

'They've done this before,' Benny murmured. The Doctor raised his head from the battered *National Geographic* he was pretending to read. 'Isaac made the cleaning-it-and-it-went-off story sound very real and panicked, but it was a script.'

'Is Joel going to be all right?' she asked.

'If he's lucky he'll just need stitches,' said the Doctor.

'I hate this,' she said. 'I hate people getting hurt around us.' She threw up her hands. 'It's not their *job*.'

'It is their job,' said the Doctor. 'Being part of Isaac's crew carries the same sort of risks as being part of the TARDIS crew. Though perhaps not on the same scale.'

'He's not a soldier,' said Benny. 'He's just a kid.'

'Albinex doesn't care about the collateral damage,' said the Doctor. 'Or he wouldn't play with nuclear weapons.'

Benny hunched forward and cupped her chin in her hands. After a moment, the Doctor put down his magazine. 'A penny for them,' he said.

'Another waiting room. I was just thinking about waiting for Cristián at the mental hospital . . . he was even younger than Joel, then. More collateral damage,' she said bitterly. 'And what they did to you at that house . . .'

'Does it disturb you that I burnt it down?'

Benny swivelled her head to look at him. It was almost as though he was waiting for her approval. 'Yes,' she said, after a moment, 'but only because it was such a normal sort of thing to do. It was the sort of thing I might do, or maybe Ace.'

'I'm getting human in my old age,' sighed the Doctor.

'Are you okay?' she said. 'I mean, having to go back there . . .'

'I hated having to be rescued,' he said. 'I hated the help-lessness.'

Benny sat up and put a hand on his arm. 'You're allowed to fall short of omnipotence, you know. From time to time. As required.'

He shook his head. After a moment, he said, 'You haven't even asked me where the two lookalikes came from.'

'Oh,' said Benny. 'I suppose I . . .' Didn't have to think about them, because they're dead now, she thought. 'What were they? Did Albinex decide to send in the clones?'

'They were genetically engineered shape-shifters from another dimension.'

'That would've been my guess.'

'They must have crossed over while Ace and I were visit-ing Llanfer Ceiriog. I expect Albinex found them and put them aside for a rainy day. Another loose thread, left untied because I didn't know about it.'

Benny leant forwards and pushed her fingers into her cropped hair. 'Jason and I should have done our own investi-gating using the time rings. I should never have contacted you.'

'I've missed you,' he said simply. 'It's been good to see you again.'

'Just like old times, eh?' she said. He smiled, and looked up as Isaac and Joel emerged from the treatment room.

'Send in the clones,' groaned Benny, as they got up. 'This whole thing is wrecking my finely tuned wit.'

* * *

It was late evening when they made it back. Isaac had ordered Joel to bed, so the boy had the Doctor help drag his desk over. He was holding the keyboard in his lap, typing one-handed, the bandaged arm resting against his chest.

The Doctor was sitting on the end of the bed, reading fanzines from the cardboard box. He clucked his tongue, absently. 'I see what you mean about the UNIT dating,' he said. 'Why don't any of these authors agree?'

'It's the D Notices,' said Joel, from behind his screen. 'You can get three different dates which all make sense, going by hearsay. I could write a killer article if you'd answer a few questions . . .'

'Ah,' said the Doctor, 'but would anyone believe that you'd interviewed me?'

'Point taken. Anyway, the Admiral would have a fit. Hey, look at this.'

The Doctor leant back so that he could see the screen. 'Ah.' His eyes flickered over the text. 'That's just what we've been looking for. Well done.'

He folded away the fanzine and got up. 'Where are you going?' asked Joel.

'Albinex's base,' said the Doctor. 'I hope.'

Tony met him on the landing. 'Did you have any luck with the bulletin boards?' said the Tzun.

The Doctor nodded. 'There was quite a detailed sighting posted about an hour ago. I'm going to go and take a quick look at the area.' He put his hands in his pockets. 'I think I'll borrow Albinex's car.'

'I'll come with you,' said the Tzun.

The Doctor looked at him, standing very still.

'Just you,' he said, after a long moment. 'And don't tell anyone else.'

'Oh,' said Tony. 'All right.'

Alekto

She appeared for the last time at eleven o'clock.

The crew were scattered about the town. Ms Randrianasolo was guarding Woodworth, who was curled on the desk, deeply asleep. Joel was at his computer, despite Isaac's insistence that he go to sleep. Graeme was soaking with the coffee pots in the sink.

Isaac was in the coffee shop, talking with his daughter and son-in-law. Jason had been expounding a somewhat Bowdlerized version of his adventures, while Benny watched the two men warming to each other. It was a boy thing, she thought. They'd been in combat together, so now they were buddies.

'Yeah,' Jason was saying, 'it happened to me on Christmas Eve. One minute I'm walking down Oxford Street, the next I'm flat on my back in an alien swamp.'

A bee landed on the table. Absently, she brushed it away, and yelped as it stung her.

'I thought I'd been abducted by Santa –' Jason stopped in mid-anecdote.

Isaac took Benny's hand and carefully brushed the sting off. 'We'll put some ice on that,' he said.

The three of them looked down at the table, where the bee was buzzing its last.

Jason jumped to his feet. 'The Doctor,' he said. Suddenly his hair was blowing, as though there was a draught in the shop. 'Where's –'

The draught became a sudden, violent rushing, almost pushing him off his feet. He sat down, awkwardly.

'I suppose it's our turn!' yelled Isaac, over the sound of the wind.

Benny gripped the edge of the table, as though expecting to be carried off in the temporal hurricane.

'I can see her,' said Isaac. He was staring up at the ceiling, as though something was hovering there.

'What does she look like?' shouted Benny.

'She looks like an Egyptian tomb painting,' he said. 'She looks like winged Isis.' He tried to stand up, reaching out as though he wanted to touch the vision.

Benny found she was blinded by the screaming wind. She was ready to have her past played back in front of her, with no corrections or additions to the diary this time. She was even ready to see her future. She wished she could reach out for Jason's hand.

Her husband yelled something. 'What?' she shouted back.

'I'm holding something,' he said.

Isaac's voice: 'What do you mean?'

'There's something in my arms. It's like I'm reaching through a window and something's being given to me.'

Benny felt a sudden, violent pain in her belly. She fell forward onto the table, tears starting from her eyes at the sharpness of it. But it was gone in a moment.

'Don't take it!' she cried. 'Whatever it is! Don't reach for her!'

'What do you want from us?' Isaac was shouting. 'Can you tell us what you want?'

Benny's blindness was becoming a searing light. The light at the end of the tunnel. They were going to die. She'd brought down some howling Fury on them. The screaming of the wind rose until it blocked out the others' shouts, blotted out her mind.

Abruptly, the sound ceased.

She blinked her eyes rapidly. All she could see was a white blur, speckled with darker colours.

'Benny,' said Jason softly.

She pulled her face up off the Formica tabletop and looked at him.

He was holding a small child.

'Benny,' he said softly. 'I think this is Keith.'

Albinex

Tony gave him directions for the last few miles of the trip.

At last they ran out of road, at the edge of a great, dark lake. The Doctor switched off the engine and got out. Tony scrambled out of the passenger seat, blinking at him.

They were nowhere near where the sky yacht had been reported.

The car lights stabbed out across the lake. A sharp wind was moving the long grass and rippling the surface of the water. The Doctor stood in the light, looking out into the darkness, his hair and jacket blowing in the wind.

'I'm here,' he said.

The sky yacht burst into existence above them, lights blazing. It lowered itself slowly, the grass and water blowing in wild circles around it, until they could see Albinex standing in one of the airlocks.

The Navarino activated a metal ladder, which uncoiled itself gracefully, its silver lines catching the headlight beams. The Doctor glanced back at Tony, and grabbed hold of the end of it. He climbed nimbly up into the airlock. After a moment, the Tzun shut off his hologram to improve his vision, and followed. He scrambled into the airlock and pulled the ladder up after him.

Albinex was holding his Russian pistol. He slapped a control panel with his free hand, and the airlock door slid shut.

There was a sudden, ear-ringing silence.

'He came of his own accord,' said Tony. 'Even though he'd worked it out.'

'I knew he would,' said Albinex. 'Wherever the Doctor goes, people around him get hurt. He couldn't let that keep on happening.' He looked at the Time Lord. 'I'm right, aren't I?'

'No,' said the Doctor. 'I came because I'm the one who's going to stop you.' He took a step forward, making the Navarino take a step back. 'Shall we dance?'

27

Fury

'This isn't right. I'm not right for you.'

Roz opened her eyes and glared at Chris. 'What's that supposed to mean?'

'I'm not the right person for you.'

'Is that why you never said anything?'

'What do you mean?' he said softly.

'I've known for a long time, Chris.'

'Oh my Goddess,' he gulped. 'Have you?'

'Yeah. I've seen it in your eyes. A few times.'

'Oh . . .'

'I just never really thought about it before. Pushed it to the back of my mind.'

Silence for a bit.

'I'm too young for you,' he said. 'I mean, I don't mean you're that old – it's me, I'm too young. You deserve someone more experienced.'

'You seem to have had quite a bit of experience, Squire Cwej.'

'You see? I'm just a Squire, I'm just your apprentice. I –'

'Damn it, Chris, that was supposed to sound sexy.'

'Oh! Well, it did. It did!'

'Look,' said Roz. 'Don't you think I'm the best judge of who's good for me?'

He looked at her with his big, blue, little boy's eyes. 'I'm not worthy,' he breathed.

'Then get your damned hand out of my shirt,' she said.

'I'm going for a walk.'

Albinex led the Doctor and M'Kabel through his space-travelling yacht to the ballroom. He'd tucked the gun away inside his jacket. He knew he wouldn't be needing it.

'So, what's it going to be?' said the Doctor conversationally, his voice echoing in the high-ceilinged room. It was the largest aboard the ship, with a wooden dancefloor and a well-stocked bar at one end. 'Thumbscrews? Forced telepathy? Suspending my companions over a vat of boiling chocolate sauce?'

'I'm not going to torture you,' said Albinex. He went to the bar, put his gun down, and poured himself a crème de menthe. 'Do you want anything?'

'I want to be a juggler,' said the Doctor absently. He was looking around the ballroom, as though trying to spot the iron maiden hidden in the shadows. 'When I grow up I'm going to run away to the circus.'

'I had hoped you'd just tell me the codes,' said Albinex, 'having come all this way.' He took a mouthful of the drink. 'But I'm not going to torture them out of you.'

'I'm so terribly disappointed,' said the Doctor.

M'Kabel looked up at him.

'No matter what you do to me,' said the Doctor, 'I'm not going to give you those codes.' He closed his eyes. 'There's nothing you can do to me. There's no pain you can inflict on me which I haven't suffered before. There's no horror you can shroud me in which I haven't endured.'

He opened his eyes again, and M'Kabel took a step back. 'I'm old, Albinex,' he said. 'I'm weary to my bones. There's nothing an embryonic upstart like you can show me which I haven't seen before.'

The Navarino gulped down the rest of his drink. 'Well then,' he said.

The hurricane snapped on as though he'd thrown a switch. The Doctor leant into the wind, holding onto his hat with one hand. M'Kabel took a few more steps back out of the way, just in case.

The ghost blossomed.

She was a point of intense colour and light, unfolding like a new rose. She floated in the raging wind, serene. A million wings uncurled around her.

The wind began to die down. The Doctor folded his arms, looking up at the gorgeous, feathered creature. Her eyes were blank, surreal. Her face was no longer human, heart-stoppingly beautiful. She spiralled inwards and out, back through time and beyond, in dimensions M'Kabel and Albinex could barely imagine, let alone see.

'What have you done to her?' said the Doctor.

'We have a bargain,' said Albinex.

'You promised her you'd restore her to normality,' said the Time Lord. 'You lied to her.'

Albinex shook his head, glancing nervously up at his pet monster. 'I'll be able to shift her back in time the one picosecond that's making the difference,' he said.

'Not now,' said the Doctor. 'Not now you've done this to her. She's gone further and further away from being human.'

'She's been exploring,' said Albinex. 'Discovering what she's capable of. Time doesn't limit her the way it limits me. Or even you. I believe,' he breathed, 'she could do anything.'

The Doctor smiled. 'Except make me give you those codes.'

The Fury looked down at him.

He held his ground as she descended. The wind rushed through his body, not disturbing the air around him, not moving a hair on his head.

She reached out her hands to him, smiled at him with blind eyes. He took her hands in his.

M'Kabel imagined he could see space-time straining around the Doctor and the ghost as they connected. The Doctor's mouth opened as her power poured into him. His eyes flickered and closed as his head fell backwards.

His hat fell off. M'Kabel jumped.

'Take him back,' Albinex told the ghost. 'Take him back to when he first learnt the codes.'

M'Kabel had the impression of rushing motion, hidden

211

under some surface skin of reality. The Doctor's eyes opened again, staring blankly into the ghost's face, as she unwound his life.

There was a sudden ripple in the room, a grinding, tearing sensation. The Doctor cried out in an alien tongue. M'Kabel couldn't tell whether it was pain or surprise or some arcane Gallifreyan emotion.

She pushed, pushed him down to his knees, fighting every step of the way. She was gripping his wrists, forcing them together, back against his chest. Their faces were an inch apart, not touching, their eyes locked.

The Doctor yelled again, turning his head sharply to one side, eyes tightly closed. She *pushed*. He cried out in that dark language. She PUSHED. His mouth opened, but no sound emerged.

I CAN'T DO IT, she said. M'Kabel flinched at the ripple of her voice through his viscera.

'What's the problem?' said Albinex.

I CAN'T GET BACK BEFORE HIS DEATH.

'His what?'

HE DIED.

'You said the regenerations wouldn't matter.'

THIS ONE IS DIFFERENT.

She let go of him, suddenly, and he fell sideways onto the floor. M'Kabel hovered, alarmed, until she floated back and away. Keeping his eyes on the ghost, he crept up to the Doctor and checked that he was breathing.

'Do you forgive me yet?' said the Time Lord, in a tiny, distant voice, and closed his eyes.

For the first time, Isaac looked ruffled.

He was holding onto his grandson. Keith Brannigan Kane-Summerfield was a bright-eyed toddler, perhaps eighteen months old. He was wearing a dark blue pair of overalls and a stripey T-shirt.

He had burst into wails when he'd first arrived, but a few cuddles and a bit of warmed milk later he was quite happy to sit on granddad's lap and look around.

Not one of them doubted that it was Keith.

'How?' breathed Jason.

He held out a finger, and his son closed his tiny fist around it. 'Va va va va va,' said Keith.

'Well, we're not going to get any answers out of *you*,' said Jason.

'The Doctor could tell us,' said Benny. 'Maybe Keith fell back through time, somehow.'

'But why? What for?' said Isaac.

Benny just shook her head. 'The Doctor could tell us.'

Roz came into the shop. She looked at the four of them. 'What's this?'

'This is our means of reproduction,' said Benny. 'We call it a "child".'

'It's my grandson,' said Isaac. He grinned, just for a moment, his eyes astonished.

Roz looked between Benny and Jason. 'What, did he bud off, or something?'

'The ghost gave him to us,' said Benny. 'We need the Doctor.'

'Bloody hell,' said Roz. 'Well, why are you just sitting here? Isn't he upstairs?' She headed for the stairs, absently doing up a button on her shirt.

'Va va VA va va!' said Keith, waving his hands around.

'I hope there's a twenty-four-hour place around here,' said Benny. 'I think we're going to be in need of nappies shortly.'

'Tell me about your plan,' said the Doctor.

He was sitting with his back to the wall of the ballroom. The glass of water M'Kabel had brought him was sitting beside him. His arms were folded and his eyes were closed.

'All right,' said Albinex.

'That was easy,' said the Doctor, opening one eye.

'I want you to know.' The Navarino sat down on the floor, a few feet from him.

He was back in his natural form; a great, suckered purple blob, a cartoon space monster. If you made dolls of him, little girls would get them for Christmas.

'I want you to know that I'm not going to kill anyone. Listen. I'm going to take control of a single cruise missile,

213

and threaten to set it off if they don't give me the resources I need. I'm going home. I'm going to lead the Navarinos.'

'Lead them?' said the Doctor. His voice was full of amusement. 'Wherever are you going to lead them?'

'We used to be warriors,' said Albinex. 'We were proud and strong. We believed in courage and honour and taking action. I still believe in those qualities.'

'So you're going to go home and bully the Navarinos into becoming your army.' He actually laughed. 'An army of Navarinos! Half of them would be on R and R and the other half would go AWOL looking for a good pub. Why would you bother with the Navarinos, when there are whole planets full of potential galaxy-conquering soldiers out there?'

'They're my people.'

The Doctor looked Albinex in the purple eyes. 'They never liked you, anyway.'

'What.'

'They didn't want to play war with you. So you stole one of their toys instead of sharing.' He gestured around at the ballroom.

'I never fitted in,' said Albinex, proudly. 'I never conformed.'

'Bully,' said the Doctor, 'for you.'

'Look,' said Albinex. 'Even if I actually set off the missile, less people would die than will die this year from tobacco.'

The Doctor rolled his eyes. 'Do you really imagine you can so precisely predict the future? Perhaps you imagine that the web of time would protect Earth. Prevent it from being destroyed, because that's the way that history goes. Well, it wouldn't. Believe me. The balance is too fine.'

He sat back again. 'Anyway, it's academic, since you won't have the codes.'

'Why do you care so much?' Albinex shook his head. 'Why Earth?'

'I'll tell you this much for free. Most planets look like quarries. Earth is precious.'

Albinex got up. He glanced at M'Kabel, who was hovering behind the bar, pretending to read the bottle labels.

She exploded into life behind him, a surreal, floating

flower. 'Where have you been?' Albinex said.

I CAN'T EXPLAIN, she said, after a moment. *YOU COULDN'T UNDERSTAND.*

'Never mind,' said Albinex.

The Doctor didn't flinch as she floated gently down and wrapped herself around him.

She unfolded his arms, holding them against the wall behind him, as they looked into each other's eyes.

She expected him to struggle. She hadn't realized yet that he didn't need to.

'All right,' said the Navarino.

She was a sizzling tang all over his body, a lemon crush that soaked into his skin and burnt him. He tried to push back, reach inside her and find what was left of the human being. She had seen his TARDIS. Where was it?

'Take him back. Find the moment.'

M'Kabel dropped the glass he was holding. The ghost was screaming.

'Hold him there!' Albinex shouted. 'Hold him! Make it last!'

I CAN'T!

With a violent burst of movement, she rushed backwards and up from the Time Lord. 'Why did you stop?' shouted Albinex, over the frantic buzzing of her wings.

IT HURT ME! ME!

She moved back further, gently bobbing against the ceiling. Albinex looked at M'Kabel, jerked his purple head.

The Tzun carefully came out from behind the bar. He stayed close to the wall as he sidled up to the Doctor, keeping his large, black eyes on the ghost as she argued with her employer.

The Time Lord was lying on his side, curled up, his skin almost as pale as a Tzun's.

'Are you all right?' M'Kabel said.

'Of course I'm all right,' said the Doctor. 'I'm always all right.'

M'Kabel helped him to sit up. The colour was coming back into the Time Lord's face. He glared up at Albinex.

215

'Good help is so hard to find these days,' he said.

'She felt what you felt.'

'Of course she did. We're the same.'

I CAN'T STAND THE PAIN HE CAN STAND, said the ghost. Albinex turned away in disgust.

'You're only young,' breathed the Doctor. He reached for the glass of water and knocked it over with a shaking hand.

'He said he was going to find Albinex's base,' said Joel blearily.

'How long ago was that?' said Roz.

'I'm not sure,' Joel yawned. 'I fell asleep at the computer. Didn't he tell anyone else?'

'Never mind,' said the Adjudicator. She snapped off the light and went back downstairs.

Benny was pouring herself a cup of tea behind the counter, while Jason and Isaac played with the little kid. Weird.

'Do you want a cup of something?' asked Benny. Roz shook her head and sat down at a table, back to the wall.

To her annoyance, Benny decided to join her. 'How's everything going?' she said, and wiggled her eyebrows.

'Nothing is *going* anywhere,' she muttered.

'That was a rather serious kiss,' the archaeologist insisted. 'I thought I was going to have to cover Joel's eyes, that first time. Goodness, I thought I was going to have to cover *my* eyes.'

'He was delirious,' said Roz.

'You weren't.'

'It was the heat of the moment!' exploded Roz as quietly as she could manage. 'I just responded automatically. There is nothing between us.'

'Yes there is,' said Benny. 'About twenty years. Not to mention the attitude gap.'

Roz made a face. 'Men,' she said.

Benny glanced back at Jason, who was swinging Keith up into the air, gently. The boy was laughing. 'You've had a bit of a rough ride where they're concerned, haven't you?' she said.

'You should talk,' said Roz. She cupped her chin in her

216

hand. 'I don't need this. I don't need it now. Why'd he decide to do this now?'

'It's been coming for a long time, hasn't it?'

'Yeah,' sighed Roz. 'He's had a puppy crush on me since he was first squired to me. Familiar pattern. Familiar bloody pattern,' she said bitterly.

'Is it just a crush?'

'I don't know. He idolizes me the way I idolized my Senior. Doesn't he know it's a cliché? I mean, doesn't he know how dangerous it is? What if they get killed in the line of duty, or . . . ?'

'What if they're on the make, and you have to kill them yourself?' said Benny, very gently.

'Let's change the subject,' said Roz.

'You could do a lot worse than Chris. He's a good man. And he's a wicked kisser.' Benny grinned.

'I'll bet he's a morning person,' muttered Roz.

'Maybe we should wait . . .'

'We can't wait.' Albinex waved a thick limb at M'Kabel.

'Um. I'm supposed to make sure he doesn't get hurt,' said the Tzun.

'Of course he's going to get hurt,' said Albinex. 'We're interrogating him.'

M'Kabel glanced at the Doctor, who was lying on the bar, his hat held neatly on his chest. 'Well, if you kill him, you're not going to find out the codes, are you?' he whispered.

'Carry on,' said the Doctor cheerfully, waving his hat. 'Why stop when you're failing miserably?'

Albinex stormed over to him. 'Do you think this is funny?' he snarled. 'This is not funny.'

The ghost, who had been sulking in a corner of the ceiling, drifted down to him. The Doctor sat up, holding his hat in one hand, peering at her. 'Are you all right?' he said.

I'M TIRED, said the ghost.

'I'm not surprised. This is hard work.'

I WANT TO GO HOME.

Albinex raised his limbs in an angry gesture. The Doctor and the ghost looked at him. For a moment, M'Kabel thought the Navarino was going to hit one of them.

'Show him what death is like,' said Albinex.

'No!' said M'Kabel.

'Bradbury did it first,' said the Doctor.

'No,' insisted M'Kabel. 'This is sacrilege. It's in the Book of Names.'

The Doctor looked the Tzun in his black eyes. 'No one may look at the face of Death,' he recited. 'No one may strike a bargain with Death. No one may make an image of Death. No one may speak the name of Death.'

'No details,' said Albinex. 'Just the moment itself.'

'Because she has no face to look upon,' whispered M'Kabel. 'And no name to speak.'

The ghost traced the Doctor's shoulder with a burning finger. For a moment, he stared into nothing, his face reflecting surprise, denial, curiosity, acceptance. Then he slumped sideways onto the bar.

M'Kabel pushed him back before his limp form could roll onto the floor. His slender fingers sought a pulse in the Doctor's throat. 'He's alive,' he breathed.

IT WAS ONLY ONE OF HIS DEATHS, said the ghost. *THE NEXT ONE*.

'Now you can rest,' Albinex told her. 'We'll try something else later.'

She should never have left him alone.

Benny had sent Jason across the road on an expedition for nappies and baby food. Keith had been too tired to eat, worn out with the excitement of his unexpected arrival. Benny had changed him and taken him upstairs to the guest bedroom, asleep in her arms. He was heavy and sweet-smelling.

She put him on the bed and watched him for a little while. Her child. She put a hand on her stomach. Had he been conceived that morning? Had the Doctor worked some magic, or was it just time?

Was she somewhere in the future, frantic over her lost baby? Or would she remember, know where he'd gone? Or was this Keith just a possibility, a memory of the future who would simply fade away?

She'd gone into the bathroom to wash her face. It was after midnight, and she was exhausted.

She shouldn't have left him.

She almost walked into Woodworth, who'd been waiting for her to come back into the room. When she opened her mouth to yell, Woodworth shoved her fist into it.

A bright light filled her field of vision as she stumbled back into the door, trying to keep her balance. It was only a few seconds before the light faded and she could function again. But in that time the torturer had run out, clutching her baby.

Benny almost tripped over Ms Randrianasolo, who was lying half in and half out of the study, very unconscious. She stepped over the black woman and raced down the back stairs, hearing the door slam ahead of her.

Woodworth headed for the road. She skidded in gravel, nearly dropping Keith, as Jason exploded out of the front door of the café and bolted down the street.

Benny sprinted after her. She wanted to shout something to Woodworth, some plea or frantic promise, but she needed all her breath for running.

It was only a coincidence that Chris walked out of the cottage at the moment Woodworth was running by. He took one look at her and hurdled the front fence, standing in her path. She veered left and into the churchyard.

Benny was through the gates even before Chris. Woodworth was stumbling between the gravestones, looking for a way out, one hand clutching the back of Keith's overalls.

Afterwards, Benny realized she had seen the strange light, an orange, pulsing glow like a low campfire, coming from a corner of the graveyard. But she was so fixated on Woodworth and Keith, barely visible by the distant street lights, that she hadn't taken any notice of it.

Chris was beside her, in his pyjamas and bare feet. 'All right,' he said calmly. 'We're not armed, and we're not going to come any closer. You're not in any danger. Why don't you tell us what you want?'

'Just you bloody keep away from me!' Woodworth snarled.

Jason had come in through the gate, followed by Isaac and

219

Roz. Where was the Doctor? Chris glanced back at them and raised a hand.

'No problem,' the Adjudicator told Woodworth. 'I'll tell you what. Why don't you let the kid come over here, and then all of us will just back away slowly? How does that sound?'

Woodworth just held Keith more tightly. 'Don't talk to me!' she squealed. 'Shut up, whatever the hell you are! All of you, you're all monsters, just *leave me alone*!'

The heartbeat filled the graveyard, suddenly, as though a switch had been thrown. They all looked around for the source of the sound. Woodworth let out an almighty scream.

One of the tombstones was coming for her.

'What the cruk is *that*?' said Chris.

The stone was huge and mossy, taller than a man. An orange light pulsed inside it as it moved. A smaller tombstone was crushed to dust beneath it as it headed for the panicked woman.

'Keith!' shouted Benny. 'Come here, Keith! Come to Mummy! Come here!'

Woodworth had almost lost her grip on the toddler, hypnotized by the stone. Keith struggled out of her arms and made a wobbling run for Benny. She snatched him up and got the hell out of the way of the stone.

Woodworth didn't try to back away. She didn't scream. She just stood there staring up at the worst thing she had ever seen.

The stone hovered for a moment, its orange heartbeat fading to nothing. Then it silently toppled forward and crushed her flatter than a pancake.

Benny and Keith both burst into tears. Jason put his arms around his family and held them tightly.

The stone flared with orange light again, *sucking*.

'Well,' tremored Isaac, 'that will save on cattle mutilations for a while.'

Five minutes later Chris said, 'Um, my feet are wet.'

Albinex had hefted the Doctor in his thick limbs and carried him to one of the staterooms. Now M'Kabel was watching him sleep. Or whatever it was he was doing.

When the ghost had offered to let Albinex see his future, days ago, the Navarino had politely refused. M'Kabel reckoned he had the right idea.

The Doctor stretched and yawned, as though waking up from a pleasant nap. 'What's in all of this for you?' he said, as though continuing a conversation.

M'Kabel said, 'Sorry?'

'I mean, is it an aliens-versus-humans thing?'

'No,' said the Tzun. 'Look, I'm not supposed to tell you anything.' The Doctor rolled his head to look at him. 'Sorry,' gulped M'Kabel.

'It must be something extraordinary,' said the Doctor. 'You've been friends with Isaac for years. And to be perfectly honest, you don't strike me as the cloak-and-dagger type.'

M'Kabel wished Albinex would come back.

'So let's see. Passage home? No, you defected, and besides, if you wanted to go home, Isaac could have organized it. Rulership of part of Albinex's conquered Earth, or perhaps Navarro? No, you don't strike me as that type either.'

The Doctor sat up, making M'Kabel jump. 'Perhaps he hasn't offered you anything at all,' said the Time Lord. 'Perhaps you're both taking your orders from someone else.'

Mercifully, that was when Albinex walked back in.

He was back in human form. He had to be: he was holding his gun again, and for that, he needed humanoid hands. 'Come back to the ballroom,' he said.

The Doctor lay down again. 'I honestly can't be bothered,' he said. 'So far, you're out for a duck. Why don't you give up like a sensible megalomaniac?'

'You can't be a sensible megalomaniac,' said M'Kabel. 'A maniac by definition isn't sensible . . .' He trailed off as they both turned to look at him. 'Sorry.'

'We can do this here,' said Albinex. 'Right here.'

The ghost appeared again. She buzzed, angrily, like a cloud of woken insects. M'Kabel wondered whether it was the Doctor or Albinex who needed to watch out.

'You still haven't worked it out, have you?' said the Doctor. 'Forcing this poor woman to distort herself further isn't going to get you what you want.' His eyes pierced the Navarino.

'Why don't you level with me? Who are you really working for? What's your real plan, Albinex?'

'Find the moment,' said the Navarino.

With a weary movement of the air, she settled down to the bed. She seemed attenuated, thin. M'Kabel was reminded of one of those miniature balloons that human children played with, one which had been allowed to drain of air for a few days. She was deflated.

The Doctor sat up. He was inside her, as though he was inside a cloud of colourful light. Her wings beat around him, slowly. 'You don't have to do this,' he said, gently. 'You're only making yourself sicker.'

His eyes went blank as she pushed him backwards. Evidently they did not have to travel far. *I'VE FOUND IT*, she announced.

The Doctor reached out a hand, as though taking something small, holding it.

'Hold him there.'

He froze. Light flashed and flared in the cloud around the Doctor. M'Kabel could see the ghost's pale face deep inside, staring at the Time Lord.

'What is it?' asked Albinex.

A NICE CUP OF TEA, said the ghost.

M'Kabel said, 'What are you doing?'

Albinex turned his fake human eyes on the Tzun. 'She's taken him back to a specific moment on his timeline. Not far.'

'You already tried that,' said M'Kabel.

'We tried taking him back to a moment of pain. But she couldn't bear it.'

The Doctor frowned, confused, as the same little moment of time played itself over and over.

'He doesn't experience pain in the same way that we do,' said Albinex. 'I doubt that he experiences pleasure the same way, either. A nice cup of tea,' he snorted. 'How much can you amplify it?'

I DON'T KNOW, said the ghost. *A MILLION TIMES, MAYBE*.

'Do it.'

ALL AT ONCE?

'As much as he can survive. Right now.'

The Time Lord's back arched, suddenly, and he fell back on the bed. The ghost stayed with him, sticking to him, swirling around, burning with an intense orange light.

AH.

'Stop!' he yelled. 'Stop it!'

Albinex knelt down beside the bed, so that his face was level with the Time Lord's. The Doctor was shaking violently, his arms thrown up in front of him as though to ward off the attack.

MMMMMMMNNNNNNNNNN.

'That's more like it,' said the Navarino.

'You're enjoying this,' said M'Kabel.

Albinex gave him a dismissive glance. 'I've got a tape recorder here,' he said.

In a single, fluid movement, the Doctor pulled his whole body into a foetal position, arms thrown over his head.

'Can he escape you?'

HE'S TRYING TO. The ghost's voice was thick with ecstasy.

'Then make it stronger.'

I CAN'T.

The Doctor said something, his voice muffled.

'What was that?'

'*Please,*' sobbed the Time Lord. He was weeping for joy.

Albinex switched on the tape recorder. 'Any time you're ready.'

M'Kabel unlocked the door of the stateroom and slipped inside.

The Doctor lay on the bed, awake. His eyes were dark and empty.

'I'm sorry,' whispered the Tzun.

He wondered what it must be like to come down from a high like that. 'It's over now,' he said. 'You've given him the codes.'

The Doctor had bitten out a long, long series of numbers. Albinex didn't let the ghost stop until he was sure he had the

223

whole of the codes safely recorded. M'Kabel had spent the last hour checking them for errors. They were all valid.

'No one can blame you. Nobody could have stood up to that.'

Behind them, the door opened. Albinex marched in. 'What are you doing?'

'I'm not doing anything,' said M'Kabel.

Albinex pushed past him and hovered over the Doctor. 'Get up,' he said. When the Time Lord didn't move, he reached down and wrenched him upright by his collar. The Doctor didn't try to resist.

'I was very worried you'd try to trick us.'

'Don't talk to me,' said the Doctor hoarsely. 'Just kill me.'

M'Kabel looked at Albinex. 'You wouldn't,' said the Tzun.

Albinex dragged the Doctor off the bed and pulled him across the room. M'Kabel caught up with them in the hallway and took the Doctor's arm, steadying him. 'Where are we going?' the Tzun demanded weakly.

'To the airlock,' said Albinex.

'We're going to let you go now,' the Tzun reassured the Doctor.

It wasn't far. Albinex slapped a panel, opening the inner door of the airlock. He dropped the Doctor onto the floor inside. For a horrible moment, M'Kabel thought they were in space.

But the sensors registered normal pressure. The outer door opened.

They were still above the lake. M'Kabel looked out, cautiously.

Thirty metres above the lake.

The Doctor murmured something. 'Last words?' said Albinex. 'I can't hear you.' He leant closer.

The Doctor lifted his head and kissed Albinex on the end of the nose. He fell back, grinning.

Albinex blinked at him. M'Kabel watched the pair of them, almost dancing from foot to foot with anxiety.

The Navarino pulled the Doctor to the door. The Time Lord peered out at the darkness. At the water, far below them,

224

the hovering ship's anti-gravity beam forcing strange ripples across its surface.

'Don't you have any mercy?' whispered M'Kabel.

Albinex glanced at the Tzun. 'Yes,' he said. He twisted his hand in the Doctor's hair and smacked the Time Lord's head against the door frame, hard, twice.

The Navarino lifted him by the collar, shoved him out into the air.

M'Kabel screamed as the airlock door slammed shut.

PART FOUR

THE END

Be like the chameleon – keep one eye on the past and one on the future.

Malagasy proverb

Falling

Towards a black mirror.

Angry eyes watching him fall. His last self. 'No. I don't forgive you. Not yet.'

The air ripped past him.

'Serves you right for killing me just so you could exist. Is it murder? Suicide? Patricide?'

Tumbling, head down, unable to get a breath.

'You've been staving off Number Eight for so long. Haven't you, "Time's Champion"? What will he be capable of?'

The mirror shattered around him with a terrible sound.

'That's the trouble with regeneration. You don't get to choose your next face.'

The Doctor surfaced.

He drew a violent breath. He thrashed, trying to get another. He couldn't swim, he couldn't remember how to swim!

But his arms and legs remembered. They dragged him forward through the freezing water, instinct pulling him towards the lights on the shore.

The water wrenched him down, wrapping him in cold. He fought his way up, surfaced again, coughing and gasping.

Come on, he told himself, what's a little chill to the Ka Faraq Gatri?

The darkness closed over him again. But it wasn't the water. The singing in his head was becoming a frozen numbness, stabbing down into his shoulders and arms. He pushed at the water as it forced its way into his mouth and nose. Keep moving, aim for the light –

Something grabbed him!

He tried to fight, tried to pull away, but it dragged him up out of the water, holding him tightly. A hand pressed against his chin, forcing his head back, and he realized after a moment that he could breathe.

He breathed, and let Isaac carry him to the shore.

Hands grabbed them as they reached the shallows, pulled them up onto the frozen ground. Isaac was kneeling, looking at him, shivering violently, pale hair plastered across his forehead.

The Doctor rolled away from him and coughed up about half the lake.

Someone draped a heavy blanket over him. When he could breathe again, they turned him gently so that he was wrapped in it, and lifted him up. He blinked up at Chris Cwej's worried countenance.

'This time?' the Doctor whispered.

The water closed over him.

28

Recovery

Chris carried the Doctor up the slope of the shore and through the long grass to the van. He held the little man like a fragile package, something expensive and rare that he didn't dare drop or jar.

Benny wrenched open the sliding door. 'Let's get him out of those wet clothes,' she said. Chris and Roz looked at each other. 'I'll do it,' Benny said.

They laid the Doctor down on the floor of the van. Joel was about to hop up inside, but Isaac put a hand on the boy's shoulder and shook his head. Benny's father was wrapped in another of the thick blankets, Joel holding his soaked jacket in one hand, his other arm in a sling.

'You all right, Dad?' she said, glancing up for just a moment. He nodded.

'Close the bloody door,' Roz said. 'The wind's freezing.' Chris slammed it shut.

Benny unbuttoned the Doctor's shirt. His skin was so cold, tinged with blue, but he wasn't shivering at all. Very bad sign. Roz helped her as she tugged the sodden shirt and jacket off. The trousers were a bit more difficult. Chris hunched in the corner, looking faintly embarrassed.

There was the network of scars over his left collarbone where an alien flower had ripped free. Lower than that, a single circular ridge of hardened tissue, the only trace of the bullet that had broken one of his hearts. There was that odd little tattoo, and there, a white mark so small anyone else might have missed it, where Ace had stabbed him.

'Wish there was a towel,' said Benny, absently.

Roz had leant into the front of the van, turning the keys in the ignition and switching on the heater. Now she took a Feinberger out of her medikit and played it over the deep gashes on the Doctor's forehead.

'Give me a moment,' said Benny.

'There's a sleeping bag behind the tent. Back there,' Roz gestured. Chris worked it free and passed it to them. They pushed the Doctor into it. Benny unbuttoned her sleeves and tugged off her denim shirt.

Now Chris really was blushing. But when Benny stretched her legs out towards him, he pulled off her shoes.

Roz tugged the zip closed. 'Tight fit,' Benny said. She snuggled up to the Time Lord, shivering all over, trying to press as much of their skin together as possible. Hanging onto him for dear life.

Roz crouched awkwardly beside them, using another Feinberger to patch up the wounds on the Doctor's forehead. He was so cold they were barely bleeding.

Someone knocked on the passenger window. Roz reached over and rolled it down halfway. 'Now what?' Benny heard Isaac say.

'We can't do anything more for him,' said Roz. 'We'll keep him warm and quiet and let him do the rest.'

'Can he be moved?'

'Probably not a good idea,' said Roz. 'He's got a head injury.'

'We're right out in the open here,' said Isaac. 'Are you sure –'

'Give it a few hours,' said Roz.

'Right,' said Isaac. 'We'll make camp.'

'Tent,' Roz told Chris. He picked it up. Isaac opened the back door and Chris hopped out. Roz stopped to spread the blanket over the sleeping bag.

Jason was peering in, Keith held inside his oversized coat. His eyes widened at Benny lying half-naked in a sleeping bag with the Doctor.

'Hypothermia treatment,' she told him.

'Er,' he said. He and Isaac looked at each other. 'Will you be all right?'

'All right,' said Benny.

Roz gave her a nod and shut the door. Benny's ears rang in the sudden silence.

She cradled the Doctor's head in the crook of her arm. 'Guess it was my turn to do the sleeping-bag bit.' His hair was still wet, soaking her shoulder. 'Guess . . .'

Benny burst into tears. 'I can't think of anything clever to say,' she whispered. 'Please don't die.'

Chris spent half an hour and a whole box of matches trying to build a fire out of damp wood.

Ms Randrianasolo fussed over the Admiral, making him sit in the heated van while she and Roz struggled with the tent. They were taking turns to hold the single torch when Isaac switched on the headlights.

Isaac and Ms R ended up in an embarrassed tangle inside the small tent, staving off the hypothermia with a hug.

It was cold and clear, the stars burning down. Roz zipped the tent shut and went back to the fire, where Chris was stretched out, trying to make the most of the pale heat.

Roz surprised him by lying down in front of him. He hesitated, then put an arm around her. They relaxed into the shape of one another.

For a long while, they just watched the fire, tracing the path of the tiny red specks that drifted down to the ground.

'We're not in love, are we?' Chris murmured.

'No,' said Roz. 'You can keep nibbling on my neck if you want, though.'

Chris sighed, his breath warm across her ear. 'I love you.'

'Yeah,' said Roz.

She turned in his arms, and they kissed again. This time Roz relaxed, let the warmth flow into her mouth and down through her body.

'You love everybody,' she told him, when they came up for air. 'You fall in love on every planet we visit.'

'No,' pleaded Chris. 'Oh no. This isn't like that. It's . . . If we're not in love, then what are we exactly?'

233

Roz rested her head on his chest. 'I guess we're two good friends who fancy one another,' she said.

'Oh . . .' Chris gave a little gasp of surprise.

'Yes,' said Roz. She pushed a hand up under his pull-over, feeling him shiver at the touch of the cold air, her cold fingers. 'You're so handsome it's bloody ridiculous, all right?' Her hand was sandwiched between them, pressing against the strong muscles of his stomach. 'Doesn't mean I'm going to shag you, though.'

'Oh, no,' said Chris earnestly. 'Of course not. I mean, whatever you like.'

'Guess you're pretty surprised to hear me say you're cute,' she said.

'Not really, not that,' he said. 'But you almost never come out and say that we're friends.'

He hugged her, the way he might hug a sister, and rolled onto his back. She nestled in the crook of his arm.

'We'd never make it as a twosome anyway,' said Roz. 'Not while we're with the Doctor. Look at Benny. She's so worried her family's going to get hurt, it's like she's been paralysed ever since we got here, too scared to jump in any direction.'

'On the other hand,' said Chris, '*carpe diem* and all that. We might not get out of this alive.' He turned his head, glancing at the van.

Roz gave a small shrug. 'Every dawn you don't know if you'll see the dusk,' she said. 'You know something?'

'What?'

'I'm not worthy of *you*,' she said. She went on before he could object. 'You don't need a grizzled old grump like me. You need someone with a few more years left in them.'

'Hey, c'mon,' he said.

'You need someone as . . . as happy as you. As optimistic.'

He held her tighter.

'You're good for me, Chris,' she whispered. 'I need you. Don't you ever doubt that.'

The Doctor was dreaming that Death had come for Benny, and he had to protect her, make her wake up, but he couldn't move. He was pinned in place while those hollow eyes watched his companion, his own half-frozen body sucking the heat out of her, the tears dried on her cheeks.

Death leant in close. He could taste the empty flavour of her breath.

She became Roz Forrester.

She had pulled open the door of the van, just enough so that she could squat beside the vehicle and look at him. Chris was standing behind her, looking nervous.

Beside him, Benny was crammed into a narrow sleeping bag. She was breathing normally, fast asleep.

'I risk your lives,' he murmured. 'I keep you in the dark. I've even lied to you. And you stay with me.'

'I'll never leave you, Doctor,' said Chris. He sounded as though he was about to cry. Benny stirred in her sleep, murmuring.

'Doctor,' Roz said. 'Are you dying?'

'No one escapes time's arrow,' the Doctor said hoarsely. Chris looked at him in astonishment. 'Do you know, I had always assumed I could beat chance and choose the moment to die. I imagined I'd rise out of the ashes of regeneration and laugh, "I *meant* to do that." But that's not going to happen. I'm not going to be in control. Surrounded by strangers. Helpless.'

'Shit happens, Doctor,' said Roz. She took his hand. 'But we'll always be there to shovel you out. You're not gonna die alone.'

'Not today,' breathed the Doctor. 'This isn't the day.'

Chris grinned. Roz smiled warily. 'Can we move you? It's very exposed here, and we're freezing our buns off to boot.'

'Albinex won't bother us again,' said the Doctor. 'Tomorrow is his day.'

They didn't know how to take that. But he couldn't keep his eyes open. Not even when Roz turned to Chris, and they put their mouths together.

The second time the Doctor woke up he was wearing warm pyjamas. There was a cat asleep on top of his feet.

He looked up from the bed. He was in his room back in Little Caldwell. It was still night. He wondered if his watch had survived the long dive into the lake.

Isaac was sitting in the chair next to the window. The small blond man turned to look at him as he stirred. Nelson meowed a complaint and hopped off the bed.

'What are your intentions towards my daughter?' said the Admiral, with one of his tiny smiles.

'How did you find me?'

'Your ghost-detector,' said Isaac. 'It was Benny's idea. Are you well? What did Albinex do to you?'

'He used that poor creature – the "ghost" – to try to get the codes from me. She would have died if he'd continued.'

'He used her? How?'

'Oh, he tried whatever he could think of. He's not much of a torturer. But you don't have to be competent to do the work . . .'

'So what did you do?'

The Doctor looked at Isaac and said, 'I gave him the codes.'

'You did what?'

'They're a decade out of date,' said the Doctor. 'He'll invade USAF Greenham Common in his ridiculous electric flying shoe, find that the codes don't work, and give up in disgust.'

'Ah,' said Isaac. 'But you see, M'Kabel will be able to extrapolate the new codes from the old.' The Doctor nodded, as though to himself. 'He's been studying the nuclear weapons computers since the seventies. Human technology is child's play to him, amusing puzzles.'

'The thing I can't understand,' said the Doctor slowly, 'is what Albinex really hopes to accomplish. His claim about returning to Navarino as the glorious conqueror just doesn't ring true.'

'Perhaps,' said Isaac, 'he believes he's working for the greater good.'

'The greater good,' smiled the Doctor. 'I used to work for the greater good, you know. But the hours were bad and the conditions were worse.'

'It takes courage to do something terrible because it's the right thing to do,' said Isaac. 'To save more lives than are lost. To see the big picture of history.'

'It takes even more courage to realize that you've made a mistake,' said the Doctor, 'and to give up a plan you've been working on for twenty years. I don't think Albinex has that courage. The question, Admiral Summerfield, is: do you?'

Isaac stood up and walked over to the bed.

'How long have you known?' he said.

'My,' said the Doctor. 'That was a good guess, wasn't it? What now?'

'Will you listen to my plan?' said Isaac. 'Give it a fair hearing?'

'No,' said the Doctor. 'I'll do whatever I can to stop you. And if you want to stop me, you'll have to kill me.'

Isaac looked at him.

'Although at this very moment,' said the Doctor, 'it may not be the best idea.'

Slowly, the Admiral turned to the doorway.

'She's been there since we began to talk,' said the Doctor gently. 'I don't think she wanted to interrupt us.'

Benny didn't even look surprised. She was leaning on the doorframe, one hand pressed to her forehead. When Isaac tried to meet her eyes, she turned around and walked away.

The Admiral glanced back at the Doctor. 'I ordered Albinex not to hurt you,' he said.

'Don't mind me,' said the Time Lord. 'I think you'd better go and talk to your daughter.'

Dad's Army

It was time. The phone calls had been made. The signals had gone out.

In Porthmadog, two stranded Chameleon scouts took the car and the likenesses of a young married couple, moving eastwards.

In London, a lonely Sirian boarded a train going west, moving invisibly through the late-evening crowds.

In La Baule, a Sea Devil pod waded ashore, following a flashing light held by a shaking human.

A group of former soldiers rendezvoused at a flat in Rickmansworth. All of them had been discharged from UNIT on psychiatric grounds. They left their guns behind and climbed into a car.

In Reykjavik, a sleek Procyonian robot moulded itself a human-looking exterior and boarded a jet.

In Liverpool, a Vardan downloaded himself from the phone system and walked through the darkening streets, looking for a taxi.

Deep in the Australian outback, a Caxtarid put down the only telephone in town, stepped outside the pub, and activated her teleport module.

They were specks on a map, wheeling inwards. From the safehouses in Berkshire and Wiltshire and Hampshire, from a motel in Maryland and a hotel in Holland Park, they came. An army of the aliens and the alienated. Heading for Little Caldwell.

Meanwhile, in space

A lone satellite, slick and black and invisible to eye and radar alike, continued its circular slide around the Earth.

Waiting for the signal.

29

The quick and the dad

Benny stood on the covered verandah, looking down into the street. The sun was coming up, a pale light filtering through the mist.

The cars had been arriving for half an hour. The engines had woken her up, sending her wandering through the house, wondering what the fuss was about and whether the Doctor was all right. And to the doorway of the spare room. And the inevitable, the unavoidable revelation.

The door bells jingled behind her. She didn't turn around, watching a Volvo parking outside the post office. She couldn't make out the driver. They were all staying in their vehicles, patient shadows.

'You expected this.'

'Of course I expected it.' She didn't look at him. 'I was awful to Jason before our wedding, waiting for him to shag someone else behind my back. It's some sort of deep Freudian thing. I expect the men I love to betray me.'

'Ever since Simon Kyle.'

'Ever since my father promised to come back and didn't.'

'The Doctor won't listen to me,' said Isaac, after a beat. 'Will you?'

'I can't stop you from talking,' she said.

'Albinex was acting under my orders,' he began. 'He far overstepped the boundaries of those orders. I sent M'Kabel to ensure that Albinex didn't harm the Doctor, but he failed.' Silence for a bit. 'We've been planning this for nearly two decades.'

'That's why we got here in nineteen eighty-three,' sighed Benny. 'Not nineteen *sixty*-three, when you first arrived.' Isaac said nothing. 'Don't stop now,' his daughter said. 'Go on. Tell me your plans. Gloat.'

Isaac said softly, 'When we learnt the nuclear missiles were finally going to arrive at Greenham Common, I switched on the transponder I kept from the *Tisiphone*.'

'And we followed its signal here. Into your trap.'

'We'd been trying to obtain the destructor codes for years. We knew that the Doctor had found them out. But we couldn't risk giving Little Caldwell away to UNIT or the Doctor.'

'My God,' said Benny. 'You knew about me. You knew I was his companion.'

Silence for a bit. 'Yes,' Isaac admitted.

'Ace told you.'

'No,' said her father. 'I knew long before that. Albinex has certain information . . .'

'You knew that I'd come looking for you, bringing the Doctor with me. You used me. My God, was Groenewegen part of your plan as well?'

'No!'

'Albinex's yacht was there when you fell into the wormhole,' she said. 'Was that part of the plan?'

'No,' said Isaac. 'Albinex told us that his ship had got caught up in the battle. He was trying to escape when his time drive malfunctioned, creating the wormhole.'

'Why Earth? Why nineteen sixty-three?'

'That had been the yacht's last warp coordinates. The Navarinos love Earth nostalgia. They were on a tour of the sixties.'

'Well. Now that you've tortured the codes out of the Doctor,' she said bitterly, 'what are you going to do?'

Another car wandered out of the mist, pulled up outside one of the cottages. Isaac said, 'In just under two hundred years, the Daleks are going to attack Earth. And we'll be waiting for them.'

'So that's why you want control of the nukes!' said Benny, turning around. 'You want to be able to fight off the Daleks!'

'No,' said Isaac. 'We're going to start a small nuclear war on Earth. Just a handful of exchanges, carefully controlled.'

Benny's mouth opened. No words came out.

'We have to keep the pace of weapons development going,' said Isaac. 'The Cold War is going to end this decade. Within two decades, there'll be massive disarmament, a move away from the military-industrial complex. There'll be peace on Earth. Then the Daleks will come, and find the planet practically defenceless.'

Benny found her voice. 'How many people are you going to kill?'

'No more than absolutely necessary,' said Isaac, and his voice was colder than the winter air.

Benny's mouth just hung open. Her father went on, 'For two decades, we've been collecting together a small army of aliens. Once our work here is done, we'll travel forward to twenty-one fifty-four and help with the battle against the invasion.

'Think about it, Benny.' He looked down at the cars. 'These people came here to pillage or conquer. Now they've made this planet their home. They're going to save the human race.' He turned to her, took her face in his hands, his gaze willing her to understand. 'What more can I do to protect Earth from the Daleks?'

Benny gasped, 'I've got another story to tell you.'

Claire

The sirens were screaming.

Bernice was seven. She was too small to understand what was happening. Only that her mummy was very scared. Only that the sirens were screaming and they made her ears hurt.

Her mummy had picked her up because she couldn't run fast enough. She was banging against her mummy's shoulder as she ran. Her mummy was crying. There was a crowd – everyone was shouting and crying.

Bernice hung onto her doll's hand. Rebecca sort of flapped out behind her mummy as she ran. Bernice couldn't see where they were going because she was facing the wrong way. All she could see was Rebecca.

She screamed when she dropped the doll. She couldn't hang on because of the running and because the sirens were screaming.

Her mother ran through a door into a big room. The room was full of grown-ups and children, all of them shouting and crying. Bernice put her hands over her ears when her mother put her down.

Her mother ran back out through the door, and it shut.

Bernice took her hands off her ears and threw herself at the door, screaming, 'Mummy!' She couldn't see how to open the door.

There was a big window in the door. She was just tall enough to see through it.

There were only a few people outside now. She could

see her mummy, running back to where Rebecca had fallen down.

There was a flash so bright that it made her eyes ring. The walls and the door rattled. She saw her mummy's bones for a moment, like in an X-ray. And then there was nothing.

One part of her started to shriek hysterically, while grown-ups she didn't know picked her up and tore her away from the window in the door, dragging her deeper into the shelter.

Another part of her understood, in a scary, cold way, that her mummy was gone now, blown up by the Daleks. But it was okay, it was going to be okay, because her daddy would come home and look after her.

30

Father makes good

Isaac went back into the shop and went behind the counter to make some coffee. He dropped the cup on the floor and knocked over the cafetière. He sat down on the floor, holding a silver spoon in one hand.

Benny did not follow him inside. He sat with his back to the sink cupboard. Shell-shocked, he thought. I'm shell-shocked, but I have to pull myself together. I have to keep functioning. I can't stop now, not for any reason.

Isaac was backing away. Why was he backing away, almost scrambling across the floor? He looked up. The Doctor stood over him, barefoot, still wearing the pyjamas.

The Time Lord absently righted the fallen cafetière. 'How much longer are you going to sit down there? We've been waiting for half an hour.'

'Half an hour?'

'Benny decided it might be best if we left you to have a think,' said the Doctor. He was holding something. Isaac saw that it was the transponder from the *Tisiphone*. 'I gather this is how you brought me here. Clever.'

He dropped the transponder, and Isaac caught it, instinctively.

'Your army is growing,' remarked the Doctor. 'There must be a few dozen vehicles out there now.'

Isaac turned the transponder around in his hands. He lifted the hatch that hid its power switch. 'Just a little button,' he murmured. His voice sounded hoarse, like that of someone who'd been crying. 'I push this little button, and it all starts. The whole chain of events. One thing after another . . . until all those lives end.'

'Surprising, isn't it?' said the Doctor. 'How important a tiny event can be. Or how unimportant. That's the thing about changing history. You have to be able to tell the butterfly that causes the storm from the butterfly that's merely pretty. But the hurricane isn't inevitable. There's still time to change the road you're on.'

'I don't believe you,' said Isaac. 'I've considered all the possibilities. I've had twenty years to think about this.'

'Twenty years to try to talk yourself into it.'

'I've got the strategy all worked out,' said Isaac. 'I've had it ready for some time. The codes give me control over every missile on Earth. I can send them precisely where they need to go . . . there'd be less deaths than the Daleks will cause in twenty-one fifty-four . . . so many deaths . . . I know just where the missiles will fall, who will retaliate and who won't.'

'Not so easy, is it? To erase her. To erase the future that gives birth to her. Now that you've met her.'

'No,' said Isaac, 'I want Bernice to be born into a future without the Daleks, without the constant fear of the Daleks . . .'

'You simply can't predict the future that accurately,' said the Doctor. 'What if one of the missiles fails to launch or explode? What if, instead of embracing nuclear development, humanity is so disgusted by the carnage that it abandons the weapons forever? The future is a kaleidoscope. To human eyes . . . besides, it's clear Albinex is following an agenda of his own.'

'Is he?'

'His time ship's engine doesn't work,' said the Doctor. 'It shattered the day he came to Earth. There's no way he could take your army forward to fight the Daleks.'

Isaac let the spoon fall from his hand. It clattered away across the kitchen floor.

'You do this sort of thing all the time,' he said. 'This isn't any different to what you do.'

246

'True.' The Time Lord looked down at him. 'But then, I'm the Doctor.'

'Albinex wanted to kill you,' Zak said.

'Albinex has gone nuts,' said Ms Randrianasolo. She leant on the counter. 'He wants to kill all of us.'

The Admiral looked pale, shaken. It was the shock of someone suddenly bereaved. Ms Randrianasolo frowned and put a hand to his forehead. It was cold and bright with sweat.

'You don't understand,' said Zak. He shook his head slowly. 'In all these years, you've looked into so many minds, hundreds of alien minds. You've never read my mind.'

'Of course not,' she said. 'Though . . . there have been times when I wanted to.'

His eyes met hers. She was taken aback by the terrible sadness she saw there. 'What's happened?' she pleaded.

'There's something you have to know,' he said simply.

He bowed his head. She sensed him dropping his mental defences. Gently, she reached in, just to the surface of his thoughts.

And stepped back. And slapped his face.

He didn't say anything as she ran up the stairs.

The door jingled. M'Kabel came in, holding his clipboard. He'd abandoned the hologram for the time being.

'They're waiting for you, sir,' said the Tzun.

The Doctor tried to smooth his shirt, but after a couple of hours in the drier it was even more rumpled than before. He sighed and pulled on his shoes.

He heard footsteps on the stairs outside. Benny came in. She sat down on the end of the bed and wept.

The Doctor went on lacing his shoe.

After a few minutes, she moved along the bed and let him hold her while she cried, great, wracking sobs that made her whole body shake.

He wondered if she'd cried like this in the TARDIS, on some occasion when his plans and lies had left her exhausted and betrayed. With no one to hang onto.

'What are we going to do?' she said, when she had enough breath.

'We'll see,' he said. 'What became of Woodworth?'

'The Ogri got her,' said Benny. The Doctor nodded. 'What are we going to *do*?'

He gave her a gentle squeeze. 'That depends on Isaac.'

Admiral Summerfield stood on the Pyramid's verandah, leaning on the wooden rail. The aliens filled the main street of Little Caldwell. Some were disguised, some weren't. Some wore human clothes, some wore uniforms, a few were naked. They were green and blue and pinkish-white and red and brown. Scales glittered in the dawn. A mix of strange scents rose, flesh and incense and chemical.

He had spent ten minutes walking through the crowd, shaking hands and tentacles. He knew almost all of them. He had saved the lives of more than half of them. He had explained his plan, given them hiding places. He had bathed their wounds and worked out their diets and sent messages home for them.

They greeted him with smiles and smile-equivalents, with handshakes and telepathic brushes, with friendly nods and trusting eyes.

Now they were silent, waiting for him to give the order.

M'Kabel stepped up beside him. The Tzun had arrived that morning, his strange face seeming strained. But Isaac knew he could rely on the little alien, no matter what. God! At least some things hadn't changed.

M'Kabel murmured, 'Everyone's here, except for a mated pair of Cygnians we can't contact. And no one's seen the Ogrons.'

'See if they're in their cottage,' said Isaac. 'They've probably slept in.'

M'Kabel looked up at him. 'What are you going to do, sir?'

'I don't know,' said Isaac. He felt the pressure of those alien eyes on him. All of them.

'Are you going to kill the Doctor?'

Isaac glanced at him in horror.

248

'If you're going to go ahead with our original plan, sir,' said the Tzun, 'you'd better kill him right away.'

M'Kabel tucked his clipboard under his arm and went to wake up the Ogrons.

Isaac turned to his army. His hands shook badly as he gripped the wooden rail. He bowed his head and took a deep, deep breath.

'There's been a little bit of a change of plan,' he said.

Joel didn't cry when Ms R told him what she'd learnt. It was just that his eyes were watering a bit. That was all.

She sat down on the floor, right on top of some of his junk, drawing her knees up to her chest. Like she wanted to just block it all out.

Joel got out of bed and went to the window. *The Admiral pushing the button, the missiles going up*. He gaped at the crowd. 'Christ,' he said. 'We're up to our ass in aliens.'

'That's what Tony was doing,' said Ms R dully. 'He had to find out whether Woodworth knew about this, or whether she was just attracted by all the aliens hidden around Little Caldwell.'

He glanced back at her. She was staring at the wall. *The Admiral pushing the button*. It's not every day you find out your friend of twenty years has been a bad guy all along. *The missiles going up*.

God! Did Benny know? She must know by now. Sorry, big sister. I guess we both lost our dad today.

Joel had only ever seen about ten different species of aliens. Now he was looking at dozens, all shapes and sizes. If only this was another adventure. He'd loved being part of this magical world, where wild things happened. Now it was dead. Now it was gone. Nuked.

Joel shook his head slightly. He still wasn't crying, though there was an iceberg in his chest. Well, he'd only been here for eight months. It didn't mean all that much.

His good hand found the window catch, and he pushed it open.

'You said,' called one of the aliens, 'we were going to fight the Daleks.'

'We might still get our chance.' Isaac's voice rang out. A leader's voice – everyone was listening. 'But we have to deal with the immediate problem. I had carefully worked out the nuclear part of the strategy. But I have no idea what Albinex plans. Whatever it is, it doesn't involve any of you.'

'So where izzy?' purred a Ra'ashet, turning its catfish face to look at him. 'Let's go rip him to pieces.'

'He's got the destructor codes,' said the Admiral. 'And our intelligence about USAF Greenham Common. He's going to launch one or more of the cruise missiles.'

'He wants power,' said a dark-coated ex-MIB. 'Five'll get you eight he points the thing at a major city and starts making demands.'

'Yeah,' said the Ra'ashet. 'So let's get over there and wait for him to show.'

'No,' said Isaac. The aliens waited for him to speak. 'We can't risk randomly changing history by revealing you. Anything could happen.'

'We've been waiting for years,' said another alien, tall, thin and lavender, a species Joel didn't recognize. 'You've been keeping us hidden and safe for all this time. You can't leave us out of it now.'

A murmur of agreement went through the crowd.

'There's something else,' said Isaac.

They fell silent again.

'Even if we defeat Albinex, we still can't go ahead with the original plan.' More murmurs. Joel rested his head on the cold glass, wondering what would happen next. Not that he cared any more.

'You said you had it worked out in every detail,' said a talking cat. 'We've been *waiting*.'

'Admiral,' purred the Ra'ashet, 'we trust you, yessss? But if you've lost your botttttttle, let us take over. We'll peel and eat Albinex and we'll get on with the plan.'

'You don't understand,' said Isaac. 'The plan itself is wrong. I've ... had some expert advice. The changes to history I thought would happen might not happen at all. We might end up destroying the planet instead of saving it. I was wrong. And I've involved you all in my wrong, wrong plan.'

250

Joel's heart pounded. He wasn't going to do it. The Admiral wasn't going to do it after all.

That was when he started to cry.

A ripple of sudden realization and fear moved through the crowd. Oh God, would they attack him? Tear him apart and carry out his plan?

Before anything could happen, another voice rang out across the packed street.

'I'd like a word,' said the Doctor. 'If you don't mind.'

31

We got the bombs

Some of the aliens gasped. Some grabbed for the weapons they'd left behind. At least two started to twitch uncontrollably. And one six-foot, fur-covered humanoid ran away waving its three arms and yelling, and drove off in its Mini.

The Doctor looked down into their faces, coolly. Teeth were bared. Tentacles were writhing. Eyes were flashing with fear and rage. At one time or another, almost every one of these people had been his mortal enemy.

'The first thing,' he told them, 'is not to panic.'

Isaac put a hand on his shoulder. The gesture seemed to calm some of the aliens. But the Ra'ashet was salivating, long feelers twitching at the edges of his mouth.

'Right now,' said the Doctor, 'I'm as trapped on this planet as you are. If Albinex starts throwing nuclear missiles about, there's a good chance that we're all going to die. All of us. Everyone on Earth.'

'Why should we believe you?' said a Kapteynian, a butterfly the size of two hands. Her voice was an angry song. 'You killed six of my scouting party!'

'I did no such thing,' said the Doctor sharply.

He raised a hand before the insect could disagree. 'There's no time to discuss it now. Why don't we deal with the nuclear problem first, and then you lot can argue about who gets to kill me, hmm?'

The aliens murmured. There was a lot of old pain there, years old, and fear, and loathing. He was the one who had stranded them here. Not their own commanders or their conquest plans or their own greed or foolishness. Him.

'Listen,' he said, more gently. 'I've been protecting this planet for years. But I've been doing half a job, leaving so many loose threads . . . and Isaac has been tidying up after me. Taking care of all of you, and so many others. Now I've got a chance to make up for that. Let me work with you to save all of our lives.'

Isaac turned to M'Kabel, who had hopped up onto the verandah, still clutching his clipboard. The Tzun murmured something to the Admiral.

'You're the ones who agreed to fight for this planet.' The Doctor looked around at them. 'This is home now.'

'Yeah, yeah,' said the Ra'ashet. 'Some of us just want a crack at the Daleks.'

'You might get it after all,' said Isaac. He held up a long strip of dark film. 'The Ogrons are gone. And these are –'

'Dalek instructions,' breathed the Doctor. He grabbed the filmstrip and ran his eyes over the harsh green characters. 'I should have known.'

'The Ogrons just left it on the bed,' said M'Kabel. 'Not too bright.'

'Albinex is working for them,' said the Doctor. 'It all makes sense. The ultimate military power. He must worship them.'

'His ship wasn't caught up in the battle,' said Isaac. 'He must have been negotiating with them. Even then. Dear God.' The Admiral gripped the railing. 'He's going to do it. He's going to start World War Three.'

'Well, what did you expect him to do?' said the Doctor irritably.

More than half of the aliens refused to have anything to do with the Doctor, even against the Daleks. Of the ones who were left, most were going to have to sit out the action anyway.

It was extraordinary, thought the Time Lord. Some of these people considered humans to be inherently inferior. Many had been involved in attempts to destroy or control the

253

human race. And yet here they were, taking orders from a short, unassuming human in a moth-eaten jumper.

The Doctor's team comprised Isaac, M'Kabel and Benny. And possibly Jason. Or not. The couple were arguing furiously in a corner of the coffee shop.

'We don't have time to discuss this,' Benny whispered. 'Albinex could arrive any moment.'

'Joel,' said Jason. 'He could look after him.' Keith was hanging around their ankles, coming out with the occasional 'Va!' in between chewing on a soft toy. 'It's not just you any more. I don't want you facing the danger alone, okay?'

She took his face between her hands. 'And if we both get blown away? Someone has to stay behind.'

'I keep getting left out!'

'That's as it should be.'

'Haven't you done enough in your life?' He caught her hand, pressed it to his cheek. 'This one's on me.'

'No,' she insisted. 'This is my job. You don't ever stop being a companion, Jason.'

She pulled him closer and kissed him. The Doctor frowned, turning away.

'Now stay put,' Benny murmured silkily. 'Or I'll wallop you with yon frying pan.'

The Kapteynian flew right at the Doctor's face. He threw up his hands to protect his eyes.

She settled onto one of his wrists. 'Listen!' she said. 'Listen . . .'

'What can I do for you?' he said cautiously, lowering his hands. She looked like a small, perfectly formed human child, with great, glittering butterfly wings.

'I want to go home,' she said. 'I sunburn so easily under this sun. We tried sunblock, but it gives me lesions.'

'Done,' said the Doctor.

The Kapteynian lifted from his hand, her wings beating languidly. She turned back and cleared her throat. He looked up at her. 'Thanks,' she said stiffly, and drifted away.

The van rolled up to Greenham Common. Joel threw open

the door and jumped down. 'The anoraks have landed!' he announced. 'We're here to save the world!'

Jason looked around at the Doctor's team. 'Oh, great,' he muttered.

'I'll find Bridget,' said Isaac. He hefted his backpack and headed into the growing crowd at a run.

'How many women did you say would be here?' Benny asked the Doctor, as they piled out of the van.

'About thirty thousand.'

There were women planting trees, women attaching banners and pictures to the wire. They were singing folk songs, voices and guitars drifting along the curve of the fence. Later they'd be shaking the concrete pillars loose and snipping through the chicken wire with bolt-cutters.

No wonder Albinex had chosen today to make his move. But if the Navarino could use them as cover, the cynical bastard, so could the Doctor's team.

Isaac came racing back, holding Bridget's hand. The young woman looked bewildered. 'She's going to get us in,' said the Admiral. 'I've explained about our crazy pacifist friend who's going to try to get himself shot.'

'Right,' said the Doctor. 'Thank you, Ms Evans!'

'We'll have to nip around the fence,' said the peace woman. 'Come on!'

Roz took Chris, Ms Randrianasolo, two aliens and the ghost-detector with her. The Doctor reckoned that the ghost would still be with Albinex; the Navarino might be able to mask the drive of his ship from their scanners, but he couldn't hide her.

The Kapteynian had donated a small computer screen, grumbling, and the Doctor had attached it to the ghost-detector. Roz held the hybrid thing in her lap.

They'd let Chris drive. He was haring it down the A339. The Ra'ashet was taking up two seats in the back. He didn't need a hologram projector; he'd done something telepathic, and suddenly he looked a whole lot like a little girl. It made Roz's stomach clench – if she squinted, she could just make out the scales and the scent of fish – but it was a bloody brilliant disguise.

The thing in the boot was too bizarre for words.

Ms R was sitting stock-still beside the alien, her eyes closed, her brow furrowed. 'Got him!' she and Roz said at the same moment.

Roz tapped a fingernail on the screen of her handscan. 'He's just come into range. At that speed, he'll be over the USAF base in minutes.'

'He's very proud of himself,' said Ms R. 'Very confident. He's . . . leaving guards on the ship.'

'Those will be the Ogrons,' said Roz.

'No problem,' said Chris. 'We'll be there in a minute ourselves.'

Alekto

It was surprisingly quiet inside the base. Bridget led them across a wide, empty field of grass. They could still hear the chanting and singing, distantly, and the growling sound of engines.

The Doctor was holding the divining rod, firmly, watching its every twitch. 'We have to keep heading for the silo,' he muttered. 'Albinex must be close by, but if we can beat him there –!' He stopped stock-still. Benny almost walked into him.

He yelped and dropped the stick. It burst into flames as it fell.

The ghost unfolded.

A vast wind blew across the grass, hammering them back. She was a great cloud of light, pale as an orange rose, her face and blank eyes hovering above them.

Tony fell to his knees. Bridget didn't scream, shielding her astonished eyes with one hand.

The Doctor forced his way through the raging wind, holding his hands out for her. Benny wanted to grab him, pull him away from the monster, but she couldn't wade through the wind fast enough.

The ghost grabbed his wrists, and they both cried out with the shock. 'Stay with me!' he shouted into the storm. 'Stay here! I can anchor you!'

But the nameless ghost was wailing. *HE TOLD ME TO STOP YOU!*

Tony stuck his hands over his ears. 'She's here!' he wailed.

'You know he's using you!' cried the Doctor. 'Stop fighting! Just relax! We can still –'

But she let him go, writhing in the air, her desperate eyes seeking.

Benny saw her coming like a tunnel of light, and there was nowhere to run.

Bridget Evans had seen women lie down in front of army trucks. She'd seen them hang onto the fence even when police truncheons were snapping hands and fingers. She'd seen women come back to the same patch of frozen land over and over after being evicted, carrying their bundles and bags.

It would take a lot to surprise her.

The floating special-effect thing shot down from the sky and surrounded Benny. The woman staggered back and yelled, pushing at the orange light. Bridget stood frozen, not knowing what to do.

'No!' roared the Doctor.

He ran to his friend. The light was like flame now, burning his hands as he tried to reach her. 'This won't work!' he yelled. 'She can't anchor you!'

I'M COMING APART AT THE SEAMS! the thing screamed. Bridget pushed her hands against her ears. Maybe its voice had once been human.

'Back off, Doctor!' shouted Benny. 'Get away!' Orange light was coming out of her mouth. 'I WANT HER HERE!'

The Doctor stepped into the fire and threw his arms around Benny.

They both screamed. She snatched at his jacket, trying to shove him away. Somehow he stayed on his feet, hanging onto her, hands locked together behind her back. '*Let her go!*' he shouted.

Benny's dad was shouting something which Bridget couldn't hear over the fire and the wind. She saw the Doctor's knees give way, his head falling back, haloed in fire.

With a *SNAP* like an elastic band in the eye, it all stopped.

32

Out to launch

Jason was hanging onto Keith so tightly that the boy was squirming. He sat in the open door of the van, scowling at the ground.

It was all very well for Benny to leave him to take care of Keith. If she didn't come back, if they failed, the boy was dead anyway.

Joel patted him on the arm in a brotherly way. 'Va va VA,' said Keith.

'Wish we could have gone,' said Joel. 'Wish we could have gone.' His voice was taut as a wire with fear. 'This sucks.'

'Benny would say I just have a lot of twentieth-century hang-ups about my masculine role,' Jason muttered. He looked up at the crowd of women. They were rugged up, talking and singing. The only men he could see were the police behind the fence.

'Takes balls to stay put,' said Joel. 'Remember, we're backup. In case anything goes wrong.'

'Yeah,' said Jason. 'Well, it gets my back up.'

Keith struggled out of Jason's grip and slid down to the ground. 'Hey you, come here,' said Jason, making a grab for the boy.

But Keith was running away across the cold ground, his little shoes sloshing in the mud. 'Va va!' he said.

Jason jumped down from the van and was after him in an instant. But the boy was – was fading, was becoming a pale figure running towards the women, then just a shadow. Reaching his arms out to someone only he could see.

'Da da!' Keith said.

And was gone.

Jason slowed and stopped, standing in the spot where his son had disappeared.

He turned back, helpless. Joel stood in the doorway of the van, watching him.

'See you later, kid,' said Jason, and marched back to the van. 'What was that you said about backup?'

Benny and the Doctor tumbled to the ground. The grass around them was scorched, the air shimmering with heat.

Isaac grabbed his daughter, lifted her head into his lap. Tony and Bridget knelt down beside the Doctor.

Bridget thought they would both be dead. But Benny was coming around. Her clothes were singed and scorched, but her flesh wasn't, as though the flames had come out of her. Isaac stroked her hair.

'I let her go,' gasped Benny. 'I let her go, Doctor. Oh God, are you all right?'

The Doctor sprang to his feet, looking around wildly. The bearded man, Tony, almost fell over with shock.

Bridget began, 'You all right, mate?' But he waved his hand at her, looking down at Benny. 'Did you see it?'

Benny sat up. 'He's already in the silo.'

'How do you know?' said Isaac.

Tony said, 'I thought she was Death. I thought she'd got a head start.' He shook his head. 'It's true what the Book of Names says. Death doesn't have a name.'

'Her name was Caroline Grey,' said the Doctor.

'She's not Death,' said Benny. 'She's dead.'

'She spread herself so thin that there was finally nothing left.' His voice rang out, louder than the ringing in their ears. 'She was a first-year archaeology student. She found an ancient Youkalian time-travel device which discharged the remnants of its power through her.'

The Doctor spun round, as though lecturing some unseen crowd. 'She grew up on Mars,' he shouted, 'where her family bred orchids, but she couldn't remember any of their names, and she was very good at origami, and she couldn't remember her own name, and her favourite flavour of ice cream was butterscotch!'

The others were staring at him. He put his hands over his face and ran them suddenly, sharply back through his hair. 'Come on,' he said. 'There's no time to spare.'

The sky yacht was parked above the forest, disguised as a low cloud. After tugging on their armour, Roz and Chris ran their handscans over the area, raising them up to the base of the ship, above the tips of the trees. You could just make out the metal if you squinted the right way.

'No obvious traps,' said Roz. 'In any case, I can't imagine anything that'll bother, er . . .'

Ms R opened the boot. The fifth member of the party came shimmering around the car.

It was a smear of red, hovering in the air, like an error made by a careless landscape artist. You could see through it, barely, the outlines of the trees diluted by its rich colour.

Roz didn't know what it was, and she didn't want to know. She just stood the hell out of its way as it blurred suddenly, leaping into the air.

Its tip slapped against the airlock of the yacht and stuck fast. It pulsed for a moment, and became more solid, wiggling itself invitingly.

Roz gritted her teeth and took hold of its sinuous body. She expected her hand to go right through it, to discover that it had no substance at all, that it was just a wisp of colour in the afternoon sun. Instead her fingers met a textured, ropy surface that gripped her as hard as she gripped it.

She resisted the urge to pull her hand away, and started to climb up the living rope. Chris followed after a moment, and then Ms R. The Ra'ashet waited, picking its teeth. Roz glanced down at it. Yeah, the red thing probably couldn't have borne its weight as well as all of theirs, she guessed.

At the top, the red thing extruded some of its rough surface to loop around her hips as she picked the lock. The Doctor

261

had pinched all of Albinex's security codes while he'd been aboard.

They had to wait while the airlock cycled, clinging awkwardly to the red thing. Roz hoped the fuzzy colour was as strong as it seemed.

'Look out!' shouted Ms R.

A hairy, warm hand reached down and grabbed her wrist and pulled her into the airlock.

'Chris!' Roz yelled. Oh great, give him even more ideas, she thought, as the Ogron tried to break her neck.

They'd slipped past patrols, avoided a jeep, and now they were standing at the base of one of the squat, cylindrical buildings. There were two dead guards at the entrance to the silo.

Bridget covered her mouth with her hand. Isaac and the Doctor knelt by the bodies. 'They were stabbed to death,' said the Time Lord shortly. 'With a long blade, by the look of it.'

Isaac shook his head. 'A sword?'

'Maybe he doesn't fancy using projectile weapons around a nuclear warhead,' said the Doctor. 'Bridget, thanks – get yourself away from here as quickly as you can.'

The young woman opened her mouth to say something, then closed it again. She nodded, and briskly walked off across the grass.

The door was open. The Doctor caught Isaac's arm as the Admiral was about to go inside. 'This is it,' he said. 'This is really the moment where you decide what you want.'

'I've made this possible,' said Isaac firmly. 'I have to stop it if it kills me.'

Benny looked at him in horror, but they were inside the building before she could say anything.

Chris vaulted into the airlock and kicked the Ogron's knee with all his strength. It roared and dropped Roz, reaching for the boy. He stuck his armoured elbow in its throat.

Ms R said something very rude in Malagasy, scrambling out of the way as the Ogron and Chris started walloping each other. Roz tried to snatch the ape-faced monster's weapon, but neither of them could get past Chris to pull the blaster from its holster.

The next thing she knew, the Ra'ashet's fish-reptile head was poking over the rim of the airlock. The alien hauled itself up, tossed Chris easily to one side, and took a big bite out of the Ogron's head.

The rest of the Ogron went very suddenly slack as the Ra'ashet chewed thoughtfully on its skull.

The telepath managed not to actually throw up. 'How many more?' said Roz.

Chris, who was getting his breath back after slamming into the wall, tugged out his handscan. 'Three,' he said. 'One's behind the inner airlock door.'

'And very pleased with his clever strategy,' added Ms R. She was breathing deeply, keeping her eyes shut, trying not to listen to the munching sounds. 'He can't see in here.'

'One in engineering,' said Chris.

'Asleep on the job,' said Ms R.

'And one up in the control room, I guess.'

Roz said, 'Er, could you pass me the Ogron's blaster, please?'

The Ra'ashet obligingly opened the holster and plucked out the weapon with a slick, scaled hand. He passed it back to her without stopping his meal.

'Thanks,' said Roz, trying to hold the gun without actually touching it.

'No problem,' said the Ra'ashet.

Good to have a weapon again. Nice chunky gun. Pity about the slobber and blood. Roz took up a firing stance, the blaster pointing at the inner door. Chris stood by the controls, ready to open it.

'Needs salt,' commented the Ra'ashet.

The missile protruded from the ground, just the tip – avionics and payload – visible, ringed by a metal railing. There were more uniformed corpses scattered on the floor. Sword wounds, and worse, chunks of flesh gouged from faces and hands.

Albinex was in his own body, wearing an archaic Navarino uniform, fierce white and green cloth stretched over his stumpy frame. There were twin ceremonial swords strapped to his back. He had dragged a desk across to the railing, and was working hard on a computer from his ship.

He glanced at them, once, double-took when he saw the Doctor, and went back to programming the weapon.

'I say,' called the Time Lord, moving towards the missile. Cables trailed from it where Albinex had slaved its onboard computers to the console. 'I've come all the way back from the dead to thwart your evil scheme. You could at least say hello!'

The Navarino didn't look up.

'Look out!' shouted M'Kabel.

Two Ogrons came at them at a run, blood and shreds of flesh trailing from their mouths.

'Check this out,' Chris said. He stepped to one side so that Roz could get to the yacht's console. 'Look at that telemetry.'

'He's tracking a satellite,' said Roz. She ran a fingernail under a blip moving across the screen. 'It looks like geo-stationary orbit. Wish I could read Navarino.'

'I'll tell you one thing,' said Chris. 'I'll bet it's not a TV satellite.'

'Daleks,' said Roz.

'Yeah.'

'We need to get our asses out of here,' said Roz.

The Ra'ashet was already standing in the corridor outside, an Ogron arm hanging from its scaly mouth. It rolled its fish-eyes at them. Ms Randrianasolo ran up behind it, holding the blaster. 'I fused the door to engineering,' she said. 'The, er, arm . . . the third Ogron's stuck in there.'

'We're done,' said Roz. 'We're outta here.'

The Doctor tripped up one of the Ogrons with his umbrella, ducking the monster's killing blow with surprising agility. M'Kabel snatched out his wand.

Isaac ran for Albinex, zig-zagging to avoid an oncoming Ogron, his eyes locked on the Navarino.

Benny flung herself after her father.

She could see Albinex tugging out his gun, a stubby Navarino gun, one purple limb working on the console. She could see Albinex pausing, aiming the gun at her father. She could see that he was too far away for her to grab the gun or to pull him to safety or to get in the path of the projectile.

She could see the future. As clearly as though she had been the ghost.

She could see Isaac tumbling to the ground, dying almost instantly as the flame-bullets from Albinex's weapon burst through him. Dying like a hero, saving the world, but not really, because it wouldn't stop the bad guy. Dying because it was all his fault and he deserved to.

She could hear herself screaming with grief, her premonition fulfilled. One of them would have to die. Because of her.

But that wasn't what happened.

Albinex raised his flame-gun, casually. Isaac was running straight at him, almost as though he wanted to be shot.

'Too late,' said the Navarino. 'Much too late.'

Something small and white shot out of the Admiral's backpack and thwapped Albinex in the face.

He swore and dropped the pistol as the whatever-it-was slapped him around the head. He tried to grab it, but it was swift and elusive, moving frantically, trying to poke him in the eye.

'*Graeme*!' shrieked the Navarino. 'You little –!'

Isaac shoved him aside, violently, and dived for the computer. Albinex roared with rage as he overbalanced, toppling over the railing and landing with a heavy splat on the concrete.

'M'Kabel!' Isaac shouted. 'I need you here!'

'Sorry!' yelled the Tzun, who was being chased around in circles by a slavering Ogron.

The other apelike humanoid had grabbed hold of the Doctor, trying to get a firm enough grip on him to snap an arm. The Time Lord wriggled in the creature's grasp. Benny started to come back down the stairs, but she wasn't going to be quick enough. The Ogron grabbed a handful of hair and

265

wrenched the Doctor's head back, baring animal teeth.

'Hey, stupid!'

The Ogron grunted and looked up. Jason belted him across the head with a pair of bolt-cutters.

The monster toppled backwards. The Doctor dropped to the floor like a cat and bolted for the computer.

'You're welcome!' yelled Jason.

Albinex was pulling himself to his stumpy feet. He grabbed at the Doctor's leg as the Time Lord shot past.

The remaining Ogron had run M'Kabel into a corner. The Tzun waved his probe threateningly, dwarfed by the mercenary.

Benny reached up and pinched hard where the Ogron's thick neck sloped into its shoulder. The creature sneezed and fell down. M'Kabel tapped it on the forehead with his wand, and it said 'Ugh', and went to sleep on the floor.

Joel gaped up at the missile. Then he gaped up at Albinex. 'Jeez,' he said faintly. 'Barney wants to destroy the Earth.'

Isaac was frantically working at the computer console. Albinex was halfway up the stairs, pulling out one of his swords, ready to cut the Admiral down. The Auton jumped in his face again. With a roar of frustration, Albinex sliced Graeme in half. The spatula squeaked and landed in two pieces on the floor.

'There's a countdown here!' Isaac shouted. 'We've got less than two minutes before launch!'

'Don't worry,' called M'Kabel. 'It can't go through the roof!'

A siren sounded. The roof started to open.

'Oh, crumbs,' said M'Kabel.

'For the glory of Navarro!' yelled Albinex. He raised a razor-sharp blade.

'Oh, for goodness' sake,' said the Doctor. He planted a finger between the Navarino's beady little eyes.

Albinex's slug-mouth dropped open. The swords clattered out of his fists. He stood rock-still on the end of the Time Lord's finger, gaping.

The Doctor turned his head. 'Well, Admiral?'

* * *

For Isaac, things had slowed down, the interruptions were filtering out. This was a pure moment, without distractions.

M'Kabel's slender fingers were flying over the console. 'We could detonate the missile on the ground,' he said.

'We'll have to do a lot better than that,' said Isaac.

The Doctor waved his free hand at the console. 'Look at the telemetry panel,' he hinted.

Isaac leant over it. 'It's a satellite. Look at that communication configuration – that's Dalek!'

'They're in orbit?' gasped Ms R.

'It's a spy,' said M'Kabel.

'Admiral . . .' said Joel, agonized. He stumbled against a wall, too frightened to keep standing up.

'The satellite's watching for the missile launch,' said Isaac.

M'Kabel didn't stop typing. 'It'll probably signal the Daleks as soon as Albinex's plan gets underway.'

'Dad?' said Benny.

'Don't stop the launch,' Isaac told M'Kabel. He grabbed the Tzun's hand. 'Don't stop it.'

'What the –' began Ms R.

Isaac looked at the Doctor, who was still holding the Navarino at bay. The Time Lord nodded.

Isaac punched in a set of coordinates.

'Everybody out!' he yelled.

They bolted from the silo *en masse*, nearly running into Chris and Roz. Albinex shot past the Adjudicators in a purple blur. 'The Daleks have a spy satellite!' shouted Chris.

'We know that!' yelled the Doctor. 'Give me a hand!'

Chris ran over to where the Doctor was struggling with an unconscious Ogron. They hefted the hairy creature between them. 'What about the other one?' shouted Chris, over the sound of rocket engines firing up.

'He's dead,' said the Doctor. 'Come on!'

They ran after the others, carrying the Ogron awkwardly between them.

'Hit the dirt!' shouted Roz.

* * *

Around the USAF base at Greenham Common, chants and songs and shouts died away into nothing as the police and the protesters and the soldiers stopped as one body, and sixty thousand eyes watched the missile climb into the sky.

The Dalek spy satellite had been idly watching the heat traces around the airforce base, wondering why there were so many humans gathered there. It saw the missile coming and woke up a bit. That was the signal. It turned lazily, its communications disc pointing outwards, aiming for the relay satellite near Barnard's Star. The one that would contact the fleet.

It had a series of coded instructions to run. Once the nuclear weapons had done as much damage as they could, it would release cleansing biological packages into the atmosphere. Human civilization would have been completely destroyed, along with the majority of the population. The viruses would take care of anything that was left, preparing the world for its new masters.

Beyond that, the satellite didn't know and didn't care what the plan was. In its own dim way it was aware that the Daleks didn't care much either. They'd been contacted, made an offer: if it didn't come to fruition, it was no skin off their implants. Earth would keep.

The satellite knew it was invisible to the planet's primitive sensors, the stumbling radar on the surface and the clumsy satellites in orbit.

If it had been bright enough to understand surprise, it would have been astonished when a cruise missile smacked into it from behind and ripped it to shreds.

Denouement

'Where's Albinex?' said Benny.

'I don't know,' said Roz. 'Get your foot out of my mouth.'

'Sorry,' said Benny.

'Last seen as a purple dot on the horizon,' said Chris.

'Are we still alive?' said Joel.

'Yeh,' said Isaac.

Silence for a bit.

'Don't say it,' said Benny.

Joel said, 'Only way to be sure.'

Albinex pressed a lumpy fist into the remote control. A hundred feet up, the airlock cycled, and the ladder gracefully lowered itself into the forest.

He grabbed hold of it and scrambled up. He had to be out of here before they got their wits together and came after him. All of them. Isaac. The Doctor. The Daleks!

He hauled himself into the airlock. He gawped at the very dead Ogron on the floor. He snarled at Ms Randrianasolo, and reached for his gun.

'Take this, you militaristic patriarchal bastard!' she yelled, and knocked him flat with a telepathic stun-bolt.

'Hmm,' she said, looking down at the unconscious Navarino. 'Not very non-violent. But satisfying.'

33

Thank you for the lovely present

A messy bed in a messy bedroom.

Joel appears in front of the camera, sitting on the bed. 'Hi,
Mom. Hi, Dad. It's New Year's Eve, nineteen eighty-three.
It's about –' he looks at his watch '– ten-fifteen p.m.

'Okay, I've got to finish off this letter. Everybody's leaving
tonight, so this is my last chance to get 'em all on tape. So I'll
be going around and doing a bunch of interviews and other
fun stuff.'

Joel reaches for the camera. Static for a few seconds, and
then:

A café full of people, some standing, some sitting. The
camera is moving down a set of wooden stairs, held
unsteadily on someone's shoulder. 'Okay!' Joel says loudly.
'Introductions. First, this is Admiral Summerfield.'

A short, blond man looks up from behind the counter. He is
wearing a black military jacket of some kind. He gives a
small smile. 'And Tony.' A taller, bearded man in a red
T-shirt smiles and says 'Hi'. 'I've told you a bunch about
them, so, here they are. Admiral, where's Graeme?'

The blond man rummages behind the counter for a
moment. 'Here you are, son,' he says. Joel's hand appears in
frame. Isaac passes him something, and he holds it up in front
of the camera. It's a white plastic spatula, glued down the
middle. 'The Doctor put him back together with some of my
aeroplane glue. So he's fine.'

270

The camera swivels round to cover one of the coffee shop's tables. 'Please, no autographs,' says an English voice, belonging to a woman in her thirties. On the table in front of her is an empty coffee cup, a battered exercise book, and a large pile of yellow stick-on notes. She pretends to hide behind her fingers. The rough-chinned man with her smiles at the camera.

'Okay,' says Joel, 'this is Jason Summerfield-Kane, and this is Bernice Kane-Summerfield. Say hello to my folks.'

'Hello to my folks,' they chorus. Jason buries his face in his hands while Benny waves at the lens.

'And what are your plans?' says Joel, in his best interviewer voice.

'We're off back to the twenty-sixth century tomorrow,' says Benny. She peels another of the yellow notes from the book. 'I've got to finish my degree. But we're planning to visit. A lot. With our son . . . when he comes along.'

Jason grins, showing off his gold tooth. 'We'll have to work on that one a bit,' he says, wiggling his eyebrows.

Benny, blushing under the camera eye, gives her husband a look. 'So long as a certain someone doesn't lose the boy again.'

Jason smirks. 'I suppose I'm lucky Benny came back, after having a chance to sleep with the Doctor.'

'You're not *still* going on about that!' says Benny exasperatedly. 'It was about as erotic as hugging a gasping fish.'

'Oh yeah?' says Jason. 'Well, there was this time that I met this –'

Benny puts her hand over the camera lens. 'This isn't suitable for parents.'

Joel pulls back. 'And next we have Christopher Cwej and Roslyn Forrester, who I'm not supposed to tell you much about except that they're from the future. I guess C19 will cut out any bits of this tape which contain stuff you shouldn't know, anyway.'

The large, muscular man with the fair hair waves enthusiastically, while the short black woman just smiles in amusement. At first you might take them for an odd couple. But their familiarity is of a different kind, the easy comfortableness of two old, good friends.

'Tell us your plans for nineteen eighty-four,' says Joel.

'Well,' says the woman, 'I plan to put a telescreen in each home and control your every thought.'

Chris groans. 'We're leaving with the Doctor, of course,' he says. 'After we see the new year in. We had a great time. Everybody here is really cool, Mr and Mrs Mintz, so don't worry about a thing!'

'That would certainly reassure me,' comments Roz, 'if my son fell through a crack in time. Tell me, Mr Cwej,' she says, turning to her friend, 'what do you think about fatherhood?'

'Well, I –' He stops, peering at her. 'Er. You don't –!'

She smiles at him. He looks as though he's about to faint.

Roz turns and looks into the camera with a satisfied expression. 'Got him,' she says.

Static.

'Sorry about that,' says Joel. 'Had to change the battery.'

The camera moves around again and focuses on a small, dark-haired man, sitting at the table closest to the front of the shop. Admiral Summerfield has joined him. They are drinking coffee together.

The man reaches up to tip a hat that isn't on his head, and settles for a shy wave at the camera. 'This is the Doctor,' says Joel, 'who's going to tell you how I ended up in nineteen eighty-three. Aren't you, Doctor?'

' 'Scuse me,' says someone behind Joel, accidentally jostling him as they squeeze past.

'We think the time distortion was caused by one of Albinex's attempts to repair his faulty engine,' says the little man. There's a definite burr in his voice. 'We're going to have to pop forward to nineteen ninety-three to see if anyone or anything else was displaced. It might have been a Fortean Flicker, or a natural phenomenon . . . stranger things have happened.'

'Absolutely,' says Admiral Summerfield. He raises his mug to the camera, as though toasting it. 'For example, the Doctor has just worked out how to make the best cup of coffee on Earth.'

* * *

272

'Okay,' says Joel. 'I'm nearly out of tape, so I better finish up now.'

The radio is playing loudly in the background. He sits back on the bed, knocking a half-empty cigarette packet onto the floor. He arranges himself so that he's framed by the camera's point of view. 'I'm going to send this tape along to C19 tomorrow,' he says. 'If they do their job right, you should receive this the day after I go missing in nineteen ninety-three.

'We're going to pretty much keep on doing what we're doing. There are still going to be aliens who need help, not to mention plenty of humans who no one else is going to believe.'

The music on the radio cuts out, replaced by a shouted countdown. 'Ten!'

'So don't worry about me.'

'Eight!'

'I can't come and visit until I'm not there, if you see what I mean, but I promise I'll walk in a day or two after you see this tape.'

'Four!'

'Of course, I'll be kind of older ... anyway, this thing's really about to run out. See you soon. Happy –'

34

The bits not on Joel's video

Benny stepped out into the cold air. It wrapped itself around her, soaking immediately through her jumper, refreshing and sharp.

Ms Randrianasolo was standing in the street, holding the ends of her woollen scarf, looking up at the Christmas lights hung outside the Pyramid. 'I found her,' she told Benny.

'How is she?'

'She'll be fine.' Ms R blew out a long, white breath. 'All Jacqui wanted was some acknowledgement of what had happened to her. No one she'd ever told had believed her. So she told me, when I found her. And I believed her.'

'Come inside,' said Benny. 'It's freezing out here.'

Ms R shook her head. 'I can't come back,' she said. 'Listen, this is going to sound awful, but . . .'

'You can't trust Dad,' said Benny.

The black woman shook her head. 'I'd never be able to trust him again.'

'Try it,' said Benny. 'I've been down this path. You can build up the trust again.'

'I'd be wanting to peep inside his skull all the time,' said Ms R. 'And I can't do that. Besides. I'm just not a soldier any more.'

'Where will you go?'

'The peace camp,' said Ms R. 'They could use another regular. I need some practice in non-violence. And I want to keep an eye on Jacqui until she's ready to move on.'

'Are you sure you want to do that? Really sure?' Benny leant on the rail, gazing down at the Malagasy woman. 'They won't listen, you know. They'll lie about you and put you in prison and beat you and . . . and even kill you.' She stopped, shuddering in the cold, not sure if she'd said too much.

'I know the history,' said Ms Randrianasolo. 'And I plan to be part of it.'

'You know the strange thing?' said Chris.

Roz was eating a pile of mince pies. 'What?'

'I realized that when we were on board the sky yacht, running around, I didn't worry about you at all. I just got on with the job.' Chris frowned. 'It's been bugging me. Why wasn't I thinking about you?'

'Nah,' said Roz. 'Same reason I can work with a red smear and a walking fish and just get on with the job. There's no room in the middle of a firefight to think about stuff like that.'

Roz glanced over to where Benny and Jason were sitting, holding hands. 'That's why Benny can't do this any more. I guess . . . I guess that's why the Doctor doesn't have anybody.'

'Job first,' sighed Chris, 'people second.'

'They still quote that at the Academy?'

Chris nodded dolefully. 'If anything ever happens to you . . .'

Roz lifted her glass of champagne. 'Here's to the future,' she said.

Chris smiled, and they clinked their glasses together.

Static. Then:

'So for the record, Doctor,' says Joel, 'how did we get away with it?'

The Time Lord puts down his coffee cup. 'Well,' he says, counting off the points on his fingers. 'Firstly, we had the problem of an escaped and homicidal alien. Right now Albinex is languishing in a spare room in the TARDIS, being made to watch *Threads* and *The Day After* until he stops ranting about Navarro's glorious future. We'll be taking him home tomorrow. He needs help.'

'What about the missile?' says Joel.

'Well, that was a bit more difficult,' says the Doctor. 'When tens of thousands of people witness something, it's hard to cover it up.'

'Nonetheless,' says the Admiral, 'Department C19 have done a marvellous job.' He smiled, satisfied. 'They cut a deal with us.'

'Immediately after the missile was launched,' says the Doctor, 'we "informed" the police that it had been a test launch, without a live warhead. They then told the protesters. I don't like to think what kind of riot might have happened if they hadn't.'

'But it wasn't a dud,' prompts Joel.

'It was live and dangerous,' says the Doctor. 'It didn't detonate when it struck the Dalek satellite, but if it had fallen back into Earth's atmosphere ... I programmed Albinex's yacht to intercept it, extend a forcefield around it, and carry it on autopilot to the sun. The Ogron Albinex had left to guard engineering was very surprised to see me. He's also in the TARDIS, in a room full of bananas. That'll keep him happy for a while.'

Isaac holds up the newspaper he's been reading, but the print is too fine to be made out. 'C19 official story was that it was a launch of an experimental plane, not a missile, and that the panic was typical of the peace movement's hysteria, et cetera, et cetera.'

'One less cruise missile,' says Joel.

'Just one less,' says the Doctor sternly. 'By your time, the base at Greenham Common is gone, but they're building Trident missiles down the road at Aldermaston.'

'The struggle continues,' says Joel.

'Indeed. At any rate, I've had a sharp word with several people, and I don't think you'll have trouble with anyone taking too close a look at Little Caldwell – for a while, at least. The Department's foremost mission is to keep secrets.'

'Friends in high places,' says Isaac.

Joel drops to a knee, giving us a sudden worm's-eye view of the two short men.

* * *

276

Later:

The Doctor is in full flow. 'I popped back to Youkali for a day or so, in search of the time device Caroline Grey found. It was hidden away in an underground chamber, along with dozens of pieces of Youkalian technology. She must have abseiled down the cliff wall. Brave young woman.'

He turns his coffee mug around in his hands. 'That particular device must have been borrowed from Osiran technology. It was far too advanced for the Youkalians. I wonder how much that sort of thing contributed to their destruction . . .'

'You mean you don't know?' jokes Joel.

'There are a lot of things I don't know,' says the Doctor. 'Contrary to popular opinion. Places and dates. And names.'

Later:

The Doctor is folding Napoleon hats out of the newspaper. 'For me,' he says, 'the best part of Christmas was decommissioning Isaac's army.' He glances up at the camera. 'Only a dozen or so wanted to go home, but I took them all.'

'Once we got the TARDIS out from the bottom of the lake where Albinex had dropped it,' points out the Admiral. 'We had to rent a tow-truck. You haven't experienced scuba-diving until you've done it in below-zero weather, believe me.'

'There were wounds that had to be healed,' the Doctor continues, 'in bodies and minds. There were diets that needed to be corrected. There were stories that needed to be listened to and accusations that needed to be answered.'

Isaac points at the Doctor. 'He had the Kapteynian eating out of his hand.'

'It was my hat, actually.'

'It was good to have your help,' says the Admiral. 'I think we work well together.'

They shake hands, over the table.

These sections of the tape were erased by Department C19.

It was just before midnight. Time to go.

The TARDIS stood outside the Pyramid, humming warmly to itself. Benny and Jason were there, holding hands, wearing long, matching warm coats. Roz and Chris were leaning on the TARDIS, chatting in low voices.

The Doctor and Isaac emerged from the coffee shop. The Doctor had a large bag of mocha, five credits and a smile. He glanced up at Joel's window, where the radio was playing away the last minutes before the new year.

The Kapteynian had refused to leave him alone, and was floating around his head and shoulders, showering his face with elfin light.

Benny let go of Jason's hand and wrapped her arms around her father. 'Do you forgive me?' he whispered.

'Yes,' she murmured back. 'Get on with your life.'

He held her tightly. 'Keep on grounding the lightning.'

When they let each other go, Isaac said, 'You'll visit soon?'

Jason raised his left hand. 'Via time ring,' he said. The band of exotic metal glittered on his ring finger.

Benny showed Isaac her matching wedding ring. 'We'll try to space it out,' she said, 'so you don't see me getting old suddenly, or vice versa.'

'Very wise,' commented the Doctor.

Isaac shrugged off his jacket. 'I want you to have this,' he said.

Benny smiled, surprised and pleased, and put on the old Spacefleet jacket. It fit her reasonably well.

Her father reached into the pocket and extracted a handful of brightly coloured glittering patches. He pinned them to the jacket, over her heart.

While Benny was staring at the medals for conspicuous bravery, Jason seized Isaac's hand and shook it mightily. 'By the time we see you again,' he said, 'I might be a father as well. Get to use that crib, eh, Doctor?'

'Best of luck,' said Isaac. 'The very best of luck.'

'Five!' shouted Joel's radio. 'Four! Three! Two! One! Happy New Year!'

Chris whispered something to Roz, who laughed and slapped him on the arm. Chris gave the Admiral a thumbs-up and they went into the TARDIS together.

'What was that about?' the Doctor asked Benny softly, as Jason and Isaac swapped quips about fatherhood.

'Oh, an old Earth tradition regarding New Year's Eve,' she smiled. 'I think they're past the snog phase now, though. I think this could be the beginning of a beautiful friendship.' She touched his arm. 'Thanks again. For everything.'

Jason took Benny's hand, smiling. As their time rings met, a soft field of sparkles erupted around them.

The Doctor looked at his feet, looked up at Benny, hesitated, folded his arms, unfolded them and put his hands in his pockets, looked up at the sky, took his hands back out of his pockets, stepped through the speckles of light and leant up and kissed Benny on the cheek.

She looked at him in astonishment, breaking into a beautiful smile. And vanished.

The Doctor, shy and puzzled and pleased, shook Isaac's hand one more time and bustled into his TARDIS. The Kapteynian buzzed about, squealing with jealousy, and shot inside. The door closed.

The Admiral watched the blue box disappear, its engines groaning as though they were held together with bits of string and chewing gum. From his window, Joel was watching too. Isaac smiled to himself. Good lad.

He was about to go back into the warmth when he heard a shout from across the road. Old Tom, a bottle tucked under his arm, meandered over. 'Happy New Year!' he said. He smelt of soap powder and humanity. 'You ought to go inside before you catch your death. Sorry I'm late, I had to finish my stocktake. Haven't missed anything, have I?'

'Not at all,' said Isaac. 'Please, come inside.'

'I wanted to ask you if you'd seen anyone mucking around near the church,' said Tom, as they went into the coffee shop. 'One of the gravestones seems to have moved right across the graveyard. I can't fathom it.'

Isaac nodded. 'Stranger things have happened,' he said.

Epilogue

I never did finish telling that story about the hermit, did I? The tale leaves an obvious question unanswered. What happens to the man when he's given away every last piece of his name?

The thing is, the only way he could give away a bit of his name was to take it out of that little inside pocket. So as he shared himself with more and more people, he got to see more and more of his own name.

Bit by bit, over the years, he learnt all the things about himself he'd kept locked away, realized what the name he'd been given so long ago really meant.

The more he gave away, the more he had.

Now tell me: what would you do if your name wasn't real? Say, if the man you got it from turned out to be a con artist (or at least, you *thought* he was)? And the fancy titles you'd fixed on the front were fakes?

It's a long road from pretend to real. But if you walk the same path as that hermit took, you can put yourself back together, you can make those names ring true. Putting your husband's name in front of your father's. And finally earning the right to put 'Doctor' in front of your own.

Doctor. Bernice. Kane. Summerfield.

Their names fit really well together, don't you think?

Acknowledgements

Paul Cornell and I wrote the plot for this book together, in a sort of reverse of *Human Nature*. Though I added bits (notably the ghost), it's still quite close to our original storyline.

Many thanks to the women of Greenham Common for their kind help. I hope I got it right! *A luta continua.*

Jon Blum contributed numerous brilliant ideas, the Prologue and Epilogue, and I love him.

The epitaphs: Jon again, Paul again, Jason Miller.

The read-through crew: Todd Beilby, Aaron Brockbank, Steven Caldwell, Peter Griffiths, Stephen Groenewegen and Kyla Ward. Thanks folks!

Special thanks to Special K.

Quick plug: contact the Doctor Who Club of Australia at GPO Box 2870, Sydney, NSW 2001.